Loss of Carrier

Russ White

ISBN: 1-4392-5850-3
ISBN-13: 9781439258507

Visit www.booksurge.com to order additional copies.

We have thought on your steadfast love, O God, in the midst of your temple. As your name, O God, so your praise reaches to the ends of the earth. Your right hand is filled with righteousness. Let Mount Zion be glad! Let the daughters of Judah rejoice because of your judgments! Psalm 48:9-11

I would like to thank my wife and daughters for putting up with me when I'm writing, and my friends for their efforts in helping me bring this book to life. I would especially like to thank Blair Kenney, who teaches the skill of writing as much as she edits. She is a bright spot in the large and confusing world of publishing.

I dedicate this book to my Mom, who instilled in me a love of reading, especially mysteries.

Prologue

Pain exploded in his side. He doubled over, his hands pressed to the skin where the sucker punch had landed, a coldness remote and fleeting at his neck. He started to straighten, but a thrust from behind propelled him into the rack of equipment, a searing pain in his head joining the pain in his side. A foot, blurry, appeared below him. A kick, and his feet lost their grip, slipping out into the air.

He grasped at the wire around his throat. It was useless. There was no way to unwrap it, to lessen the constriction. His fingers dripped blood from the effort to unplug the cable. It was no use. The pain in his side was still resonating through his body, fueled by the panic of his lungs working against the noose around his neck.

He pushed his arms out, trying to grasp something, anything. The cables around him didn't offer any purchase, and he couldn't find the handles he knew were there. He kicked. His toe gained purchase, but his arm wouldn't pull back out from the tangle of wires. He pulled his arm harder, and his foot slid off the tile floor into the hole again.

Footsteps. Silence. Rows of light, shutting down one at a time. Soon it would be dark, the total darkness of a room with no windows. The darkness of a coffin. He tried to cry out, but no sound came. Every movement he made tightened the wires around his neck, closing his throat against the air he needed.

Why? What have I done? Tomorrow I will die, not today. Pray. But what? To what? I'm not ready to die. Tomorrow I can ask Jess. I can't…

Darkness.

Chapter 01

Jess nudged his truck into his usual spot. A new sports car, its maroon paint polished to a deep shine, put his truck's dull green paint to shame. Short swatches of rubber, passing for tires, stood in contrast to wide whitewalls and garish polished chrome wheels against polished hubcaps.

The new car must be Carl's. It was just like the car he'd bought last year. And the year before. And, in fact, every year since he'd met Carl. How could Carl afford to buy a new car every year? He sighed and bumped his truck's door closed, carefully sliding the key into the lock and turning it until he could feel the click. There was no way the paint on his truck was ever going to look like the polished surface on Carl's car, but still, no point in adding new scratches.

As he turned in behind the tailgate of his truck, he glanced over at the new car again. Water spots marred the polished surface. "Water spots? How did it get wet?"

"Talking to yourself again?"

Jess's keys dropped to the asphalt at his feet as he turned and found himself facing his boss's secretary. "Linda! I didn't see you there. Good morning."

"Don't be jealous of Carl. He has his own problems, you know, new car every year or not."

He frowned. "It's just puzzling."

"And no puzzle can rest unsolved around Jess Wirth, can it?" After a moment of silence, she continued. "He lives with his parents in Chapel Hill. No rent, no bills. Other than that car, and, of course, all the dates he brags about, he doesn't have to pay for much of anything." She sighed. "You'd think a twenty four year old man would be a bit more grown up. You're about the same age, and you act like a gentleman."

"Maybe that's because I've lived a bit of a rougher life than he did." The corners of his mouth reversed direction, forming a smile. "You're like the class mom, aren't you? You should pop him across the knuckles with a ruler. Maybe he'll come to his senses."

She turned and looked at him. "Are you saying I'm old?"

"Well, I had noticed a little gray recently—"

"Lo'mighty, my hair's been gray since you were just a child. But now the ruler idea, I might take you up on that. If I do, you better watch your knuckles, too." She laughed.

Jess laughed with her and shook his head. "I would never call you old, Linda. Perhaps aged to perfection would be a better description. Anyway, I was just wondering why Carl's new car is wet."

"It rained?"

"Not while I was on the way in to work. Carl is usually very careful about allowing his car to get dirty, especially just after he's bought it." They climbed the steps at the front of the building in silence, Jess glancing at the small logo engraved on the glass doors as he held it open for Linda. The little letters below the logo proclaimed, "OptiData Management," and then, "We manage your data, you manage your business."

As Linda continued towards the elevators, Jess made his way through the maze of cubicles, finally turning in at his doorway. As he stepped into the space, he wondered how he'd ever ended up in network engineering. He considered the life he would have preferred, working outside in forests and fields as a county agent, like his grandfather.

His thoughts turned to the boat show, opening at the state fairgrounds first thing in the morning. At least a boat show would brighten up his weekend. Especially since this weekend he was going to look for a new personal watercraft. A boat was always possible, but the feel of the motorcycle allowed him to have something on the water that he never allowed himself on the road since his rougher days had passed.

He dumped his laptop case on the desk, wound his way along the cubicle walls, and stopped to rap on Carl's whiteboard.

No answer. Carl wasn't anywhere to be seen, although his laptop, the screen dark, was cabled to the desk. Jess walked in and touched the case—cold plastic met his fingers.

In the break room, Jess's morning turned bad quickly; not only was there no coffee made, but the pots weren't even in the machines. He pulled them from the little drying rack the cleaning lady, Benita, put them in every night, settling them in their rightful places on the dark brown burners.

After dumping fresh grounds from a little sack into the machine, he wandered back over to his cubicle, hating to waste time waiting for the coffee to brew.

Back in his cubicle, Jess slid his laptop out of its case and pulled its locking cable through the center of an old brass propeller leaning against the side of the cubical wall. It would be funny to watch someone try to steal his laptop with that brass propeller attached. They wouldn't be able to run very fast, anyway.

Popping up a Web browser, he checked the weather for the weekend. Then he skipped back a day and replayed the maps from the night before. It had stopped raining at the office around one in the morning. His mind raced back to the parking lot, thinking about the water spots on Carl's car.

Breaking his train of thought, he punched the messages button on his phone. An all-too-familiar, and all-too-annoying, voice popped out. "Jess, this is Jamie in network operations. We got a problem, row fifty-three, rack twenty. I've poked it from this side, but no juice, so it looks like it's on your end." More information about the server followed, along with a trouble ticket number.

His phone rang. The number on the screen was Linda's. "What's up?"

"Hey, Jess. I'm going home. There's nothing going on around here today. Gerard left a message on my voice mail saying he wasn't coming in. He stayed out late at the spring bash last night. He sounded like he was in rough shape."

Jess pressed his palm onto the desktop, irritated he had forgotten the yearly bash Gerard threw. "I can't believe I forgot that. This place is going to be empty today. I drove all the way down here for nothing."

"I forgot, too. You and I never go to it, so why would we remember? It's silly he does it on a Thursday night, anyway."

"Yeah, I know. Well, I'll see you on Monday."

"You okay here by yourself, Jess? Don't stick around long."

"Are you crazy, Linda? If no one else is coming in, I'll clear up this one server problem the network operations folks called me about, and then I'll get out of here and head to the lake. That server probably just needs a reboot—shouldn't take but a minute or two to clear it up. I'll have my cell phone with me if anything comes up."

After dropping the receiver on the cradle, Jess headed over to the elevators. As he waited for the elevator to arrive, he wondered where Carl could be. He must already be down in the data center.

Jess considered his distorted reflection in the elevator doors. Jess was medium height. Carl was definitely on the short side, but what Carl lost in height, he made up for in almost everything else—the top part of an exclamation point, wide at the top, a thin waste, and powerful muscles bulging under whatever he wore to cover them.

Jess stared at his own clothing in the reflection. The corners on the collar of his polo shirt were definitely starting to fray since it had seen better days. Frumpy cargo shorts, close-cropped hair, little round glasses, and hiking boots completed the picture. While he didn't think of himself as out of shape, he certainly wasn't one of those ripped weightlifters like Carl or the guys he saw showing off on the lake all the time.

But then, Jess liked himself just like he was. He didn't have any reason to be showy, like Carl. Who wants to spend every waking moment worrying about what you look like, anyway? Aren't there more important things in life?

The doors slid open, breaking the mirror in half, leaving the emptiness of the elevator in front of him. Jess stepped in and pressed the button labeled B. He'd always thought the button should be labeled D, for dungeon. And they should supply oxygen tanks, like divers wear, for the trip down. He sighed. Without the data center, though, he'd be out of a job.

Within a few seconds, Jess stepped off the elevator and walked up the ramp onto the raised floor, stopping at the door leading into the data center. He pulled his badge away from the yo-yo on his belt and slapped it against the card reader next to the door. While he waited for the door to click, he read the signs posted nearby. The first one said, "Danger! Halon fire extinguishers in use. If the alarm sounds, please exit this room as quickly as possible to avoid suffocation." They were asking people to please avoid being suffocated by the halon in the fire extinguishers? Did anyone really need to be asked politely to not suffocate themselves?

The second sign said, "Danger! Class 3 lasers in use. Do not look directly into lasers used on equipment." At least this one didn't say "please." The light on the card reader turned green and emitted a low beeping sound to signal access granted. A few seconds later, the door clicked. Jess reached over and pulled it open. He stepped inside into a world of darkness, lit only by thousands of multicolored twinkling status lights.

As he moved his foot forward into the dark, it hit something. "*Ouch!*" Whatever it was, it skittered across the floor, leaving a throbbing pain in Jess's toe.

Wondering why the lights hadn't come on automatically, he felt around the wall beside the door. His fingers moved across the roughness of the wall, finally finding the cool plastic of the switch panel. Jess started moving the switches around, trying to figure out what combination of the switches would turn the lights on.

As rows of lights started popping on, a dreary world of gray floors and gray racks in a windowless gray room replaced the darkness. He knelt and untied his boot. While he massaged his toe, he considered the switch on the wall. The sensor that was supposed to turn the lights on automatically appeared to be working, a little red light blinking occasionally to say it knew the room was now occupied.

As his eyes adjusted to the increasing light, Jess stared, concentrating on odd shapes littered around the normally smooth raised surface. Large floor tiles, each one about two feet square, were piled up all over the room, leaving gopher holes in an expanse of gray yard. Within each hole, a subterranean city was exposed, a rat's nest of wires, bundled neatly enough, but running at all sorts of odd angles, making a maze of huge proportions.

Why are there so many tiles pulled up? Jess wondered. Every person who got access to the data center had to go through the safety briefing, which included a big point about not pulling more than one up at a time. His toes didn't seem to be hurt, so he slid his boot back on and started tying the laces. The source of the pain in his toe was directly in front of him—a set of mouse ears. It was a simple device, two suction cups joined by a metal bar, used to lift floor tiles into and out of place. Why had the mouse ears been left in front of the door?

Jess sighed. It would take hours to clean this mess up, and there was no way he could leave before it was done. He'd have to fill out a safety report adding a half an hour to his time in the office, at least. At least Gerard wouldn't be screaming at him for this mess. Retrieving the mouse ears from where they lay, he knelt close to the door, suctioned the first tile, and set it in place.

Staying on his knees, he slid across the cold, smooth floor, towards the next tile upended out of its spot. The work was slow, and the tiles were heavy, but he plodded down the rows of racks, finally reaching the last out-of-place tile at the fifty-second row. Jess's shoulders complained as he lifted himself from the floor after setting the last out-of-place tile in the main corridor back into place. *Now for a look at that server so I can get out on the water.*

He rounded the corner into row fifty-three, focusing on the rack numbers, looking for the failed server. A tangled mess of cables poured out of the rack the server was in, a floor tile removed and leaning against the rack on the opposite side at an odd angle. It looked like…

"Hello?"

No answer. Jess was drawn down along the confined space between the racks of equipment, afraid of what he was going to find, but certain he needed to discover what was there in that tangle of cables.

Long, dark hair, pulled back in a ponytail. Shirt sleeves pulled up so the little red eyes of a tattooed dragon looked out at him, as if the dragon could offer some protection for its owner. The dragon's owner, Carl, was suspended by a pair of twisted and deformed Ethernet cables, his brightly polished shoes hanging in the air above an opening left by a pulled up floor tile. Scratch marks, angry and red, welled up along Carl's neck around the cables. His arms were buried in a mass of cables on either side, as if he had reached out to grab on, perhaps to try and hold himself up in some way. The cables were strong enough to hold his weight, but they were not easy to grab and hold on to. A smashed cell phone rested on the floor by the rack.

Slipping from his hand, Jess's coffee cup fell to the floor and broke, splattering coffee and ceramic shards back up onto his legs. He backed out of the narrow space, rushed over to the corner of the data center, knelt there, and threw up. He stayed there for a moment, trying to calm down, to make his stomach settle, to think, to stop shaking. His mind returned to the scene of death.

Bright yellow cables against a blue shirt? Carl never would have approved of *that* color combination. Why was his face so white? His eyes should be closed, not open. Why hadn't one of the security guards seen this and reported it to the police? The lights were off, and the cameras were useless in the dark.

Of course, the cables wrapped around Carl's neck explained why the server wasn't working. Loss of carrier. How did those cables end up plugged into the wrong jacks? One end should have been in the server, rather than both ends being plugged up high into the patch panel along the top of the rack.

He needed to do something.

Mechanically, he pressed the buttons for 911 on his cell phone, but nothing happened. He tried again. Jess let out a breath. *Slow down. Think.*

Cell phones never worked in the basement of the building, especially in the data center. His hand released the phone, and it fell to the floor with a dull thud. He looked at his hand, shaking, empty. The cell phone didn't break. Why had Carl's cell phone broken? This floor wasn't hard enough to shatter a cell phone that way. Who would want to murder Carl? What if the killer were still in the data center, watching Jess now, waiting for a chance to…? Goosebumps lined Jess's arms, and a cold chill washed across his forehead.

He needed to do something.

The door. There was a phone there. He could call the police. His stomach wretched again. He hurried through the grayness, trying to get the images of Carl out of his mind. Finally, he was close enough to pick up the phone; he reached out towards the receiver.

Then he remembered this phone didn't handle emergency calls correctly. He would need to know the address for the building when the operator answered. What was the address? Five minutes ago he could have rattled it off. The memory nagged at the back of his mind, sitting there. He couldn't reach it.

Jess jumped clear out of his skin as the phone rang, the forceful sound loud above the low hum of the equipment. He lifted the receiver and placed it against his ear. His heart thumped loudly.

"Jess, this is Brian. I was just going through the cameras for my morning check and saw you running towards the phone in the data center. Is everything okay?"

"Carl's down here, Brian. He's dead. You better call 911." Jess heard his own voice speaking, but it was distant, mismatched from the thoughts in his head.

Silence. And then Brian said, "Wait! What did you say? I thought I just heard you say Carl is dead. Are you feeling okay, Jess? You don't sound good. You're not pulling one of your practical jokes, are you?"

"Brian, hang up and call 911. I'm serious!" he shouted. Then he added, more softly, "Carl's dead, Brian. Please call the police." The phone clicked. Dial tone. He stood staring at the signs on the door, fixated on the incongruent "please" printed there in bold red letters. Did he really need to say "please"?

Chapter 02

The door pulled out of Jess's hands unexpectedly, leaving him sliding down the ramp, grabbing desperately for the handrail to regain his balance. It clicked closed behind him, a touch of finality in his race to get out of the data center. He held on for a moment and then moved forward again, bumping into a box at the bottom. The entire stack tumbled onto the floor in front of him. There was no place here to sit and wait for someone else to arrive; he would have to keep moving.

The walls seemed to press, hemming him in, his stomach churning at the thought of being stuck in the basement with Carl's body. The elevator doors, reflecting the light, beckoned, but there was no time to wait for the car to make its way down from wherever it currently was. The stairs at the end of the hall would be faster.

He climbed, his knuckles white on the cold steel railing, eyes fixated on the light coming from above, avoiding looking through the spaces between the stairs where risers would normally be.

Brian met him as the stairs emptied out into the hallway, helping Jess out through the doors, supporting him as they passed through the lobby and finally out onto the patio, into the fresh air.

Jess sat heavily on the steps in front of the building, the coolness of the Carolina morning flooding his lungs. Each breath not only brought in life, but it also took with it poison, lifting his spirits and covering the searing memory with a light gauze of time.

Brian spoke, his voice devoid of its normal strength. "You okay? It's pretty freaky, sitting out here like nothing has happened while Carl's body is down there."

"I'm getting better. I think being outside has settled my stomach some. I had to get out of the basement. It was so small all of a sudden, and I felt like I was going to—"

"I'm glad you didn't try to wait down there. I don't see how you could stand it. I called 911 and Gerard both. We can just sit and wait until someone shows up; it shouldn't be but a few minutes."

Those few minutes stretched into an eternity. The scene replayed itself over and over—the tiles falling into place, getting up to look down the row of servers, the yellow cables, the shoes hanging into the opening in the floor. Some part of his mind was trying to cope with reality, but he needed to stop the tape from rewinding.

A car door slammed, breaking the pattern of thoughts. Gerard was jogging up the ramp beside the stairs and then brushing past. As he passed, Jess glanced up, into his face. The eyes were red-rimmed and glassy, full of tiredness. The face was out of place for Gerard, but before he could ask, Gerard had passed into the building, the doors swinging slowly closed behind him.

Brian was clearly annoyed with the brush-off. "Not even a good morning?"

Gerard must have been up late—or rather, early. The spring bash, of course. He had been up early and probably had a smashing headache as well. No wonder he looked bad.

"You okay, Jess?"

"Sorry, just thinking."

"It's okay. I can't believe he's rude like that."

"Technically speaking, it's not been a good morning." Jess turned back away from the building, looking at, but not seeing, the trees sparsely planted throughout the empty parking lot.

"He still doesn't have to be that way about it."

Gerard's voice came from behind them. "Hey, Brian, get these doors unlocked and call some other folks in to watch the building entrances, would you? The cops should be here any minute. Might make things move faster if we keep the doors unlocked."

Jess turned just in time to see one of the glass doors closing, silently spinning on its hinges. He turned back to Brian, whose face was reddening from below his neatly ironed collar to the edges of his close cropped gray hair. A military uniform would have matched his well toned physique and demeanor better than a white button down shirt and tie.

"Not too shocked, is he? I mean, just a little slacking off in efficiency wouldn't hurt, would it?"

"Gerard? He's unflappable. I'm convinced nothing gets to him," Jess replied.

"Unflappable? Almost inhuman. I wonder if he's cleared out his voice mail and e-mail already?" Brian had intended it as a joke, but it fell flat.

"His life is this business."

"And girls. He was a lot like Carl when he first came to work here. I can't believe I'm one of the few people left from the old days, before that private investor bought the whole operation and put Gerard in charge."

Jess thought back to the day Brian had started working there. It was after Jess has started, and that was after the management changeover. "I thought you'd only started here a short while back."

"Oh, sure. I left and come back. Gerard likes me, so he's always willing to put me back in charge of security when I come back. The only real difference between then and now is he didn't drive a fancy sports cars. Used to be, he drove a battered minivan."

"Like my pickup, huh?"

Brian snorted. "Your pickup isn't battered in any sense of the word, Jess. Old, maybe, but not battered. And his minivan wasn't old, it was just battered. I'd guess the only reason his sports cars always look so nice is because he pays someone else to do the work."

"Anyway, you'd better hop to it and head inside before he pokes his head back out here and really starts screaming."

Twisting as he stood up, Brian stepped up onto the porch and headed for the doors. Jess watched him as he put his badge against the reader, but he turned back to the parking lot at the sound of car wheels on the pavement, the sound of someone hurriedly turning into the drive. While the door closed behind Brian, Linda navigated her car into a spot.

She walked up to the steps, stopping in front of Jess. "How are you doing?"

"I'm doing okay. I don't know if I could stand going back in there right now, but out here, I'm okay. Gerard called you back in?"

"No, Brian called. He figured the police would want to question me, and I figured you could use someone to talk to, so here I am."

"Thanks, Linda."

"It's no problem." She sat down next to him on the steps. "I only live fifteen minutes from here. I was just thinking about sitting down at the sewing machine when the phone rang."

Jess withdrew into his own mind again, going over details, trying to sort out what must have happened, what a shame it was to die so young, and what would happen if he died. Would there be a hole in anyone's heart if he didn't show up for work one morning?

She looked over her glasses at him, her gray hair falling down across the dark skin of her forehead. "What are you thinking about?"

"My life. I'm not close to anybody who works here. In fact, I'm not even close to many people who don't work here. I wonder if anyone would notice if I went like that. What sort of world do we live in now? People live their lives in such close contact but without really knowing anyone else."

"Death makes you think about life, doesn't it?" Linda remarked.

Jess nodded in reply.

"Don't be hard on yourself. You've come through a lot, and you've done okay. God created you, and he'll pull you through 'til He's done with you. That's what we always used to say when we hit hard times." A tissue gently dabbed at his face, removing a tear that had settled on his cheek.

"Nothing here that couldn't be fixed by a good dose of faith seasoned with a dash of family."

She always drove into his singleness whenever he was under stress like this. It was her way of saying she cared, to remind him of what was important. "You mean a girl. I did have a girl in my life. It didn't work out too well, as I recall."

"Girls and families aren't the same thing, you know. We've had this talk before. Finding a girl would be the place to start in building a family. Families don't just grow on trees any more than money does. Now, as for the past, it's the past, not the future. You need to let go."

"Oh, I know. But where do you find a girl nowadays? The bar scene? A personal dating site? At work? The problem is the people are all the same. It's all about the experience, the feelings, the chemical reaction. Everyone wants to know what they're going to get, and they want it now. There's no interest in the long term, putting work into a relationship for a lifetime."

"You ask me, you're starting at the wrong end of the stick if you're looking for a family. Don't start by trying to find a girl to fall in love with—start by trying to find a friend." She brushed the hair off her forehead, revealing a wise collection of wrinkles. "Have you tried the produce aisle? Always lots of fresh stuff in the produce aisle, from what I see. And at least you'd know she eats her veggies."

She laughed.

At first, Jess found the sound wrenching, in conflict with his dampened feelings. But then, his mood breaking, he joined in. He tilted his head up, catching the sun low on the horizon, suddenly happy just to be alive and outside.

A black-and-white car pulled into the lot, a long strip of colored lights across the top. It was followed by a plain white truck. Jess thought about how long the sport-utility was as it slid into the parking lot, finding several spaces unoccupied to pull into sideways. The police had finally arrived. The vehicles disgorged their contents—police officers hauling various bags, cases, and lights—into the parking lot.

"They'll probably keep us here for hours to go through all sorts of questioning. They always suspect the person who found the body, don't they?"

"You're disconnected, Jess. Out of touch." The crinkles at the corners of her eyes bunched up as her mouth found its way into a smile. "Mysteries today aren't about people any more than the rest of life is about people. Things are always solved by some new technical wonder. There aren't any old-fashioned detectives any longer. We've left them in the past, along with our morals." She sighed and continued. "But, there it is—time only runs one way this side of the River Jordan."

"What if they arrest—"

"They won't, not right now, even if they think you had anything to do with it. They'll probably give you a day or two, at least, to feel bad about whatever you've done before they come and get you." She laughed again, prompting several of the officers to look up from their work to stare at them, as if the laughter was somehow out of place.

Air fluffed on Jess's neck, and footsteps sounded behind him. He turned to find Gerard standing on the porch in front of the building's entrance.

He began to pace. "They take forty-five minutes to get here, and then they take half an hour to come inside once they're actually here? They could have used their sirens and gotten here faster. Don't they realize we have a business to run? This whole mess is keeping us from getting down there to clean things up."

Turning around to look at him, Linda said, "Isn't Carl already dead? There's no rushing about that's going to change anything. That milk's already spilled. Rushing isn't going to put it back into the bottle."

Gerard stopped and glared at Linda. "Who called you in, anyway? I suppose it's just as well; the police are going to want to question you, anyway." His feet started clicking against the polished concrete porch again. The police officers continued arranging their equipment in the parking lot. "Come *on!* Get this investigation started so we can clean this mess up! We have a *business* to run here."

At long last, four officers broke away from the truck and paced over to the base of the stairs. Jess looked directly into the eyes of the man in the front, and older man in a frazzled gray suit matched with a red tie worn soft around the edges.

Breaking his eyes from Jess, sweeping the group in general, he said, "Good morning. I'm Detective Harris. Which one of you found the body?"

"I did."

The detective glanced at Jess and then turned his attention to Linda. "How do you come into this?"

Linda explained she was in the building earlier in the morning, had left Jess alone in the building, and had come back when called.

He finally turned his attention to Gerard. "And—"

Gerard interrupted. "I can't believe it took so long for you to get here. I have a business to run. You might as well come in. I already have a conference room cleared out for you."

Not waiting for the officers to follow, Gerard moved back into the building. The officers standing behind the detective trailed him through the door. Detective Harris stood for a moment, a quizzical look passing over his face. Finally, he mounted the stairs and passed into the building.

As Jess and Linda sat in companionable silence, several more police officers passed them as they moved equipment into the building. Finally, two officers shrugged on long white coats as they passed up the stairs, a slight breeze pushing them along as they disappeared inside. The white jackets brought the scene in the basement to Jess's mind once again; he tried to bury the thoughts while he waited.

"Jess, they want to see you in here." Jess turned just in time to see Gerard on the other side of a partially opened glass door. He stared as the door finished closing, anxiety building in the pit of his stomach. Glancing at Linda, he rose, heading up the stairs and over to the glass doors. Jess slapped his badge against the reader, but the motion wasn't answered with a small beep.

Linda's voice came up from behind him, saying, "The door is unlocked..."

Gerard hadn't waited for him. The heavy wooden door between the lobby and the hallway was just closing behind him, so Jess rushed over to catch up to him. Gerard led Jess to a conference room, the windows opening up over a lake ringed by squat brick, concrete, and glass buildings. Research Triangle Park didn't allow the buildings to rise above the tree line, so the buildings tended to fall into a repetition of designs.

Gerard cleared his throat with a low bruffing sound and turned around sharply on the ball of his foot, standing sideways between the table and Jess. "This is Sergeant Stone. I think you met Detective Harris outside." He then fell silent. Sliding out of the conference room, he left Jess alone with the two officers. Jess heaved a sigh of relief.

Sergeant Stone glared at him through squinted eyes. Jess thought he looked like a ferret rather than a man, incongruently wearing a sharply pressed uniform. The leather around the sergeant's waist gleamed. Only combat boots in boot camp could have matched the shine.

Detective Harris looked rather more placid as he indicated the chair. Once Jess had taken the seat indicated, he understood how the detective's tie had come to have soft edges. Detective Harris fidgeted with the tie, looking a little disconnected, wearing an expression of the older military men Jess had known. *Retired on active duty*, Jess thought. *He'll want to clear this up and get out of here. It's Friday.*

Detective Harris said, "Tell me, as closely as you can, what happened this morning."

"Well, I came in to work a bit early, like I always do, to clean up any calls that were opened the night before. Gerard doesn't like to have any major cases open when he gets in. He says it disturbs his first cup of coffee and upsets his stomach—"

"Okay, we don't need that much detail to start. Why did you go down to the basement?"

"I had a voice mail when I got into the office from Jamie, down in the network operations center. She said there was a server down and I should go check on the trouble ticket and clear it up as soon as possible. Generally, that means first thing in the morning, before I start on anything else."

Detective Harris started to speak, but the sergeant broke in. "Is the message still there?"

"I would guess so. I...I didn't delete it, anyway. I never do until after I've solved the problem." Detective Harris held a quizzical look on his face, so Jess continued. "It's a personal system I have to keep me from losing track of important problems."

Sergeant Stone slid a phone across the polished surface of the conference room table, turning it as he shoved it in front of Jess. "Think you can play it for us from here?"

"Sure, hang on a second." Jess hit the speakerphone button and then dialed in to the main number. He dialed his own extension and stepped through the menu options to retrieve his voice mail. A bit nervous, he punched in the wrong password a couple of times. Finally getting into his mailbox, he pressed 1, as instructed by the canned female voice, to play his saved messages.

Sergeant Stone's eyes narrowed. "You always have that much trouble getting into voice mail?" Jess wondered if he could even see when he screwed his eyes down that hard.

"Well, honestly, only when I'm using a real telephone. I normally use the phone from my computer." A look of surprise crossed the sergeant's face. "I am a computer geek, you know. Would you like me to play the message now?" Detective Harris nodded. He pressed 1 to play back all of his messages.

"Jess, this is Jamie in network operations. We got a problem, row fifty-three, rack twenty. I've poked it from this side, but no juice, so it looks like it's on your end."

Detective Harris looked satisfied, but he said, "We'll check with Jamie to make certain she was actually on duty and that she can corroborate the timing of the call. Mind telling us what was wrong with the server before you describe what you found down in basement?"

"Sure, it was a loss of carrier, that's all."

"What does that mean?"

"'Loss of carrier' means the cable is either cut, damaged in a way that prevents it from carrying a signal, or unplugged. Typically, each network interface emits some sort of a constant signal, called the 'carrier,' across the cable plugged into the interface. When the cable is damaged or destroyed, the carrier signal is lost, bringing the interface down." Jess continued, half to himself, "Dying is a lot like a loss of carrier, isn't it? Your soul unplugs from your body, and then you go to see GodI wonder if Carl was happy or unhappy to see God? It's always hard to tell when you're on the outside looking in..."

Sergeant Stone broke his contemplation. "Why not call it a disconnected cable?"

"Well, why do you say you're putting an all-points bulletin out on someone when you could just as well say you're trying to find them?"

Laughing, Detective Harris said, "Point taken. I assume this doesn't relate to what happened, does it?"

"I actually don't know whether it relates or not. I was just—"

"—answering the question," Detective Harris finished for him. "So what Jamie said led you to believe the cable was unplugged?"

"Well, not really. Jamie can't really see what's going on in the data center because she's in the network operations center about a half an hour from here, on the north side of Raleigh. I started by trying to connect to the server in several ways, but when I couldn't, I decided I should to go down there to see what was going on with the physical connections."

"Why not just go down there in the first place?"

Jess didn't want to tell the detective the place was dreary and depressing. "Well, there's not much room to work in the data center."

"It looked like there was a lot of open room—"

"No, I mean there aren't any chairs or desks or anyplace to put a laptop while you're working. Flat spaces collect junk. Junk in a data center would be a bad thing all around."

"Could you have seen the cables using the security cameras?"

"No, I don't think so. At least I've never tried to use them for that; I don't think you can see that level of detail in them. Besides, I'd have to run up to the security office to look at the camera output. The data center isn't much farther, and I could fix the problem from there if there was one."

The detective seemed put off by this answer. "Wouldn't someone with the access you have to the company's computers have access to the security camera recordings from your desk?"

"No. Gerard is very strict about who can access what sort of information on the network."

Detective Harris considered this for a moment and then continued. "So you did some things to try and solve the problem from your desk, and then you went down to the data center. And what did you find out?"

"The lights were off. I stubbed my toe on the mouse ears—"

"Was it normal for the lights to be off?" Detective Harris asked.

"Yes—well, no. You see, there's a sensor in the room that turns the lights on when you walk in."

"And they didn't come on when you walked in?"

"No. So I felt around the wall for the switch and started turning the lights on."

Detective Harris made some notes on a small pad of lined green paper sitting at an angle on the table in front of him. "Did you see anything unusual when you turned the lights on, or did everything look normal at that point?"

"There were a ton of floor tiles pulled up. I don't know why they were pulled up, but most of them were in the main aisle."

Detective Harris looked up from the notepad, locking onto Jess's eyes. "It's unusual for the floor tiles to be pulled up?"

"It's dangerous. The rule is you're supposed to only have one up at a time, and then you're supposed to put them all down before you leave the room, for any reason."

"And then?"

"I started putting the floor tiles back down. It took me a while. You have to use the mouse ears to pick each one up and set it back into place."

Sergeant Stone broke in, apparently irritated. "Why did you do that instead of attending to the server first?"

"I couldn't walk to the server without putting the tiles back to walk on. Besides, safety first."

The sergeant's fingers drummed on the table in front of him. It was an unsettling sound, but then he probably intended it to be. "What are mouse ears?"

"They're, well, its two suction cups fastened to a metal bar. They look like mouse ears."

The sergeant's drumming intensified. "I certainly wish you hadn't tampered with so much—"

Detective Harris broke in. "Okay, let's not go too deep in the condition of the evidence and what should or shouldn't have been moved. Let's try to get through the rest of the events."

"I hung up the mouse ears and went back down to the row the server was on. When I walked into the row, I saw Carl there, hung from the Ethernet cables. His arms were through some of the cables, as if he..." Jess trailed off, starting to feel queasy.

Detective Harris came around the table, bringing a trash can with him while motioning for Jess to bend over in the chair. Jess stayed bent over until he felt a little better for a bit, and then he sat back up. "It's fine, Jess. It's going to take a while to get over that initial shock of seeing someone you know dead like that." Settling back into his chair, Detective Harris continued. "Now, tell me, did it look like an accident to you?"

Jess knew the question was rhetorical. There was no way it had been an accident, and he knew the detective could easily see it couldn't have been. "No, I don't see how it could have been an accident. The cable had been unplugged from its normal jack and plugged in someplace else. No, it wasn't an accident, that's for certain."

"Okay, thanks. I think we have the rest, so we can build an almost complete picture now. There are a couple of things we still need to check on, but we can wrap this up pretty quickly. It looks pretty simple to me."

"Do I need to stay in the building or something? Am I free to go?"

"You're free to go, Jess," Detective Harris said. "I don't think we'll need you again unless we need you to testify, but I doubt it."

Jess stood up, stretching the tense muscles in his legs. He turned on his heel and started moving towards the door.

Detective Harris continued, saying, "It's a pretty clear-cut case of suicide."

Jess spun around again, almost knocking the chair over. "*Suicide?*" He stabilized the chair and continued. "Carl wouldn't kill himself."

Detective Harris lowered his voice to match the quiet in the room. "That's a common reaction, but all the facts point in that direction. Mr. Mattingly, your manager, says the victim had a run-in with a girl last night. He and the victim left a company party at around eleven, and he sat outside with the victim to calm him down. Mr. Mattingly eventually followed him home to make certain he was okay."

Harris looked down at his notes before continuing. "This morning, the victim came in to work as usual, before anyone else got here. Mr. Mattingly tells me the victim was normally here before anyone else, anyway, so that's not unusual. He then proceeded to the basement and hung himself. Of course, we'll check these times with some other people who were at the party, but that much seems clear."

Jess was only half listening, his mind going through the events of the morning, trying to make sense of them.

"And Mr. Mattingly says the victim was depressed lately, so that fits. And then there's the note," said Harris.

"The note?"

"Oh yes, like most suicide victims, the victim left a note. In e-mail. We printed a copy out so I could keep it in the file."

"Can I see it?"

Detective Harris shrugged and sifted through a pile of papers, finally choosing one and sliding it across the table.

Jess, stunned, picked the paper up and read it through. The individual sentences certainly seemed like they were written by Carl, but the flow, the way the sentences were put together, they didn't have the right rhythm. Unconvinced, Jess laid the paper back on the table. "The water spots on his car—"

Detective Harris didn't let Jess's response become a complete sentence. "I know this must be hard for you. It's always hard to accept that someone you know and like committed suicide, but there it is."

"It's not a matter of my liking Carl, Detective, it's just that—"

Indicating the door, Detective Harris said, "Then I'm glad it's not your case. That's the way we're going to report it, so it's over and done with."

Jess stepped into Carl's cube and sat down. Carl's laptop was still there, looking forlorn with a cold, dark screen. The walls were a mishmash—a calendar of pictures of pretty girls, a waterfall of industry conference badges, pictures of all his cars, one year after the next pinned one on top of the other. Pictures of Carl standing next to famous people Jess didn't recognize. It was personalized, and yet it didn't say anything about Carl himself. Who was Carl, really? What would the office be like without him?

"Hey, get out of here!"

Jess spun in the chair and found Gerard standing in the cubicle's entryway.

"What?"

"I said you need to get out of here. It's not like you and Carl were close or anything, were you? Something going on I didn't know about?"

"No. Sorry, Gerard. Just thinking, that's all."

"Well, go think someplace else, would you? You're just going to drive yourself crazy sitting there thinking about this thing. I need you to be on top of your game on Monday morning. With Carl gone, there's going to be a lot of work to do. Get out of here—go do something other than work for today."

As Jess brushed past Gerard, he turned to look one last time into the cubicle, assuming it would be cleaned out by the time he got to work on Monday. The whiteboard was erased, and the new messages light had gone out.

Jess walked back outside and sat heavily in the same place he had been sitting before. Linda was no longer there, but her car was still in the lot. Instead of leaving, Jess decided to wait until she came back out.

He felt the doors opening behind him; a few moments later, Linda sat beside him. "I know *that* look. What's bothering you?"

"What are the odds Carl would commit suicide? It doesn't fit. There's something wrong."

"Gerard said he was depressed, and the detective said there was a suicide note."

"Did you notice him being depressed? Did you read that note? It wasn't Carl's."

She sighed. "We can't ever tell what's going on inside another person. Gerard knew Carl better than anyone else around here, so we can't do anything other than trust what Gerard says, can we?"

"I suppose you're right. But something doesn't add up. This whole thing just isn't elegant. His car was wet, so it had to have been sitting there all night. He didn't make coffee, which is way out of character for him. His voice mail hadn't been checked this morning. The lights were off in the data center. I don't get it. It just feels wrong to me."

"And then there's the way he committed suicide. Who would have thought of hanging yourself from some cables in the data center?" Linda sighed. "I know, you're probably right; it doesn't add up. But does life ever add up? Think about it, Jess—what can you do? You don't have access to the evidence, and you don't have any authority. You shouldn't get involved."

"I don't like loose ends."

"And no puzzle can rest unsolved around Jess Wirth, can it?"

"All the signs point to him being here all night."

"Maybe he did come in here last night and committed suicide then instead of this morning. What difference does it make?"

"Then why did the detective say Gerard had followed Carl home to make certain he got there safely? No, things aren't fitting."

"Jess, I think you should let this go. There's nothing you can do here, no matter how much you think the pieces don't fit. Go do something special this weekend. Go out on the lake for a while or buy something. Things will look different on Monday morning."

The doors burst open behind them; Detective Harris slid between them on the steps. Jess turned to see Sergeant Stone holding the door open for the two men who were wearing long white coats and carrying a stretcher covered in a sheet. He traced their progress down the ramp beside the side of the steps.

"Detective Harris?"

"Yes?" The detective turned away from the men carrying the stretcher into the lot, towards Jess.

"I was just curious about what time Carl died. I'd hate to think..."

"That he was wrapping those yellow cables around his throat while you were inside? That data center's kept cold, really cold, like a refrigerator. There's no way of telling how long he was dead, other than it was sometime between ten o'clock last night and this morning when you found him."

Jess trailed the group out into the parking lot and stood unlocking his door.

"Hey," yelled Gerard, "I know what you should do! You should go get a new truck this weekend. Look at that car Carl was driving—why do you think he got all the girls, anyway? Stop doddering around in that old thing and get something worth looking at. Maybe the girls will actually pay attention to you then."

Jess started to say something back, but he decided it wasn't worth getting into an argument with his boss over his choice of lifestyle. Jess remained standing there, thinking, while Gerard got into his car and drove off. Linda wandered over.

"Just let it all go, Jess. It's not worth it."

Jess smiled at her. "We'll see what turns up on Monday."

All the way home, though, details about Carl's death troubled him. The feeling was like those he had when dealing with an out-of-place point in a network design, a misplaced piece of code, or scripts that didn't quite do what he wanted. He'd often felt the same uneasiness when reviewing network changes or proposed configurations that just didn't make sense. Something was definitely out of place here. *Elegance*, he thought, *the defining barometer of all engineering projects*. This suicide wasn't elegant; it had too many loose ends, too many holes.

He started to formulate a plan.

Chapter 03

Leah stared at the e-mail opened on her computer screen, her chair squeaking as she rocked back and forth. "Do you think we should change our plans at all? I feel like I've read this e-mail a hundred times, and I can't sort out what impact this is going to have on our investigation."

Daniel peered over her shoulder. "You're going to gut me with that chair if you don't calm down a little."

"Sorry." Leah stopped herself from rocking the chair.

"Okay. So our primary suspect committed suicide. His body was discovered this morning by one of the other employees."

"Odd sense of timing," Leah switched to another application, looking up the name of the detective assigned to the suicide case. "Think we should ask the detective a few questions?"

"I don't know if we should."

"Oh, yes. The mole. A tip they'd received indicated one of the local police officers was tied into the mess Homeland Security had sent them out to investigate. "I doubt its Detective Harris, though." She turned to face Daniel, the chair giving a squeal of disapproval. Daniel's face held an expression matching that of the chair.

"Why don't you think Detective Harris is the mole?"

"I just don't."

Daniel smiled. "You're going to have to do better than that."

"He's an old family friend. I don't think he would be mixed up in something like this."

"Before, or after?"

She sighed; this was a topic she hated to discuss. "Before my parents died."

"Have you talked to him since then?"

"No." She knew he'd only asked to emphasize the point. He knew she hadn't talked to anyone from her past once her parents died.

"Things change."

"Sometimes, yes." She weighed her next words carefully. "But Detective Harris isn't someone who's likely to change."

"Never postulate ahead of the facts."

"Thanks, Sherlock. So, what's our next move?"

"You're asking me? You're running the case. Do you think Carl might have known we were getting ready to trace down where the stolen data was coming from?"

"We don't know if he was definitely involved, do we?"

"I'm certain you're hoping he wasn't. He seems like your type. Fast cars, lots of partying..." His lips turned up into a wolfish smile.

Her hands clenched on the chair arms. Leah wanted to slap him, but she had to make do with glaring across the black rims positioned in front of her eyes. It was late, and she was tired. No reason to get into an argument right this second. She rocked a few short times, and then willed herself to stop. "Never postulate ahead of the facts. Isn't that what you always say? Anyway, his death might be the end of the situation."

"It might. Or it might not. It would be convenient, but we can't tell at this point. Maybe we should go see our resident computer geek. He might have come up with something by now." Daniel padded out of the cubicle and down the hallway. He *was* like a big cat, sleek and certain of himself. Too certain of himself.

Leah closed out her e-mail and shut down her computer. What was the name of the conference room Thuan had reserved? The Aardvark? No, they weren't in there. The Inspector? No, no one was in there, either. The Pink Panther. The lights were on—that was it.

Thuan was there, his head lowered behind the screen. She knew he was typing from the movement of his arms, but there was no sound. It was eerie the way he moved his fingers across the keys without making any noise. Daniel was standing, hunched over so he could see what Thuan was doing.

"Slowpoke." Daniel didn't glance up as she entered the room.

"Anything happening?"

"It looks like there's chatter."

"What's the deal?"

Thuan glanced up, over the top of the laptop. "A thousand identities or so. It's all planned for tomorrow. It looks like medical records, credit files, and some other odds and ends correlated into identity records."

Leah sighed. "Well, either our suspect wasn't really involved, or this is stuff that was put together before he committed suicide."

Daniel studied her. "We all wish these identities weren't being stolen in the first place. Getting cold feet?"

It was terrible to be relieved at someone's death, but if the identity thefts had stopped, it would have solved a lot of problems. And it would have shut down the investigation before she had to make the hard decisions she knew were awaiting her.

"A little, I guess. Was there a delivery method specified this time?"

Thuan shook his head. "Just the usual jumble of nautical terms. The messages are too cryptic; there must be a back channel besides the e-mail accounts we've been monitoring."

Leah considered this. Nautical terms. The presence of so many nautical terms had been the reason one of the people sitting in this room had been at every boat show in the Raleigh area for the last year. Tomorrow it was her turn. It wasn't that she minded the boats, but she did mind standing on her feet all day. And the guys. So many men asked her out on dates when she was working a booth at the boat show. Not a one, so far, had been what she was looking for. If she had even been looking. "I suppose I'll have to go on tomorrow anyway, then."

Thuan smiled. "It is your turn, isn't it?"

She grimaced. "I suppose the data could be carried out by hand and deposited someplace at the various shows. Carl Sparks did buy a Jet-Ski recently. A nice one. According to the dealer, he paid cash for it."

Daniel said, "He could have been using that new Jet-Ski to deliver the information by boat someplace on one of the lakes around here. There are three or four to choose from. And hundreds of miles of shoreline."

"Yep," Leah replied. They had been over the possibilities before. Leah had even spent time on her PWC wandering around the hundreds of miles of shoreline Daniel had alluded to. They had all spent hours poring over topographical maps, trying to figure out where someone might meet to exchange data disks. The problem was there were just too many good spots. "Are we certain it's not coming out through the network?"

Thuan glanced up from his laptop again. "If it is, I can't see it. Most of their traffic is encrypted, though, so it could be hard to see from here."

"How much do we know about the suicide?" Daniel asked.

Leah checked the screen in front of her again. "Not much. The report hasn't been entered into the system yet, so we can't see it."

Daniel looked over Leah's shoulder at the screen in front of her. "Detective Harris is a bit old-fashioned, isn't he? Most folks would type their initial report into the computer, rather than doing it all on paper to be entered later. If the data is still coming out, then we need to reconsider our suspects and change our focus. Who else inside the company seems technically competent enough to get this data?"

Images of each of the employees flashed through her mind. "The only two left are Gerard Mattingly and Jess Wirth."

"Mattingly is the general manager or something like that, right?"

"Yes, he manages the whole place. The person who committed suicide reported to him, in fact," said Leah.

"You think Mattingly would know how to get this data and get it out of the network?"

"He ran the network before he moved into management, so I think it's possible."

"Couldn't it be anyone if the data is being physically carried out the door?" Daniel asked.

"No," Thuan said, "you have to know where to get the data, in terms of where the data is on the servers. And you have to know how to format it, to correlate it so it all makes sense. This isn't something just anyone could do."

Leah said, "I think we should focus on those two, for now. I'll know more when I start working at OptiData on Monday. We might as well wrap up here. We're not going to find anything else out tonight."

Thuan pressed a few buttons on his laptop and unplugged it from the wall.

"Leah, want to go out this week?"

"No, Daniel." He apparently had no idea how she felt about him. He seemed so perceptive, and yet he didn't seem to understand how much she disliked him. She could deal with it at work, but dating him? No way.

"No? C'mon."

"No."

"I promise I won't bite."

"No."

He shrugged and turned, moving out the conference room door.

"How many times has he asked you?" asked Thuan.

"At least a hundred over the last two years, it feels like."

"Good thing he's not your boss. I think you tolerate him sometimes, and other times he drives you crazy."

"How do you know that?"

"Just a feeling I had. I was wondering if you turned him down for your career, or if it's just Daniel himself you don't like."

"Both." Leah didn't mind giving up her personal life for a while in order to build a career. It was what all the rookies were expected to do, anyway. There was time enough for a family later, once you moved into a desk job. It was the relationships on the side that developed from this practice she didn't like. Friendships with privileges, they called them.

"Kinda figured that. You've not accepted a single date since you came to work here."

"You've never asked, have you?"

"I'm too smart to." He smiled and snapped his laptop cover closed.

"Have a good night, Thuan. Don't stay too late."

"Thanks, Leah. Have a good night."

Leah trudged down the hallway to her cubicle. She slid her laptop into its case, pulled her keys out, and headed out to the parking lot. She would have to choose which of the two suspects to pay the most attention to when she got into place on Monday. Of the two primary suspects, Jess Wirth seemed to be the more likely one. He had more to gain, less to lose, and better access to the equipment the data was stored on. The lights on her Jeep flashed as she hit the button on the key to unlock the door. In the light, she could see Daniel leaning against the side of her truck.

"What is it, Daniel?"

"Please go out with me next week. I'm not your boss; you don't have to worry about it impacting your career or anything."

"I've already said no, Daniel."

He sighed and moved out into the parking lot. "I just don't get it, Leah. One date isn't a big deal."

"And I doubt you ever will."

Chapter 04

Jess started awake, the loud beeping of the alarm clock interrupting his sleep. He rolled, pulling his hands away from his neck and slapping the top of the clock. Was it already time to get up?

Why could he remember the dream he awoke to? He normally didn't remember dreams. And in this case, he didn't want to. He was trapped in a long, narrow space, his hands bound to something, not able to move. A thin yellow cord was pulling tight around his neck. He grabbed at the cord but was unable to free himself.

For an eternal moment he was trapped there, struggling in his dream, when the beeping alarm had saved him, pulling him up into consciousness. As his mind cleared, the fragments of the dream morphed into memories of finding Carl's body.

He slipped out of bed, shook the memory off, and jumped into his clothes. Was it a good idea to buy a new PWC today? He had been planning this for months, waiting for the boat show rather than driving down to the marina he normally did business with. The prices were sometimes good at the boat show, and he could shop around to make certain the PWC he had picked out was right, or if there was something else he needed to look at.

He continued arguing with himself as he downed some breakfast, and finally, as he drained the last of the coffee from his mug, he added one more reason to the list—to forget about finding Carl's body for at least one day.

The ticket booth was a small, dilapidated wood frame building, white paint peeling from every flat surface. He slid his money through the window. The lady inside, looking tired, picked it up. She counted it carefully, took a sip of coffee from a paper cup, and tore a ticket from a big roll. She pushed the ticket through the window.

He walked three steps to the door and handed his ticket to an older man sitting in a brown folding chair. "Why do they bother selling tickets over there, if you're just going to collect them a few feet away? It's not much of a walk between the two."

"Well, I don't want to handle the money."

It didn't make sense, but he wasn't about to convince them it would be better not to hand the ticket out at all. He headed through the double doors and out into a forest of masts. On his right was a forty-five-foot yacht, the dark blue strip curving from the stern to the bow and finishing up in a perfectly matched stripe on the truck parked in front of the boat.

Jess strode up the gangway and onto the deck. A full-color brochure bragged the boat came with a "full-service galley, complete with a knife block that will hold knives *at any angle*."

"Interested in a new boat?"

Jess considered the brochure for a few more moments and then glanced down at the price. He took his breath in. That much?

"Um, no. More than I can afford."

"The truck comes with it. Show special."

"No thanks."

Jess trotted down the gangplank and headed for the small hallway connecting two of the buildings. The forest was behind him now, and hundreds of power boats, marooned on blocks of wood and foam, were in front of him.

The first marina in his path didn't have any PWCs on display, but he stopped anyway. Looking didn't cost anything, did it? Stepping up a set of stairs, he walked along a carpeted platform that was set between boats arranged stern to stern on either side.

Picking up a brochure for the boat he was standing in front of, he began to sort out the seating options. It didn't make sense to him how they could claim a boat this size could carry eight people; the hull just wasn't large enough, no matter how you arranged the seats.

"Hi! Can I help you with something?"

Jess turned to find a young lady in loose jeans and a polo shirt standing behind him. She must work at the marina, given the marina's logo embroidered where the pocket would normally be. Her dark brown hair fell to below her shoulders, and her eyes were gray.

"Hi, I'm Leah. Are you looking for anything in particular?"

Gray. A most amazing shade of gray.

"I notice none of these have props." He pointed to the eighteen-foot open-bow runabout in front of him. "What do you think would work well for that one?"

"Well, it always depends, of course."

She was probably stalling for time. A lot of the folks working at the boat shows didn't know anything about the boats themselves. They were either temp hires, just for the weekend, or they were folks pulled out of the back room someplace, usually an admin assistant or a finance person.

She jumped off the platform and examined the foot of the stern drive, reading the label mounted there. "This is a two-hundred-horse stern drive with a one-point-six gear ratio that runs at around four thousand rpm. I'd probably put a twenty-two-inch three blade on it. You could go higher I think, but with that hull at that weight, you'd not be able to pull turns well. It would tend to cavitate and dump off plane if you pulled the wheel over hard."

Okay, so she knew something about boats. She'd certainly proposed a plausible prop faster than he could have, and without looking at any charts or tables.

She climbed back on the platform. "So, is that what you're looking for?"

"No, not really."

"Let me see. You're probably more of the deck boat type, I'd guess. Planes like a runabout, but has the space and stability of a pontoon when it's anchored. Have you ever looked at a deck boat?"

"I don't think I've ever looked at a deck boat. Can you show me one?"

She headed down the platform; Jess trailed behind her. Stopping at another boat, she said, "This is a twenty-foot modified V with a one-ninety in it. The gear ratio is a little higher, so a twenty-two-inch prop would probably work here. Probably a four blade would be best on this one. Is this something you'd consider?"

A cute girl who knows about boats. And gray eyes.

"Cat got your tongue?"

Someone snickered behind him. Jess turned to see another salesman walking up behind him. He passed so he was behind Leah and stopped there. "She often has this effect on guys. Pretty amazing, isn't it?" He winked at Jess and said, "She's single, too."

Leah turned. He could only imagine the sort of look she must have given him, but when she turned back, she was smiling again.

"Sorry. I'm really not looking for a boat today. I'm really just looking at new PWCs." He took a brochure out of his pocket and handed it to her. As he pointed to the model he'd spent time researching, he said, "Do you sell these, or anything similar?"

Leah took the paper from his hand and considered it for a minute. "No, we don't any longer. And the brand we carry now doesn't have anything comparable."

The salesman looked over her shoulder, examining the brochure as well. "Funny, we quit selling that brand about six months ago. Just before we stopped, there was a guy who bought one. He paid cash. I remember it because it was so odd, someone walking in and buying something like that cash, counting out the bills on the finance guy's desk. Another thing I remember is he wanted it to be maroon. And he had some odd looking tattoos, too."

Maroon PWC. Cash. Tattoos. "Was his name Carl?"

The salesman moved up past Leah so they were in a triangle, facing each other. "Yep, that was his name. How do you know him?"

"I work with him. Or rather, I worked with him." Leah looked surprised.

Now it was Jess's turn to poke a little fun at her. "Cat got *your* tongue?" He smiled.

"No, I was trying to figure out where I'd heard that name before. Wasn't he in the papers just this morning?" asked Leah.

"Yeah, well, I'd rather not talk about it right now."

She looked at the other salesman. "I don't remember him. I must not have been there the day he came by."

"It's not like he was your type, anyway. Not that I can figure out what your type is."

Leah smiled. "I keep it secret. Otherwise, every guy in the world would know just what to say to steal my heart. Anyway," she said, turning to Jess, "so you and this guy worked together? I remember now. His name was Carl Starks. Didn't he commit suicide or something?"

"According to the police, that's what happened, yes."

"Well, I'm sorry to hear it."

"Yeah, sure. We weren't close or anything, but it is still a bit of a shock. I wish y'all sold a PWC I could look at to compare this model to, though."

"There's nothing out there that compares directly. If that's the one you want, then I'd get that one; I wouldn't spend my time looking at anything else."

"Well, thanks anyway."

"Hope to see you around!" Leah turned away, leaving him to wander off the platform on his own. As he walked down the steps, he glanced up to see a large banner hanging from the ceiling with a familiar logo. The marina he normally did business with had their floor space just a short walk away.

Heading over to their area, he browsed through the boats and then moved into the PWCs. Finding a model similar to the one he had researched, he climbed on and started looking at how the controls were laid out.

"Jess! What are you doing here? You're not looking at a new PWC, are you?"

"Hey, Mike." This was the salesman Jess normally dealt with, so he felt no need for formalities. "As a matter of fact, I think I am. I've not splurged in a while, and my PWC is getting pretty ratty looking. How much does this thing weigh?"

"This one is seven hundred and fifty pounds dry weight. I think your truck could handle it, though I've always said you shouldn't be pulling a PWC with that thing. You need a four-wheel drive."

Jess pulled his leg over the seat and leapt lightly to the ground. Handing the shiny brochure to the salesman, he pointed to one of the pictures there. "Do you have this model?"

"They discontinued it. The one you were just on is the replacement. It's a four-cylinder one-point-eight-liter four stroke. How does it feel?"

Jess pulled up the seat, checking out the storage space underneath. It seemed roomy enough, plenty of space for a couple of hanks of line, some bumpers, and lunch, at least. "This looks nice, but is there anything equivalent I should be looking at?"

The salesman smiled. "Now you know I wouldn't sell you second best, don't you, Jess?"

Jess laughed. "Oh, I'm certain. All you salesmen are alike. Do you have one in stock? I'd like to spin one before I trade my old one in."

"What color are you looking for?"

"Red, I think. The old one is blue. Time for a change."

"You want to run down this afternoon and look at it? I'll call them and see what we have. I'll also make certain you get the show price down there. No point in coming here first unless you get the discount, is there?"

After a few moments on the phone, the salesman returned. "Yes, we have one in stock. It already has a GPS and a depth finder mounted. Is that okay?"

"What sort of GPS?"

"One of the new fancy ones that overlays a satellite photo map onto the topology map."

"Well, I guess it won't hurt to look at it."

"I'll give them a ring back and tell them you're coming. Say five o'clock?" the salesman said as he walked away again to place the call. He came back a few moments later. "Are you going to want financing?"

"How much are we talking?" The salesman quoted a figure. "No, I don't think so. I'll bring a check with me." As the salesman walked off, Jess looked up to find Leah looking at him. The moment he saw her, she turned and walked quickly away.

The salesman stepped up in front of Jess holding a piece of paper ripped from a small pad he was carrying. "Bring a cashier's check for this amount. We'll deal with whatever's left on a personal check, so we can have you on the water tomorrow rather than Monday."

On his way out, Jess stopped by a stand selling life jackets. He carefully selected one that would match the color of his new PWC and took it up to the long table where the salesmen were standing.

"This doesn't look like it would be comfortable to swim in. Would it be?"

The salesman replied, "No, it's designed for riding on a PWC all day rather than for swimming. More of the bulk is up in the shoulders, which thins down the bottom side for better comfort. Most people buy one for riding and another small one for swimming, or they just toss a couple of throws on their PWC." The salesman indicated a rack of small, round, throwable floats.

Indicating the life jacket on the table, Jess said, "I'll take one of these and two of the throws."

Chapter 05

Jess woke up on Sunday morning after a peaceful night of rest. No dreams about Carl, Ethernet cables, or the data center. He looked at his clock. There was plenty of time to hit the early Apex Grace, pick up a sandwich, and eat lunch on the lake. Especially since he'd left the new PWC hitched up to his truck last night rather than backing it in under the carport like he usually did.

In fifteen minutes he was drinking a cup of coffee with one hand and steering with the other. Skipping church would have been an option if it weren't for his mother's constant admonitions to go and meet a nice girl. Not that it had ever worked before, but he didn't want to disappoint his mother. Well, the pastor's grandkids would miss him if he didn't come to church on a regular basis.

The back pew on the right side was empty, so he slid just past the end, watching the people as they moved in through the two sets of double doors in the back. The back pew was perfect for this morning. Not that he didn't want to hear the sermon, but he really wanted to be out on the lake.

After the sermon, the ushers moved down the aisles, passing the offering plate from pew to pew. Jess took the plate, dropped a check in, and handed it back. Past the usher, on the other side of the church, there was a very pretty girl sitting in one of the back rows. Maybe his mom was right after all.

No point in hurrying to get out on the lake, was there? The pastor always said they should say hi to visitors, after all.

He glanced to his left. The back pew in the center section was empty. It would be easy to work his way across the sanctuary and take up a position directly behind her so he would be in between her and the doors when the service ended.

The worship team's drummer kicked into a soft backbeat. A measure later, the acoustic guitar player joined in, and the worship leader stepped up to the microphone. Better to wait until the chorus—people were less likely to notice him moving across the back of the sanctuary then.

"...better is one day in your courts..."

Jess scooted across the first aisle, in front of the first set of doors, into the center section of pews.

"...better is one day in your house..."

He slid across the pew so he was just behind her but across the aisle. She had black hair pulled up into a ponytail. She looked vaguely familiar, but he couldn't place her from behind. He would probably recognize her when he could see her face.

"...better is one day in your courts, than thousands elsewhere..."

He picked up in the singing, impatient for the song to end, ready to jump out so he could be between the girl and the doors as the song ended. As the acoustic player strummed the last chord, he leapt out off the end of the pew, into the aisle, and into someone else who was moving quickly towards the doors.

"Hey, Jess. In a bit of a hurry?"

"Um, no, not really. Sorry about bumping into you, Pastor David. How are you?"

The pastor put his arm around Jess and dragged him outside the doors to get out of the way of the flood of people starting to move past.

"I'm fine. I saw you pulled in trailing a new PWC. In a hurry to get out on the water? It sure does look like nice weather for swimming today."

"Yep, that's the plan. Great sermon today, by the way."

"Thanks. One of the best lessons we can learn on love, I think. Hey, why don't you come to dinner on Tuesday night? It's been a while since we've seen you, and I'm working on some material for a new small group. Maybe you could help me with some of the preparation work?"

"Sure, why not? What time?"

"I'd say around six thirty. Is that okay? You're not flying anywhere this week, are you?"

"No, I'm not traveling this week, so that should be fine."

The pastor looked around at the crowd of people. Some were milling around expectantly, waiting to talk to him, and others were engrossed in their own conversations about their plans for the coming week or some point the pastor had made in his sermon.

"Okay, see you on Tuesday."

"Yep, see you then." Jess turned and scanned the back of the church through the doors. Not seeing her, he turned to the parking lot just in time to see her disappearing into a car parked up close to the door in one of the visitor's slots. If it weren't for bad luck—well, whatever. If she visited this Sunday, maybe she would be back next Sunday.

Jess took it easy coming out of the little cove the New Hope boat ramp was located in. There was a sandbar across the inlet, between a small, tree-covered island and the point opposite. The water wasn't low enough for the sandbar to be a problem today, but ever since he'd had to maneuver around a large cabin cruiser stuck there, its keel completely out of the water, he'd always been careful just in this spot.

The motion of the map on his GPS screen caught his attention. He reached down and pressed a button to set a waypoint. He'd never been lost on Jordan Lake, but there was always a first time. Just over the bar, he twisted the handle, popping the PWC up on plane. Turning to his starboard side, he headed up through the channel and into the main lake.

He passed under the Highway 64 bridge and waved at the wildlife officers out watching for people disobeying the No Wake signs attached to buoys floating on the funnel into and out of the spaces between the concrete abutments. As he skipped up the lake, he noticed a cove he'd not been in before on the GPS. The entrance was small as he passed it, but it opened into a substantial area. He shifted to his port side, thinking this would be a good spot to explore.

The cove did open up into a space large enough to ski in. He traced the shoreline, watching the depth finder carefully, looking for places to either stop and swim, or where he might be able to spin the PWC in circles to build up a wave pool he could jump across.

Fascinated by the GPS, he began tracing the shoreline farther up the lake, figuring out how to use its various functions. The menus were a little confusing—probably the result of trying to pack so much into such a small space.

Reaching the Farrington Bridge, he scooted under slowly, obeying the No Wake Zone signs, and moved up into the shallow water at the north end of the lake. He dropped anchor in a small cove just to the side of the eagle-watching station. After eating his lunch, he tied one of the throw floats to the PWC, pulled off his bulky life jacket, and dove into the water. He floated, watching the bald eagles pick up small silver fish in their great claws.

Chapter 06

Leah sat and drummed her fingers on the matte tan surface of the conference table. She looked across the table at Daniel and Thuan. They didn't normally have meetings on Sunday night, but this case had developed a little differently than she had expected. The information she'd learned this weekend might change the way they approached the next few months of investigation, so it was best if they actually sat face-to-face to discuss it before the week began.

Leah just wanted to get it over with. "Interesting weekend."

Daniel said, "So, tell us about it, Leah. You were tailing him all weekend. What happened?"

"I saw him at the boat show, of course. It seems like the man who died on Friday bought a new PWC, cash, just a few months ago." Turning to her left to face Thuan, she continued. "Can you check into that? Call the marina and see if they can dig up the records? I'd like to know what happened there, if possible."

Daniel pushed Leah back onto topic. "And then?"

"Apparently, Jess bought a new PWC this weekend, on Saturday afternoon. I trailed him and overheard him talking to one of the other salesmen," said Leah.

"How did he pay for it?" asked Daniel.

"He was planning on paying cash."

Daniel said, "That's an interesting coincidence. Hey, Thuan, when you ring the marina in Sanford can you see if the salesman remembers him being nervous or anything like that."

Leah waited until Thuan had finished taking notes. She hadn't noticed before how they always assigned everything to Thuan to do. "I followed him to church on Sunday morning. He almost made me out there, but he bumped into the pastor and was detained long enough for me to get out."

"Close call," said Daniel.

"You're kinda hard to hide, honestly," Thuan said.

"Thanks, I think," she replied.

"So, what happened after that?" Daniel continued. "I know you went out on the lake, but you've not told us what happened there."

"Yes, I ran down to the lake and put in at another boat ramp. I lost him for a while, but I caught up with him at the bridge under Route 64. The wildlife officers were out, so the traffic there was a bit worse than usual. They really slow people down when they're watching for wake violations. He ran into a cove north of the bridge and traced the shoreline from there all the way up to the Farrington Bridge. After that, he just did the normal stuff—hanging out in the water and watching the eagles, I suppose."

"It's odd. He traced the shoreline?" asked Daniel.

"Yeah, slower than he ran up the rest of the lake. He kept looking down at his GPS constantly."

"Like he was looking for someplace to drop something. Did he stop and investigate the shore at all? Pick up rocks, things like that?"

Leah shook her head. "Not that I saw."

Daniel considered this and asked, "Did he drop anything?"

"No. He could have just been scouting for locations, though."

Thuan said, "Like geocaching, I suppose. You just look around for something unusual, a rock or something, someplace to hide a small package, not the GPS coordinates, and then leave it there."

"Yeah, like geocaching," Leah responded.

Daniel said, "Maybe that's how they're getting the information out. It would be really hard to find a USB key or disk stuffed in a small waterproof container along that shoreline."

"Yeah, it would be. Very hard. If that's what he's doing, we'd have to just watch him and hope he leads us to the spot. My PWC is a little too obvious, though. We need a couple of fishermen who can just happen to be wherever he is all the time, casting their lines out."

Daniel replied, "That's a good idea. I'll see what I can arrange. It still seems like it would be easier to push the data out through the network connection."

Thuan looked up from his laptop. "I'm still watching that, but I've still not seen any indications. There's just no correlation between the traffic patterns and the stolen data that I can see. I've analyzed it every way I can think of. I've even been into the building and been over the network with a fine-tooth comb. There's nothing unusual in the way the network is connected. I went over the data we captured off the unencrypted side of the Internet connection, and there wasn't anything there of interest. There's just nothing I can see that points to the data being stolen that way."

Leah sighed. "I supposed we'll have to wait 'til next week to know more."

As Leah drove to the temporary apartment she was using, she considered the enigmas this case presented. They weren't any closer to finding out how that data was being stolen from OptiData's servers. They knew it was coming from there, but how?

And what about Jess? Was he a credible suspect? He certainly seemed like it, at this point. Buying new boats with cash wasn't a normal, everyday occurrence. And the way he had gone along the shoreline was odd, too. And the day before, at the boat show, he'd made a comment about Carl's suicide. He obviously didn't think it was a suicide. Why? He wasn't likely to have said anything in public if he was involved in a murder. But what made him think it wasn't a suicide? Was it connected to the data thefts? Jess would be one person to really keep her eyes on.

Chapter 07

Jess sat and listened as the voice mails reeled off his telephone. It shouldn't be possible for a Monday to be worse than usual, but this one certainly was. He sipped his cup of coffee, suddenly feeling tired. His phone rang. He watched the light blink, but he didn't pick it up. It would have been one thing if Carl had taken his work with him. As it was, Jess had to do both their jobs, at least until they could replace him.

How would this impact that new project? It would probably set it back by a couple of weeks. And what other work was Gerard going to pile on?

Plop!

"Find the three or four best résumés here. Bring them up to Linda so she can schedule interviews. I can tell you're underwater here already. There's too much work for one person to do, so we need replace Carl pretty fast. Make this your top priority."

Jess mumbled under his breath, "As if Carl can be replaced. As if we want another Carl."

"You're not precisely the socialite of the month, and we still put up with you." Gerard stalked off.

It would take a while to find someone qualified to replace Carl. Network engineers were easy to find. The problem was finding someone who really knew networking. And then Gerard would want someone who was certified. Certifications impressed customers. Customers paid the bills. It would be hard to do.

After clearing a space on his desk, Jess looked at the first résumé on the pile. No. He placed it on the cleared space and moved to the next one. No. Slowly, two piles built up in front of him. The phone rang, interrupting his reading.

He glanced up at the display, more out of habit than a real desire to find out who was calling. An outside number. Jess exhaled, placed the remaining résumés sideways across the piles, and settled the headset over his ear.

"Hello?"

"Jess Wirth?"

"Yes, why?"

"Jessica Monington *Southern Wake Observer.* Do you have a minute to talk about Carl Stark's death?"

"No, not really."

The voice on the other end of the phone continued anyway. "We're doing a longer follow-up piece on his death. Exciting time you had on Friday, huh? You found the body, right?"

"Yes." Jess kept his voice flat.

"Any impressions you want to give me from the experience? Something to add color to the story?"

"No."

"Hmmm...Did you know Carl well? What sort of person was he? Did you two travel a lot together or know each other socially?"

"Carl and I didn't exactly run in the same crowd."

"There was a suicide note, right? Did you read it?" asked the reporter.

"Yes."

"What was in it?"

"I don't think I should tell a reporter what was in the suicide note."

"Do you think this guy would have committed suicide over a girl?"

"No more than I would commit suicide over a broken string on my guitar, no," replied Jess.

"So you don't think it was over a girl? Can I quote you on that?"

"No, and no. Listen, I'm really busy. Could you call Carl's manager, Gerard Mattingly? He'll have a lot more information than I do."

"You two couldn't stand each other? Is that it?"

"Please call his manager." He could hear her continuing to talk as he pulled the headset off and hung it up on a hook stuck into the soft cubicle wall. He pushed the headset button and picked up the pile of résumés. Instead of reading, his mind wandered. He got up and headed towards the break room. He needed a glass of water, or something, to get his mind settled. As he stepped into the room, Benita looked up from cleaning one of the sinks.

"Good morning, Jess."

"Hi Benita. How are you today?"

"Good."

"You normally aren't here this time of day. You're normally gone by now, or you come in much later, right?"

"Yes, but I don't like being in this building alone anymore."

"Carl? He committed suicide, Benita. The police don't think there's a murderer walking around the building or anything like that. They've closed the case." If it was a suicide.

"Why do you think Carl was alone in the building when he died?" asked Benita.

"The police say he died in the morning, before work," said Jess.

"Oh, I didn't know that, I had always assumed—"

"Assumed what?"

Benita thought for a second and continued. "No one ever talks to me. Even the police didn't bother to question me. And Gerard, when he does talk to me, he never says anything nice."

"Gerard likes getting under people's skin, Benita. I wouldn't take that personally."

"He and Gerard were here the night before you found him, late at night. I usually don't come in until around two or three in the afternoon, and then I leave around two or three in the morning. Gerard and Carl came into the building around midnight. Neither of them had left by three, when I left. I saw Gerard in his office, working on the computer, and I saw Carl's car in the parking lot, in the rain."

"You're certain it was Gerard and not just someone else who was sitting in his office?"

"Yes, I looked twice to make certain it was him. I always wonder if someone would break into this place to steal something. There's all these computers lying around, so I always look to make certain I know who it is if someone is here. I was just on my way out, and he was there, working in his office."

———

His trip to the break room hadn't settled his mind at all. *But I really need to get on with sorting through this work.* He looked down to read the résumé on the top of the pile again.

Plop!

A newspaper fell on top of his two neatly arranged piles, setting them in disarray.

"Do you ever look at the newspaper?"

"You know I don't read that one, Gerard."

"You should. You might recognize people when they call you."

Ignoring the newspaper, Jess looked up at Gerard. "Why should I care?"

Gerard put his finger on the folded page, drawing Jess's eyes to the picture of a girl.

"And?"

"She's cute. And she's single. I checked."

"And you're married."

"I'm meeting her for lunch tomorrow. It doesn't cost anything to look." Gerard picked the paper back up and strode out of Jess's cube. Jess sorted the résumés back into neat piles, hoping he would have some peace until lunch, at least.

As Jess slid his lunch bag out of the drawer he'd placed it in that morning, he heard a rap on his whiteboard behind him.

"Hey, come out into the real world for a minute and meet this nice young lady," said Linda.

Putting his lunch bag down, he stepped out into the hallway and found himself face-to-face with the girl from the boat show. He didn't remember her name. "Well, you have caught a prize. She spent her weekend amazing people with her ability to pick the right prop for a boat off the top of her head." He shook Leah's hand and then said to Linda, "I didn't know we were selling boats now. Or did you happen to find her hanging out in the lobby with nothing better to do, so you decided to drag her around and introduce her to everyone?"

"So you two know each other already?" asked Linda.

Leah scrunched her face up in thought. "Let's see... You were asking about PWCs, maybe? So many people pass through the marina sales floors at a boat show—I can't possibly remember all of them."

"Yes, I was looking for PWCs. You were showing me the deck boats instead," Jess said.

"Right! Did you buy a new PWC at the show?" Leah asked.

"Yes, from my normal place, one of the marinas down in Sanford. I had it out on the water yesterday, in fact, trying out the GPS and trying to get used to the way it handles."

"Which lake?"

"Jordan. I ran up past the bridges and hung out by the eagle sanctuary for a while."

"Cool! I love it up there, but the water is too shallow for bigger boats most of the time."

"You know, I'm sorry, but I did forget your name."

Linda interjected. "Jess, this is Leah. Leah, Jess."

"Ah, that's right, Leah. I remember thinking it was a very pretty name when we first met at the show."

"Thanks. You didn't tell you me worked here."

"I didn't know you would be here on Monday, or I would have told you all about the place, like who to avoid—pretty much everybody except Linda."

Linda laughed. "And you, Jess."

"Isn't this the place where that guy Carl committed suicide? You said something about it at the boat show, didn't you?"

Linda replied, "Yes, but you don't need to be worrying about that. The less we think about it, the better."

Leah turned to Jess. "Do you think you could show me where sometime? I mean, not to be morbid or anything, but it is kinda interesting."

"I suppose I can take you down there sometime and show you the place, yes. You should probably know your way around the server room, anyway, in case you ever need anything down there. You're not here to work on the network, are you? I could sure use some help, but Gerard must have been working fast to find a replacement for Carl this quickly."

Linda answered before Leah could. "Now, don't you just wish she was going to work on the network! No, she's going to be taking over project management for a few projects around here. Don't worry, I'm certain at least one of them will be one of yours, so you'll be seeing plenty of her, Jess." Linda winked at him.

"Linda has warned me that you can be a bit sarcastic, though."

Jess glanced at Linda before continuing. "I'm only sarcastic to people I like. The more I like you, the more likely I am to pick on you. The real sign of dislike is being ignored."

Leah laughed. "Okay, I'll remember that. So any sarcasm launched my way is a sign of affection? You won't mind if I drop by, occasionally, for a dose of sarcasm?"

"Sure, why not? It would be a change from staring at the computer, anyway."

Linda interjected, "Most folks around here consider Jess to be a bit unsociable. You don't pay them any mind, though, Leah. Jess is fine, and he's the best technical resource you'll have for *any* of your projects, not just the ones he's working on. Anyway, we should move on; there are a few other people you need to meet before we grab a bite to eat." Linda started down the hall. Turning, Leah started to follow her.

Jess stepped out of the cube for a second to catch Leah's attention."Hey, Leah, can I ask you something?"

She turned her head. "Sure."

"Do your eyes change color depending on your mood?"

Leah blushed. "Actually, they do. What makes you ask?"

"Oh, my mom's eyes are pretty close to the same color and they change colors, so I figured yours might, too. They're very pretty." As she walked away, Jess considered asking her out on a date, but then he discarded the thought. She was way out of his league, anyway.

Setting his lunch down, he looked over the pile of work on his desk and the pile of e-mails in his inbox. There was only one way out of this mess—he would have to work late pretty much every night this week to try and catch up. That meant picking up dinner on the way home rather than making his own and stopping by to see his landlady, Ms. Parker, on the way home tonight. She was generally observant and would worry if he wasn't pulling up in his driveway in some semblance of his normal schedule. Tuesday night, at least, he wouldn't have to cook since he was going to the pastor's house for dinner. Sighing, he opened his bag and read e-mails in between bites.

Friday of the same week, just before lunch, he was sitting in the same position, looking through what felt like the same long list of problems to resolve. He had just closed one problem and was looking for another one to start on. There was nothing he felt like starting on a Friday afternoon left in the list of problems. He picked up the pile of paper trouble tickets and sifted through them. Nothing there, either.

Maybe make an early day of it. It had been a long week. But there was something else he wanted to look in to—figuring out Carl's death. He still wasn't convinced Carl had committed suicide. He considered the list of things he wanted to check and decided on one. Carl's voice mail light had been lit when Jess walked by his cube that morning, but it was off later when Jess had sat down in Carl's chair. He wondered what was in Carl's voice mail box.

He began sorting through his notes from old trouble tickets, either putting them in a pile to be scanned in later, or balling them up and shooting them into the garbage can. He didn't find what he was looking for, so he next turned to his computer. Here there were notes from older trouble tickets, if he could just find the right one. He quickly scanned the tickets, until finally—"Aha!"

He opened a new window on his computer's desktop and started a session to the voice mail server. Referring to his old case notes, he carefully typed in a username and password. On hitting the enter key, he was greeted by a menu that would allow him to modify users, back up voice mail boxes, or modify the voice mail server's settings. Happy they didn't change the password on this server very often, he clicked on the button to modify users.

No, what he was looking for wasn't there. He considered the menu for a moment. It certainly wouldn't be under the option to modify the system settings, so it must be under backups, no matter how illogical that might be. Clicking there, he found himself confronted with a long list of all the voice mail users in the company. Scrolling down to S, he found Carl's name and clicked on it.

The prompt read, "(B)ackup or (E)xport?"

Jess chose export. A dialog box popped up, asking him where to save the file. He navigated to a folder on his local hard drive and pressed the button to proceed. He then examined the screen showing each call Carl had received and the number from which the call had originated. Carl had not received any calls from Thursday around lunch. It didn't make any sense.

He thought back to last Friday morning. Carl's voice mail light had been on. Since Carl didn't ever go home without clearing out his voice mail box, and Carl was at work on Thursday, what happened to the voice mails?

Jess double-clicked on the file he'd downloaded from the voice mail server. Several dealt with cases, and there were the ubiquitous calls from salesmen, and then, finally, a very upset girl.

"Carl! This is Joanna. You promised you would call me about going out this Friday night, and you haven't! Do you want to see me or not? If I find out you're taking someone else in that new car of yours..."

Rap! Rap!

Jess quickly clicked the stop button and turned to see who was in his cube.

Leah was dropping her hand from the whiteboard, looking around his cubical. "Hey. Are you busy? I heard someone talking in here...Joanna? Does she work here?"

"No, no one else is here. I was just listening to some old voice mails is all."

A look of understanding spread across her face. "You're not listening to your old voice mails, are you? You're listening to someone else's." They stared at each for a moment.

She continued, breaking the silence. "It's Carl's voice mail, isn't it?"

What story could he come up with that she would believe? "Well, I was trying to make sure all the problems had been logged into the help desk system. In case anything had not been taken care of, it would need to be logged in. It's not like I can listen to just the voice mails that deal with cases."

"Oh." Her words implied acceptance of the explanation, but Jess could still read the doubt in her eyes.

"Is it lunch time already?"

Leah smiled. "Yes, already. You must have been so engrossed in Carl's old girlfriend's rant that you weren't watching the time."

Jess laughed. "Well, it is interesting, isn't it? I mean, if I stood a girl up, I wouldn't have anyone to date for another six months!"

"Well, honestly, I think you're too much of a nice guy to stand anyone up. Besides, it's not *that* bad, is it? Aren't you going out this weekend? Today is Friday."

"I might go hang out on the lake, but I don't have any plans with anyone, if that's what you're asking."

She smiled. "Well, that's too bad."

Was she prompting him to ask her out? He bit his lip, trying to sort out what he should do. He let the moment pass.

"Anyway, besides lunch, it seems like Gerard has assigned me to a new project to add some more bandwidth to the Internet connection. I don't understand what all these devices do, and I can't seem to find any explanations I can understand on the Internet, either. Think you can help me?"

"Sure, fire away."

As she sat down, he turned and closed the application he'd been using to listen to Carl's voice mail. He swiveled his chair around to see her pulling a few items from her lunch bag.

"There are a couple of terms from the program documentation I don't understand. I get the feeling it's going to take me a while to learn this stuff. Anyway, what exactly do routers and firewalls do?"

"Let me think how to explain." He pulled out his thermos of leftover chicken noodle soup and set it on the desk beside him. Next was bag of potato chips and then a couple of pieces of Scharffen Berger dark chocolate.

"At least you don't skimp on your chocolate. But soup and potato chips, in the middle of the spring?"

"Leftovers. It was easy, I guess."

"Sounds like you need someone to pack lunches for you if you can't be any more creative than soup on a hot day."

"Okay then, smarty. For bonus points in creativity, let's see what you have in your lunch." He smiled.

The bag crinkled as she reached back inside to pull out the last item. Holding it up, she said, "Peanut butter and jelly."

He laughed. "A peanut butter and jelly sandwich isn't any more creative than leftover soup. Want to trade?"

"I happen to think peanut butter and jelly can be very creative if you..." Then she started laughing as well. "Okay, point taken. And no, I don't want to trade." She opened the bag and took a bite out of the sandwich. "Now tell me about routers and firewalls."

"Imagine a big network of roads with no signs telling you which way to go to get anyplace. Routers are like policemen standing at the intersections between the roads, telling each driver the right way to go."

"It sounds terribly inefficient. Every driver would have to stop, and there would be lines for miles."

"Unless, of course, you had a tag on the front of every car that told the policeman where the driver was headed."

"Oh, so the policeman just reads the tag and points the direction the car needs to go. Boring life for the policeman, though," Leah remarked.

"Which is why we let computers do the work. They seem to excel at really boring things," said Jess.

"How do the policemen know how to get to the various destinations? In the real world, we have maps, but you can't have a map of a network, can you?"

Jess turned for a moment and pulled out a small, simplified diagram of OptiData's network. "Yes, you can have a map of a network. This one is ours, for instance."

She took the map and studied it for a moment between bites of her lunch. "You don't program this map into every router, do you? That would be a lot of work."

"No, of course not. There is a special program that builds a map of the network running on every router in the network. The program uses a routing protocol to automatically figure out where everything in the network is."

"Okay. And you're saying each of these little cars carries information, instead of people?"

"Yes. Packets. Does that make sense?" asked Jess.

Leah replied, "Yes, thank you. What's a firewall, then?"

"Well, it's a lot like a router, only the policeman is replaced by an airport security team."

She laughed. "Okay, that makes sense, if I can just think about it that way all the time."

Jess slurped a few spoonfuls of soup, making Leah laugh again.

"Didn't your mom ever tell you slurping's rude?"

"Is it really?"

"Don't give me that! You *know* it is. Oh, why do I bother? Anyway, let me ask you about Carl's death. The police ruled it a suicide, didn't they?"

"Yes."

From the look on her face, Jess could tell she was weighing her words carefully. "You're not convinced, are you?"

He was taken aback. Had Linda told her about his doubts? How else could she know? *How much should I trust her when I know so little? I don't know her very well.*

Leah studied his face, watching the thoughts pass through his mind. "Want to talk about it?"

He decided to play for time. "It's not a big deal."

She lifted her head and looked directly into his eyes, unnerving him even farther. "You don't think you can trust me, do you?"

Jess carefully placed his soup spoon on a napkin. He tried to hold himself steady, to appear nonchalant as his mind reeled. Had Linda talked about his divorce with Leah?

He flashed back to the buildup of scenes. The beginning, how it had been so carefree, and how he had trusted her. Their marriage, his fiancée walking down the aisle, followed by a trailing white train. The initial arguments, spending time working through them, trying to build a relationship.

And then the day he came home early to find another car sitting in his driveway. Rushing in, worried about what was wrong. And finding his wife with another man. The pain still struck him in the center of his chest, a fist pounding out his life and his trust. The immediacy of the pain, like it was just yesterday, struck him. It was really several states, and several years, in the past.

"Are you okay?"

Leah's words brought him back to the present. He tried to think about the turns the conversation had taken, trying to figure out what the right answer would be, not wanting to give any clue to the pain he still felt. Yes, that's right, she had just asked him about trust.

"It's not that. I'm just not convinced either way. I'd like to tie up some loose ends and see where they lead before I make up my mind."

She indicated his now blank computer screen. "Old voice mails are one of the loose ends?"

Now that she knew this much, what harm was there in admitting the truth about the voice mails? "Yes."

She looked into his eyes again. He couldn't look away from her. "Jess, I hope you don't get in over your head. These sorts of private investigations often spiral out of control. Maybe you should hand it over to someone who knows what they're doing."

"Like who? Who would believe me, anyway? The detective certainly didn't."

She sat in silence for a moment before answering. "I'll have to think about that one." She crinkled up her paper bag, threw it in his garbage bin, and smiled at him. "See you Monday. I hope you have a good weekend."

Again, the moment hung in the air. Should he ask her out? Again, the moment passed. "You, too."

"I'll try. Going out to dinner tonight, but it doesn't look like anything promising."

Why did her words sting? Turning back to his computer, he created a new folder. Pulling up the folder's properties, he marked it encrypted. He moved the copy of Carl's voice mail into it along with a copy of the screen he had captured from the voice mail system which showed the number and time stamp for each of the messages Carl had received. Finally, Jess created a new text file in the folder and started writing notes to himself about Carl's death. He saved it and encrypted the file again. This time, he used a different piece of software than he had used to encrypt the folder—just to make certain no one would be able to get into his little collection of information before he could sort it out.

Chapter 08

Jess could hear Jamie bubbling up the aisle between the cubicles, her voice echoing through the floor as she said hello to people, like a lemur bouncing along through other people's lives. Couldn't she be just a little quieter on a Monday morning? As she approached his cubicle, he turned to the doorway in anticipation of her arrival.

"Hey, Jess! It's great to see you!"

"Here for a meeting? I didn't know they called meetings for the help desk folks over here because it's so far for most of y'all to drive."

"A two-week rotation. *Two weeks!* Can you believe it? I love being here."

"I didn't think you liked working in Research Triangle Park. I thought you liked the building up in North Raleigh better."

"My son is in football camp just a few miles from here. Working in the Park means we can make it over for the game every night with the generator and blow-up bee we bought for his team. Isn't that great?"

"I didn't know you liked football, Jamie."

"What gave you that crazy idea? I *love* football!"

"Well, the last time you were here, you said—"

"Whatever. Did I tell you my son made MVP in the town team this year? He's made MVP every year now!"

"That's good. How's your daughter?"

"Oh, she's fine. She made the cheerleading team for her brother's football team, so she has something to do at the games, anyway."

"Um, that's good, Jamie."

"Well, I should be getting down to the security office. If you need anything from security, let me know."

The presentation for this project was in front of his face, but he had a hard time concentrating on it. The myriads of lines running all over the place in the network diagram reminded him of a rat's nest, and the rat's nest reminded him of Carl.

Opening the encrypted file he had started several days ago, he looked at the notes he already had. There wasn't a lot there so far—just some jotted notes, a weather map, and the audio file of Carl's old voice mails.

Maybe it was fortuitous Jamie's son was in a football camp that brought her down to this part of town. It would be easier to shake information out of Jamie than the other folks in the security office. He picked up the phone and dialed her number.

"Yo! This is Jamie!"

"Hi, Jamie."

"Hi, Jess! Hey, want to meet us out on the lake on Saturday? All of our friends seem to be busy. You could throw some balls to my son, and—"

"Sorry, Jamie. I'm not really planning to run out there this weekend." Jess ignored the backhanded invitation.

"Don't tell me, you have a date! My son has a girlfriend now—isn't that exciting?"

"Um, no, Jamie, I don't have a date. And isn't your son a little young to be dating?"

"He's thirteen! That's practically grown up nowadays!"

"Anyway, there is one piece of information you could help me with, if possible."

"Shoot!" Jamie said.

"Can you tell me the last time Carl badged into the building?"

"I don't know if we're allowed to tell anyone when people badge in."

Jess had already planned for this contingency, so he forged ahead without a pause. "Oh. I see. Well, that means I need to find some other way to figure out if this file was backed up correctly."

"Oh. It's for the network. I thought maybe you were just snooping around. Well, I still can't tell you, but...Remember those two visitors you had yesterday? What time did we call you to come get them from the lobby?"

"It was just at lunch time. Why?"

"Oh, just checking to make certain they were recorded in right. Anyway, it's a good thing they didn't come in around the same time at night, isn't it?"

"Then no one would have been around to pick them up from the lobby. I certainly wouldn't come in for a meeting." What was she talking about? And then he understood. "I see. It was that late when Carl came in?"

"Yep."

"Thanks, Jamie."

"Sure thing! Glad I could help! And remember, we'll be on the lake this weekend."

Jess pulled his headset from around his head and hung it on the wall. It was always a relief to hang up when he was talking to Jamie. He noted the information he'd just gleaned from Jamie in the file and saved it. Sensing someone else was in his cubicle, he turned towards the opening into the hallway.

"Leah! You startled me..."

"Mind if I sit and eat lunch with you?"

"No, not at all. Have a seat." It was becoming a habit, but it wasn't a habit Jess minded. As she started digging stuff out of her lunch bag, he continued. "How'd the date go on Friday night?"

"Maybe I should eat lunch someplace else today."

"No, please don't. I'm sorry. Was it that bad?"

"I won't be dating him again." She sighed. "Linda was right."

Jess took a bite out of his sandwich. "About what?"

"The geeks here really are all jerks. They're so full of themselves."

"I'm sorry." He took two more bites, chewing them slowly, before she answered again.

"It's not your fault. Friends?"

"Sure. Friends." Why did all the girls he know end up as just friends? "There's something else on your mind, isn't there?"

"This project I'm working on," she replied.

While guy problems were out of his league, he could certainly help her with a project. Feeling better, he asked, "Something you need help with?"

"I just don't think it's going in the right direction. Everything points in one direction, but I'm certain something is wrong. There's something I'm missing, and I can't seem to put my finger on it."

"Yeah, I've been there before."

"How would you handle it?"

"I look until I find a more elegant solution."

She laughed. "A computer network in a tuxedo?"

"Oh, it's not like that. If you've been an engineer for a while, there's a feeling that develops, a feeling about what should work and what will never work. There's also a different feeling you get when you realize you've missed an important concept or detail. I suppose it is a bit like fashion, in a way. If you saw someone wearing a tuxedo and a baseball cap to a wedding, what would you think?"

"Not too elegant."

"You would know that the baseball cap is not elegant, but you might not be able to exactly explain *why* a baseball cap wouldn't go with a tuxedo, right?"

"I suppose not."

Jess crunched his lunch bag up and tossed it in the garbage can. "When you design a network or a piece of computer software, it's hard to let it go until you've made sure that it's elegant—at least if you're a good engineer. So, what did you bring for lunch today?"

"Oh, some salad. I felt like I needed some healthy food today."

"Hmmm...you look healthy enough to me."

"Oh, shut up, would you? Are you guys all alike?" She laughed before continuing. "Aren't you going to tell me who you were talking to when I walked in?"

"If you walked a little louder I'd make certain I was finished with my conversation before you made it to my cubicle. Could you shuffle your feet or something when you're walking down the hall?" The look on her face said she was not amused by his answer. "Jamie, in security. I had some questions about when someone badged in."

"Carl?"

Jess was silent. He didn't think it would be a good idea to let someone else in on what he had collected about Carl's death. Who could he trust?

"Why would you need to call security about that? Can't you just look at the records yourself? Doesn't the badge reader system run over the network?"

"I don't have access to that system. Unless there's a trouble ticket, that is, and someone gives me the password."

"What else runs on the network around here?"

"The security cameras, the telephone system, the music piped into the elevators—pretty much everything."

"The sun?"

"No, I think God's in control of that one."

"I didn't think geeks believed in a power higher than their intelligence."

"Oh, I do, Leah. I do."

"So, what did you do on Friday night?"

"Nothing."

"No date? No girl?"

"The only girl in my life is Linda."

She laughed. "It can't be that bad."

"It is, trust me."

"Oh, come on!"

"I've not been on a date in a long time. Not a real date. At least since my divorce."

"Linda told me some stuff about that. A lot of people are divorced now, Jess. You made a mistake. We all make mistakes. As long as you learned what you did wrong and you don't repeat it, there's nothing wrong with being divorced. At least I don't think it should disqualify you from the dating pool." She looked up from her salad. "You don't seem all that horrible to me."

"It was bad, Leah. Worse than Linda knows."

Putting her fork carefully in the plastic container on her lap, she looked up at him. "I'm sorry to hear that, Jess. But no matter how bad it was, isn't it worse that it's stopping you from living your life? Maybe it's time to let it go. If God's forgiven you for this, then why should you let your past impact you this way?"

After a few moments of silence, she continued. "What was that file you were closing just as I sat down?"

"Oh, nothing."

"I'll bet that nothing was about Carl, wasn't it? I do wish you'd let me see it. I'm always interested in this sort of thing. I might even be able to help you, you know."

Not knowing what to say, he didn't answer.

"Please, Jess, don't be like this."

She tossed the remains of her lunch into the garbage can and slipped out of his cubicle.

Chapter 09

Leah tried to figure out what to do as she walked from Jess's cubicle towards her own. She had a lot of work to do. It was hard holding down two jobs like this. She changed direction, heading to Linda's cubicle instead. Maybe Linda could help her make some sense out of Jess. She needed to find some way to pry what he was keeping in those files out of him.

"Hi, Linda." She sat heavily in a chair stashed in the corner.

"Enjoy your lunch with Jess?" Her voice was muffled. She was in the back of her cubicle, kneeling on the floor in front of a filing cabinet. She was pulling papers from a pile sitting on the top of the cabinet, stuffing them into the folders hanging in the open drawer.

"So, tell me, when *was* the last time Jess went out with anyone?"

Linda turned and looked at her. "Now why would you want to know a thing like that?"

"I don't know. He just seems like a bit of a loner."

She turned back to her filing, the pile on the top of the cabinet quickly getting smaller as she worked. "He is a bit of a loner, but he gets on with people just fine when he wants to. Just has a hard time trusting folks is all."

"Was the divorce *that* bad?"

Linda deftly finished the rest of the pile on top of the filing cabinet, pushed herself up, and sat in her chair. "Not many people know. He doesn't talk about it. I know he went through a real rough time after that—had all sorts of problems. It was just after he got out of the military that he divorced, but I'm certain there were problems long before that."

Leah decided to take another tack in trying to figure out Jess's history. "Where'd the green truck come from?"

"Oh, I think I should let Jess tell you that one. You're just striking out today, aren't you? I don't know much about the divorce, only the results. And I'm not telling you about the green truck." She smiled as she leaned over, shuffling more papers on her desk, sorting them out so she could file them.

"Not many people drive around antiques like that."

"Nope." She straightened the papers and continued. "Carl used to give Jess a really hard time about it. They got into a few arguments over the truck, Jess not dating girls, and things like that. They didn't get along too well, those two."

"Really? I would have expected them to be close, being the only two folks working on the network in the company."

"Then you expect wrong. They got along about as well as oil and water, those two." Linda thought for a second and said, "You want to know more about Jess, then meet him out on the lake sometime. You probably won't get him to ask you out on a date. I'd venture to say he's about the only one around here who won't. But I think you already know that."

Leah blushed. She had gone out with, or planned to go out with, most of the guys in the building. But it wasn't because she liked any of them. Formal interviews would have been more effective than the dates, but she couldn't go to that point yet. They needed a break, a line they could follow, before they started using what would be considered normal procedures.

"Yes, I suppose most of the guys here have asked me out. Even Gerard."

Linda rolled her eyes. "Of course. He's married, but he says looking doesn't hurt. And he asks girls out that are far too young for him. That one will never grow up, I don't think."

"At least he brought up the divorce, though. Maybe he'll open up a little."

"Oh, don't start thinking that. It's going to take a lot to make Jess Wirth open up again, I'm afraid."

"So it was that bad, huh?"

"Given the tailspin he went into after, I would say so. Pastor David and his wife are probably the only thing that kept Jess from crashing hard."

"Where were his mom and dad?" Leah felt bad about prodding for information this way.

"His dad hasn't spoken to him in years. He doesn't talk about that part of his life much, either. His mom was there, yeah. But Pastor David was the one that really pushed him along, though."

Linda picked up the sheaf of papers in her hand. Turning, she spun her chair so she was facing the filing cabinet. From the chair, she could reach the bottom drawer. It didn't look any more comfortable, but it was a change, anyway, from kneeling.

Leah thought they looked like check stubs. It wouldn't make any sense for Linda to be handling real checks; most all that sort of stuff was handled through electronic transactions now. She wondered what these could be for.

"So what happened to the girl?"

"She's off in California, last I heard. Living with the other guy, if you know what I mean."

"Oh. Then it wasn't his fault."

"There's plenty enough blame to go around in any divorce. But you've not been there, so it's hard to understand. It's not the way God intended, all this divorcing we have now."

She continued her filing and then said, "Give him time, if you're really interested, Leah. Meet him on the lake. He's different when he's not at work. Or meet him after church. He eats lunch or dinner with the pastor a couple of times every month, and he does other stuff around the church."

"Oh, I'm not in a rush. I have a career to take care of first, anyway."

"Just like all the girls now. Rush around having a career, then rush around having babies, and then complain about rushing around."

Leah laughed. "I suppose so. Are those check stubs you're filing? I didn't think OptiData even had a check printer. Isn't everything done through electronic transactions?"

Linda finished the second set and turned back to her desk. "Well, not everything. These are exceptional service bonuses. When someone does something 'above and beyond,' as Gerard likes to say, he has a special check cut so he can give it to them personally."

"Interesting. Who do you think holds the record for getting the most of these?"

"Carl, by far."

"In amount, or in frequency?"

"Both. Carl used to get these checks every couple of weeks. There were some of them that were large. And the company even pays the taxes on them."

Bonuses? Leah considered this for a moment. Bonuses would be easy enough to scam, or to pay someone for work on the side, wouldn't they? "Are there records about why employees are awarded these bonuses?"

"Forms are filled out for each one. It's one of the only things around here that's not automated. The folks in IT have tried to automate it several times, but Gerard never seems to be satisfied with their proposals."

"Gerard seems to be pretty picky, isn't he?"

Linda filed the last paper and pushed the drawer closed. "He's persnickety about some things but not about others. It's always hard to tell with Gerard what's going to get him upset and what doesn't faze him at all."

Leah worked until late in the evening. She walked out to the lobby and peeked through the doors, looking at the cars in the parking lot. Gerard and Linda were both gone. She badged back in through the lobby doors and headed up the elevator.

Dropping just below the level of the cubicle walls, she took out a small pick and inserted it into the lock on the low, tan cabinet Linda had been filing in earlier in the day. A few moments later, the lock popped open, and she slid the bottom drawer open.

She quickly found Carl's file and slipped the check stubs out onto the floor. As she leafed through them, she added up the numbers in her head. The result was a figure much larger than Carl's salary, based on his regular direct deposits into his checking account. Where had this money gone? He hadn't deposited it in any of the accounts they had pulled histories on, so there must be some other account, someplace Carl was putting money they hadn't yet found.

Next she pulled Jess's folder out and checked the stubs there. There were a few bonuses, but not nearly as much. She made some notes on a small piece of paper so she could have his bank records checked to see if he normally deposited these checks.

Knowing she couldn't use any of this as evidence, she pushed the stubs back into the folder, slid the drawer closed, and pushed the lock back into place. If it came down to it, she would have to get a warrant or have the records subpoenaed. For now, she just needed enough information to try and track this money down through other channels. She considered all of this on the drive to Chapel Hill, back to the apartment she was using while she was in town working on this case.

Thuan was sitting across from her at the kitchen table, his laptop open, looking at something.

Daniel opened the conversation. "So what do you think of Wirth as a suspect?"

"The facts seem to point in that direction. He had the motive. He and Carl didn't get along at all. He has the knowledge to be stealing the data, and he's definitely hiding something. He's a loner—there's no one in his life to track his movements. On the other hand, it doesn't fit." Leah considered what Jess would say about being a suspect. "It's not elegant."

"Elegant?" Daniel looked over at the top of Thuan's head, searching for an answer. "What do you mean?"

"It just feels like there's something more here, something deeper. The problem runs higher up the chain."

"Why do you say that?"

"Well, what did we find in Jess's bank accounts?" Leah asked.

"His normal paychecks and some extra deposits here and there, maybe once every couple of months. Savings moved to another accounts, nothing unusual, until the PWC. But that doesn't mean he wasn't pulling in money on the side and stashing it someplace else or taking in cash."

"Right, but we've looked, and we can't find it. And I don't see any evidence of it in the way he lives." She slid the handwritten note across the table. "Those extra deposits, they might match some of these."

"What is this?"

"Bonus payments. Turns out Gerard likes to do things the old-fashioned way—he pays bonuses with physical checks. This is the last year or so of what Jess received."

Daniel picked the paper up, glancing along the dates and amounts scribble there. "How did you get this?"

"Don't ask. We can subpoena the records later if it turns out to be material. For now, just use this as a guide. See if it matches. It'll help us look in the right direction, provide some focus."

Daniel slid the paper over towards Thuan. "Okay, I won't ask. But be careful. We don't want to blow our case."

"I know. I'm careful."

"And you have a list for Sparks?"

Leah shook her head no. "There were a lot. I added them up in my head. It's more than his salary last year."

Daniel whistled. "That's very interesting. We didn't see that in his bank accounts."

"I think we need to find out where those checks OptiData paid Carl went."

Thuan didn't look up. "I'll look into it tomorrow, see what I can find. He must have had some sort of regular way of cashing them and banking the money—we just have to find it."

Daniel offered, "Try his parents, of course. We didn't really check his entire family, just his accounts."

She showed them out the door and ended her long day with a cup of tea and a few pages from a novel she was reading.

Chapter 10

Jess could feel the onset of hotter weather as the sun rose in the east, the sky brightening across from his right as he drove from Apex in towards Research Triangle Park. It was going to be a dog day, he could tell, the first of a long season of dog days. At least it was Friday. Tomorrow there would be plenty of time for lunch on the lake and maybe a run by the shooting range in Holly Springs.

Smoke suddenly billowed up over his windshield, blocking his view of the road and filling the cab with the distinct smell of burnt rubber. Gripping the wheel tightly, bracing for an impact, he let his foot off the gas, pushed the clutch to the floor, and eased off towards the side of the road, scanning the scant set of gauges in front of him for signs of trouble. Nothing appeared wrong there.

Red lights flared in front of him, drawing his attention back towards his windshield. The smoke cleared, the rear of a dark, four-door sedan rising quickly in reaction to the driver braking hard. Sliding left, the driver barely missed a car in the left lane. Jess lost sight of the car as it passed on through the smoke, down the highway.

He steadied the wheel, continuing his movement off onto the shoulder. The source of the smoke was the tire on a white van, belching out burnt rubber. The van rocked as the air was released from the tire in a rush. The van inscribed a black arc of rubber across the asphalt, the driver losing control as the van started into a spin.

Just as the nose of the white van pushed into the grass along the shoulder, the sport utility vehicle in front of Jess plowed into it, striking at the passenger side door. Metal screeched as the big truck pushed the van forward, the mass sliding across the grassy strip into the parking lot of a business alongside the highway.

In the quiet after the storm, Jess worked to recover his equilibrium. A car moved past, and then another, each car increasing in speed. The world was filled with sound again, people moving past the accident towards the rest of their day.

His hand still shook when he grabbed the shifter to put the truck back into gear. Slowly, he moved up the grassy shoulder, pulling into the parking lot. He stopped in a corner, well away from the big white truck embedded in the side of the van.

Climbing out, he stood for a second, allowing his legs to adjust, watching the driver of the white sport utility vehicle exit and sit on the grass. The driver's cell phone was against his ear. Jess assumed he was calling the police.

He focused on the van. The passenger's side was completely crushed; there was no getting in that way. He looped around the front, pulled open the driver's side door, and looked in. There was a girl slumped against the steering wheel. Jess touched her shoulder, shook her.

As the woman in the driver's seat turned, her eyes full of fear, Jess recognized her in a flash of shock and sorrow. Benita. He had to get her out of this van, now.

Fumbling his pocketknife as his ears picked up the first hints of sirens, he opened the blade and cut her seat belt, freeing her from the van. As she fell out into his arms, he steadied her, directing her to a spot on the grassy stretch along the side of the road, as far away from the traffic as possible.

"My husband..."

Jess realized there must be someone in the van, but he doubted he could do anything about it. There was no way to reach anything on the passenger's side of the vehicle, so he stayed there.

"My husband..." Her voice rose with the noise, matching the volume of the sirens on the approaching emergency vehicles. Shock was coming on, but Jess didn't think he could leave her there. Certainly she would try to get up and go back to the van, which would only make things worse.

"The police are on the way. They'll get your husband out."

She buried her head in her hands and wept.

The first police car slid into the lot, followed closely by a fire truck. The officer leapt out.

"There's someone trapped in the van. The passenger's side."

The officer nodded. "Does she need medical attention?"

"I think she's going into shock."

"Stay with her; I'll get a blanket."

The officer moved to the front of the fire truck and said a few words to the driver. He then headed to his car and opened the trunk.

Firemen swarmed over the truck, pulling a hose out, readying valves, and settling the hose so they could quickly wash the interlocked vehicles. Two more men jumped off the back of the truck, carrying a huge pair of hydraulic scissors.

The steel back doors on the van complained, but they finally gave way to the pressure of the tool. An assortment of paint cans spilled out of the back of the van, splitting open, leaving a rainbow of colors, incongruent on the gray asphalt.

An ambulance swept into the parking the lot, the doors swinging open before it stopped. A gurney was flung out, followed by two EMTs in blue jumpsuits.

A screech rent the air, steel being pulled from steel. Two firemen appeared from the back of the van, carried Benita's husband gently to the gurney, folded its wheels, and pushed it into the ambulance.

One of the EMTs was looking around the parking lot, obviously searching for the van's driver. Jess signaled him over and shook Benita, who was now wrapped in the blanket from the police officer's car.

"They have your husband out. They probably want you to go to the hospital with him to do whatever paperwork is needed."

She nodded numbly and rose to her feet. The medical technician took her by the arm and led her to the ambulance.

"Hey, bud! Which car is yours?" Jess pushed himself to his feet and pointed to the green truck.

"Lucky. I don't see any damage. How were you involved?"

"I was three cars behind the van. It blew a tire."

"We saw the seat belt was cut. That must've been your work. It's good you stopped. You could've gotten hurt, but it's good to see someone stop. Not many do anymore." The officer pushed a brown clipboard in his hand. "Fill this out. We might be in contact if we need something more, but I think just filling this out for now will be fine."

"Will the man from the van live?"

"I don't know. I'm not a medical expert, but he has extensive injuries."

"What will she do?" He hadn't intended to say it out loud as the thought crossed through his mind.

"They're illegal aliens. The van isn't registered, and her license is a fake. The local INS folks will probably deport her when all of this is said and done."

Jess climbed up the steps of the building slowly, rode the elevator upstairs, and headed for Linda's cubicle. Leah was there when he stepped in.

Linda saw him first. "Late this morning, aren't you? Everything okay?"

"I passed by an accident on the way to work and stopped to help. It was really bad; a big white sport utility plowed into the side of a van."

"Ouch, sounds bad."

Leah turned to face him. "I only got to work a few minutes ago, too. The traffic was terrible. You were there, at the accident? It looked really bad. Was anyone hurt?"

"Benita's husband."

Linda gasped. "The cleaning lady? Is she okay?"

"I think she's okay, but I don't think she'll be in today. I figured I better come up here and tell Gerard so she doesn't get in trouble."

"I'll let him know." She disappeared into Gerard's office.

Leah said, "I'm sorry, Jess. I'm certain you feel bad."

"Yes, I do. But there's not much I can do about it right now. When I bump into Benita again, I can offer to help, but for now, the best thing would just be to get my nerves calmed down a bit and go bury myself in work."

"I understand the feeling."

Linda popped out of Gerard's office. "Jess, let me get you a cup of coffee or something. Don't move, just sit there for a bit and listen to Leah and I chatter. When you've calmed down, I'll give you permission to leave. There's nothing we can do for Benita right now."

"I'll go." Before Linda could protest, Leah was up and out of her cube. After she returned and handed the cup of coffee to Jess, she sat in a chair and continued as if Jess weren't there. "So, I was curious about the girl that Carl was dating. I mean, he must have been really attached to her to commit suicide because she broke up with him."

"It is a puzzler, to tell you the truth. I wouldn't have put Carl down as someone who would commit suicide, that's for sure. I didn't believe it all 'til I saw the note."

Wheels started to spin in Jess's head. The suicide note. He needed another look at that suicide note. Something about it wasn't right. But how?

Leah said, "So, who *is* this girl? She must feel terrible."

"Gerard's niece. If she's at all like her uncle, I doubt she feels badly."

"Have you ever met her?"

"Oh, yes, she's been through here quite often. She's a real looker; I can see why Carl would latch onto her. What I don't know is how Gerard would feel about Carl dating her. She's a good bit younger than he is, from what I remember, just out of high school."

"Are they close then, Gerard and his niece?"

"She thinks he's the best thing since pickled peaches. Tells all her friends how important her uncle is, president of a big company and all, with lots of people working for him. Follows him around like a puppy when she's in the office."

"So, do you think she'd start an argument with Carl on purpose if Gerard wanted her to?"

"Where are you getting these ideas from, girl? Have you been talking to Jess about Carl's suicide?" Linda winked at Jess, who was nursing his coffee in the other chair.

Jess soaked the information in, keeping his silence so he wouldn't break the flow of the conversation.

Leah laughed. "No, I was just interested. It seems so strange to me, hearing what people say about Carl, to think he would have committed suicide over a girl. I suppose you don't know much about their relationship? Did she lead him on?"

"Not that I noticed."

Jess broke in at this point. "Linda, do you have a copy of the suicide note?"

She turned from Jess and looked at her computer monitor for a few moments. Finally, she sighed. "I suppose it won't do any harm if you have a copy of it. It's still in Gerard's e-mail." The printer sitting on the low, tan filing cabinet behind her whirred to life, spitting out one page. She reached behind her, pulled the paper from the tray, and slid it across the desk to Jess.

After lunch, Jess headed to the break room to refill his water bottle for the afternoon. Stepping in, he bumped into Benita, who was standing at the counter, crying.

"I'm so sorry, I was just—" She looked up and realized it was Jess who had bumped into her.

"I can't imagine why you're at work today. Your husband was taken to the hospital just a few hours ago."

"I need the money. If I don't get paid, then I can't buy food or pay the rent on our apartment."

"How is your husband?"

"I don't know. When I left, he was in bad shape, but I've not called since then."

"Benita, I can call my pastor, and we can get you some money to tide you over, to help. We could also take up a collection here at work. At least a few of us would contribute."

Her eyes filled with tears. "Just pray, Jess. I don't know what I'll do if my husband dies."

"You should be there. I wouldn't want your husband to be alone right now."

"To die alone. I know," said Benita.

"Don't assume the worst, Benita. I'll be praying for your husband. I hope he gets better. I will take up the collection at work and talk to my pastor about raising money through the church. If there's anything else I can do, let me know."

"Thank you, Jess, I will let you know. I know I can count on you if I need something."

———

Jess stared at the suicide note for some time. *Something caught my eye before, but I can't remember what it was. There is something out of place, but what is it?*

On a hunch, he opened his e-mail, selected all the e-mails he could find from Carl, and saved them off into a big file. He opened the file, and searched for several words from the first sentence in the note.

There. There's the first sentence. He searched again, this time for several of the words in the second sentence. *There's second sentence.* Feeling certain he was on the right track, he moved through the suicide note, finding each sentence in turn. *This suicide note is made up from pieces of Carl's other emails. What are the odds?* Logging in to the e-mail server, Jess navigated through the directories where all the mail files were kept. He found Carl's e-mail file and copied it over to his desktop. On double clicking the file to open it, he was presented with a password screen.

What would Carl use for a password? Maybe something about Carl thinking he was God's gift to girls. Or maybe it was something to do with his new car. At least these were places to start.

He tried *airooncar*. The password screen popped back up again. Next he tried *gift2girls*. No, that wasn't it, either. But their e-mail server required some sort of special character in every password, so he needed to add those in. Periods were always the easiest.

He tried *maroon.car*, *gift.2.girls*, *maroon.1*, *maroon.moon*, and *gift.2.girlz*.

What could it be? Hackers liked to turn letters around backwards and use a number in place of the backward letter. Jess tried *g1ft.2.g17l2*. Bingo.

The inbox was the first to pop up. There was lots of e-mail, just like Jess's inbox. The last e-mail was on Friday around lunch, probably when Gerard had finally shut down Carl's e-mail account. The more recent e-mails were from girls, announcements that had been sent to the whole company, or spam.

There was a gap in the timestamps, though, from Thursday night around midnight until Friday morning around three o'clock. Most people probably didn't get e-mail at that time, but Carl received plenty of automated announcements and plenty of spam, so the gap was discernable. Why were there three hours of missing mail?

The sent mail box was the next one on the list. There was the same three hour gap, and no suicide note. Jess picked the note up and examined the header information, the information about when and where the e-mail had been sent from. It showed the e-mail had been sent from Carl's mail account at six in the morning.

Again, he searched through Carl's sent mail folder. There was no e-mail containing the suicide note at six in the morning. There was other e-mail, but no suicide note.

He picked up the printed copy of Carl's e-mail again and considered the header fields more carefully. The originating address didn't look right. Jess closed Carl's e-mail and quickly moved the e-mail file into the encrypted file and folder he'd created to hold information on Carl's death.

As well as the e-mail address, the e-mail header contained information about the actual computer the e-mail had been sent from, in the form of the computer's IP address. Finding the IP address of the computer from which the e-mail had been sent would be a strong indication of who had sent the e-mail in the first place.

Jess opened a file containing a list of IP addresses. Each IP address had a computer listed alongside it. Scanning the list, he found the IP address of the computer from which the e-mail had been sent. Gerard's. Jess sat for a moment, stunned. He carefully folded the copy of the e-mail and shoved it down into his pocket. It would be easier to hold onto if he scanned it into an image file, something that was easier to do at home.

Jess badged into the data center, dropped his backpack on floor just inside the door, and walked into the main aisle. Turning around as the door clicked closed, he looked at the sign posted there, considering the dire warning for a moment. Walking back, he opened the door from the inside and used a cardboard box to prop it completely open. If the halon extinguisher system went off while he was in there, he could get out faster if the door was already open.

He picked up the phone next to the door and dialed the number for security.

"Hello?"

"Hey, Brian, this is Jess. I'm going to run a quick test on the fire system activation circuits down here in the data center." He waved to Brian through the camera above the door and continued. "Just keep an eye on things for me, would you?"

"Sure thing, Jess."

"Thanks." He walked over to the red button covered by a plastic box hanging on the wall. There was a small green button there, just above the red one. He opened the plastic cover, held down the green button, and took a deep breath, holding it in. Quickly, he pressed the larger red button. Once he released both buttons, he let his breath out and watched the green button closely. It flashed several times and then went dark. He dropped the plastic cover back in place and picked up a clipboard hanging on the wall beside the red button used to activate the extinguisher system. After marking the date, the time, and his initials, Jess walked around the box and through the door, taking the box with him as the door clicked shut behind him.

Shouldering his backpack, he headed home for the day.

Chapter 11

Benita stole into the conference room, nervously looking around the hallway before closing the door and turning the blinds to their closed position. The phone sat on the long, shiny table, her future lying in the response to a single call, a few words spoken, a moment in time.

She pushed each digit in the hospital's number gingerly. Holding the phone to her ear, she waited for the connection to the nurses' station to complete. When the nurse answered, she explained she was married to the man in room 143A, and she asked how he was doing.

"Ma'am, I think it's best if you come to the hospital. We've been trying to get in touch with you for about twenty minutes."

She hung up the phone, knowing full well what they were trying to get in touch with her about. He had died alone.

There was no money to pay any of the bills, of course. And with only her working, there was no money to pay the rent or feed the children. She could go back to the old country, but what would that gain her? All of her family had either died or disowned her. Either way, she had no one to turn to.

Dropping her head onto the cold, hard table, Benita wept.

Sometime later, she stood up. She had made it through hard times before, and she would make it through again.

She watched the people filing out of the office at the end of the day as she emptied the garbage cans in the lobby. None of them looked at her, noticed her red-rimmed eyes, or even said goodnight.

She would finish this day's work, ask for her pay, and head back south. Her husband's people would at least take the children and watch after them, even if they were no better off than she was. She could make her own way as best she could until she had put her life back together enough to take them again.

Jess had said something about taking up a collection or getting some money from his pastor. That would help her make it back to her husband's people, anyway. At least there were some people in the world who would still help and who didn't treat her like a fixture on the wall of the office building.

She put off emptying the garbage in the big room with all the computers until the last thing. Since that man Carl had been found there, she didn't relish the thought of going into that room. She didn't want anyone to see her nervousness, and she also didn't want to walk in and find someone else there. She was happy, at least, that this was the last time she would ever need to go into the basement.

Emerging from the elevator, she walked up the gray ramp, wondering why it was there. Selecting a key from the ring on her belt, she unlocked the doors and walked into the data center, admiring how clean and orderly the room was. There were lots of cables tied into orange and yellow bundles tied against the gray racks standing in rows. At least this room was kept neat, no food in the garbage cans, no spilled drinks left for her to clean up.

The bold red letters on the door reminded her of one of the many reasons she didn't like coming into this room. The place felt dangerous with its warning signs and the low rumble of the equipment. She stepped halfway out and found a box to prop the door open. She didn't like the thought of being trapped inside this room. Moving towards the back corner along the first row, she picked up the first garbage can. She replaced the bag, tying the old one up and tossing it towards the door. There was another pair of garbage cans along the back wall and then the one next to the door, and she would be done for the night.

There was a sound. Was it the door clicking shut? Turning, she moved quickly towards the front of the room to see what had happened to the box. Then a loud siren screamed in her ears. She tried to run.

In slow motion, like a dance, ten or fifteen of the floor tiles lifted from their places, flipping over or twisting in the air before settling to the ground. She tripped into one of the holes left by a flying tile, falling, the searing pain running up her leg. She got up, moving fast, paying closer attention, praying for strength. Her breath was shorter now. It was hard to breathe, like the oxygen was being sucked from the room.

She made it to the door and looked out the two long, thin windows there. Someone was standing on the outside, watching her. She banged on the window, but the face remained impassive. She tried to grab the handles, to turn them, but she was weak, and the handles felt like they were blocked from moving by something. Finally, out of breath, she sank to the floor.

Chapter 12

Jess sat in a small metal chair, waiting. He had looked at his clock when the banging on the door to his apartment started two hours ago. Five o'clock. In the morning. He resisted the urge to lay his head over his folded arms and go to sleep.

The initial flaring of his anger had died. No one had bothered to tell him why he had been dragged out of his apartment. The only thing he could get out of the barked replies to his questions was that he was being taken to the station for questioning in a murder case and that he wasn't under arrest *yet,* but that he would likely be placed under arrest once he arrived there, pending some information someone was waiting on.

He wondered what the effect of the noise had been on Ms. Parker, his landlady. His apartment was just three rooms carved out of a larger house in the Arts and Crafts style, accessed through a door that led out onto the back porch. He imagined he would have some explaining to do if and when he got home, and he would likely need to go looking for another apartment. It was a shame, really, since he got along with Ms. Parker so well.

He reminded himself, again, that neither anger nor fear was going to help things at this point. That they had come in an unmarked white truck bothered him. It was a good thing he had actually been awake, rooting around in the kitchen for something to drink, when they pulled up. If he had been awakened by the banging when they set on the door, he might have feared for his life. Glancing around the room, he noted the mirrors starting about halfway up along one entire wall. They weren't normal mirrors, of course; they were one-way mirrors, set up so someone could observe an interrogation, or other proceedings in the room, without being observed.

The door clicked. Goose bumps rose up on his arms. Fear wouldn't help anything, either, so he settled himself, bracing for what was to come next.

Sergeant Stone strode in, banging the door closed behind him. He sat in a chair opposite Jess, facing him over the gray steel table.

"What am I being held for? They said questioning when they pulled me out of my apartment. What am I being questioned about that couldn't wait until tomorrow?"

"We have witnesses that say you left work around five o'clock this afternoon. Can you verify that's when you left work?"

"I left work at five o'clock. But you've not answered my question. Should I call a lawyer at this point?"

"What did you do when you left work?"

"I went home, ate dinner, and started reading a book."

"That's it? You didn't meet anyone or go anywhere?"

"No, I didn't meet anyone or go anywhere."

"It's Friday night. You didn't go out with a girl?" His face wore a sneer as he said this, mocking Jess.

"No. You drag me down here to ask questions, but you won't give me any information." Trying to hold his anger down, Jess began to emphasize each word, enunciating each one as a separate exclamation point. "Who was murdered?"

"Did you see anyone as you were leaving the office?"

"You know what time I left the office. You've already said you have witnesses. Who was murdered? Am I being charged with something?"

"I suspect you already *know* who was murdered. This would go a lot easier if you just told me the truth."

"I *am* telling you the truth. Am I being charged with something?"

"Are there any witnesses who can vouch for your whereabouts tonight?"

"No!"

Sergeant Stone's eyes narrowed. "Yelling won't get you anyplace with me, son. I will gladly spend tonight ripping your life apart without you. I will dig up enough to prove you did this, one way or the other. It's easier all around if you just come clean."

Jess relaxed, breathing out his anger, and waited. It was going to be easier to play along for a bit, giving as little information away as possible, until he could pry out what Sergeant Stone had brought him down here for.

"Who was the last person to see you at work?"

"Linda."

"And did you go back to the office last night?"

"No."

"Are there any witnesses to your movements last night?"

"None that I can name. My landlady would have seen my truck in the driveway. It's hard to miss."

"It's easy to get around without driving, so that doesn't prove anything."

Jess shrugged. It was time to prod Sergeant Stone, to try and turn the tables a bit. "I suppose I could have used my PWC to get to the office. Is that the sort of thing you're suggesting?" The sergeant's face turned beet red.

"Drop the sarcasm, too. It won't work. You went back to work to see someone. It didn't work out like you thought it would, did it?"

"I went home and cooked up some fried chicken for dinner. After that, I cleaned up and sat down to read a book before going to bed. Would it be helpful if you knew what I drank?"

"Okay, if you want to play it that way, what was on television?"

"The last time I watched television, I think it was a rerun of *The Avengers.*"

"What station was it on?"

"I don't remember, given that was at least ten years ago."

Sergeant Stone's fist slammed down on the table, making the book jump into the air. "This would be a lot easier if you would just come clean with me."

"I already have. I left work, went home, ate dinner, and read. I didn't watch television; I haven't watched television in at least ten years."

"You are *lying!* This nonsense is just going to cause you more trouble. Come clean, son."

"I am not lying, Sergeant. I don't think it's possible for me to get into more trouble by telling the truth."

"What if I told you someone saw you going back to the office?"

A knot formed in his stomach. Jess hadn't gone back to the office, but he also knew witnesses could be manipulated to fit the circumstances. Eyewitnesses are only as good as their eyes, their memories, and their motivations. They generally aren't as reliable as people think.

"I would say that person is either lying or mistaken."

"Why should I trust you?"

"Because I *know* what I did tonight."

"What *were* your plans for tomorrow?"

"I *am* planning on running up to North Raleigh for a cowboy action shoot, a competition, at Sir Walter Raleigh Gun Club."

"Well, you aren't now. You're moving to a cell and staying here until Detective Harris decides to come in. Luckily for you, it looks like he's coming in tomorrow morning. Otherwise, you would be here all weekend."

"What am I being held for?"

"You are a material witness to a murder, at the very least. I'm certain you are more than that, but we'll have to spend some time developing the case more fully. I hope Detective Harris can talk some sense into you in the morning, make you come clean."

"Don't I get to at least call my lawyer?"

"Son, I'm not charging you with anything. You're being held for questioning. You're not under arrest." Sergeant Stone stopped for a moment to add emphasis to the next word. "Yet."

"Aren't you at least going to tell me who was murdered?"

Sergeant Stone moved to the door and knocked. An electric lock clicked, and he stepped out into the doorway. Jess could see an officer standing just behind him, blocking the way in case Jess tried to run. "Benita. Maybe that will shake your brain cells loose for your little talk tomorrow morning with the detective."

Anger and sadness overcame Jess. Hot tears slid down his face, dripping onto the coldness of the steel table. Hadn't

Benita's children had enough for one day? Their father and their mother both dead. What would happen now? And how could Sergeant Stone hold him like this, without arresting him?

"How...how did she die?"

Sergeant Stone looked at him. "You already know that because you did it." He pulled the door closed behind him, leaving the sound of clanging metal ringing in Jess's ears.

Chapter 13

Leah started. The ringing of her cell phone cut through the gauze of sleep. Leah rolled and picked up her phone, checking the time on the front. Six in the morning. It rang again. She flipped it open.

"Hello?" Her mouth was dry. She rolled to the side of the bed and sat up, not recognizing the room she was in.

"Leah? Did I wake you?"

"Yeah, but it's okay. Who is this?" Memories started to flood into her mind. Ms. Parker had called her around three in the morning, in a panic; Jess had been taken off in a white truck with no markings. Her mind went back to her interview with Ms. Parker a week ago. She had assumed Ms. Parker would know the ins and outs of Jess's life well enough to be helpful in their investigation. *I did tell her to call me if anything unusual happened. I just wasn't expecting to be Jess being arrested at three in the morning.*

Leah had rushed from Chapel Hill to Apex to try and sort things out. She had called every police department in the area, but no one had any record of Jess being booked or arrested.

Homeland Security would be really angry if she blew the investigation into this identity theft ring up, but whatever had happened, it had happened under the radar screen. Leah found things happening under the radar screen disturbing.

The voice drifted back over the cell phone, bringing her back to the present. "This is Detective Harris. Sorry. I suppose I rise a little earlier than most people."

What else can I do? I've tried everything else I can think of. She had finally called Detective Harris, leaving him a voice mail on his cell phone. It was a risk. Daniel said everything can change, but she couldn't see Detective Harris changing. *Certainly he's not the person in the Apex department tied up with this mess. I hope not, anyway.*

"It's okay, really. I'm normally up—well, not quite this early. I had a late night, or rather an early morning. Sorry for calling you out of the blue, but I remembered you knew my parents pretty well. I thought you might still work at one of the local police departments around the Raleigh area. That was back when you were a sergeant."

"Yes, Apex, currently. I was with the county for a while, but I shifted back a few years ago to stay closer to home. You were only, I'd say, ten, when your parents passed away? I was promoted to detective a while back."

Had it really been fourteen years since her mom died? Tears threatened to overflow her eyes. She needed a tissue, but she didn't know where to find one. Spending the night in Ms. Parker's spare bedroom had been a matter of necessity. There was no way she was driving back to the apartment she was using by the time they were finished hunting for Jess.

"I'm sorry, Leah, I didn't mean to—"

"It's okay. Really." She composed herself while she waited for him to continue.

"I understand you're looking for Jess Wirth?"

"Yes. He was apparently picked up around midnight, and I can't seem to figure out where he was taken. I'm assuming it was a local force."

The white noise of his sigh came through the phone. "One of the officers in the local office brought him in for questioning in a murder case. He went, shall we say, overboard a bit."

"Oh. I see. Who is in charge of the case?"

"I am. He's in custody here in the Apex precinct. I'm on my way over to question him. My, um, overboard officer is, well, anxious to charge him with the murder."

Her stomach rumbled. If she didn't get something to eat, a headache would follow, and then she wouldn't be able to do anyone any good. "Maybe we should talk about this over a cup of coffee and something to eat. I suspect I have information that might pertain to your case."

"Could it wait until after I've questioned Mr. Wirth?"

"I would prefer to talk to you before you question him, if possible." Another sigh broke through the receiver. She decided to play the personal angle as well as the professional. "Besides, it would give me the chance to do a little catching up after all these years." Leah listened to the silence for a few minutes, hoping he would come around and meet her before questioning Jess.

"Six thirty at the chicken and biscuit place in Apex."

"I'll be there." She flipped the phone closed and started dressing. Foremost in her mind was the question of how to handle this. Would Daniel approve of this course of action? She had to do something. If they arrested Jess for murder, it would blow the case. She had to find out what evidence they had, see how solid the case was. She didn't want a murderer on the street, but she also knew that Jess wasn't a likely murderer. A data thief, perhaps, but not a murderer.

Getting there before the detective, she sat along one of the walls in a corner, positioned so she could see as much of the parking lot as possible and both of the doors. On the tall, white plastic top table, her chicken and biscuit sat. The place they had decided to meet was a run-down, eighties-style building featuring décor from the fifties inside, although the idea of deep frying boneless pieces of chicken to be served on a bun hadn't occurred to anyone until at least the mid-sixties.

An older man walked in and waded into the sea of chrome and bright red. She'd taken the liberty of finding his picture on the Web, so she recognized him instantly. She waved him over to her table.

"Detective Harris! It's great to see you. It's been years."

"Yes, and you've grown into quite a beautiful young lady."

Her face was hot for a moment. "It only seems to attract the wrong sort of guys, nowadays."

He didn't seem to notice her embarrassment. "Okay, so I'll start with the hardest question of all. This might seem impertinent, but what's your relationship to Jess Wirth?"

"Why?"

"You wouldn't believe the number of people who try to get someone they're involved with off the hook by offering false evidence, corroborating an alibi, and so forth."

Her face warmed up again, but this time there was more than embarrassment. Pushing her anger out in a low, forceful voice, she said, "*This has nothing to do with any relationship I might or might not have with Jess. Do you honestly think I would leave you a voice mail in the middle of the night to come out here to discuss my feelings?*"

She half stood, but reconsidered. This was her only link to finding out what had happened last night without pulling official strings she didn't want to pull right now. She hesitated, poised between sitting down and walking out.

Detective Harris put his hand up, signaling her to stop. "It's never a pleasant thing, pursuing a line of questioning you suspect will make people mad. But it's easier to get the cards out on the table from the start."

She sat down, releasing the energy, letting the anger drain. After carefully unwrapping her sandwich, she took a bite. "Nothing to eat?"

"I've already eaten. I always eat early. I would like to grab a cup of coffee, though."

Nodding, Leah continued to take bites out of her sandwich as Detective Harris waded through the morass of people towards the counter. He returned, carrying a very large cup of coffee. He blew the steam off the surface, poured several creamers in it, and continued.

"If you didn't call me because of an existing relationship with Jess, then why *did* you leave me a voice mail in the middle of the night?"

She produced a thin bifold from the front pocket of her sweat pants. Opening it so it would stand on its edge, she set it on the table and slid it across to the detective.

He examined it at length. "I see." Folding it closed, he slid it back across the shiny tabletop towards her. "Department of Homeland Security, cybercrimes division. You've certainly made your way in the world since I last saw you. I'm surprised you chose a career in law enforcement, though, after what happened to your father."

She was silent, not wanting to let the conversation get sidetracked onto the subject of her parents.

Sensing her hesitation at changing the subject, he continued. "Of course, it changes a number of things. Has my department been informed you're working in our backyard?"

"No, not yet."

He was clearly irritated. "Mind telling me why?"

How much could she trust him? She was going to have to trust him enough to find out what had happened and to see if it had any bearing on her case. "Mole."

She was met with a look both startled and incredulous. "In our department? Here in Apex?"

"Yes. Someone in the local department is tied into what we're chasing."

"Who?"

"I'm really sorry, but I can't tell you."

"You're afraid I might let the cat out of the bag, and whoever it is will go to ground. Or you don't know. Or it's a little of both. Makes sense. I suppose that means I can't tell anyone up the chain that you're in our backyard, can I?"

She shook her head no.

"Okay." Although his words said he understood, his face still said he was irritated about the situation. Leah couldn't blame him. She was playing a game of cat and mouse, trying to get information when she had little to give in return. She would be irritated in the same circumstances. "So, what's your interest in Mr. Wirth?" he asked.

"He's a likely suspect in a string of identity thefts."

A low, unnerving whistle escaped from his lips. "If we hold him, then you can't chase your investigation."

"Right."

"And what if he murdered someone? Isn't that local jurisdiction?"

"Yes. But I'm not convinced he did. I was hoping you could give me enough details about when and where. Maybe we can figure out what happened."

"Interesting proposal."

"Look, I know this is hard. We can't really work together on this, for now. If things change, I can promise you I will fill you in. Until I know who the mole is, though—"

"The mole might be me, too, might it not?" He sighed and paused for a moment, thinking. "Okay, we'll do the best we can with what we have. This is what I have. Last night, at two fourteen exactly, the fire extinguishers were triggered in the data center at OptiData. That's where Jess works, but I assume you already know that."

Leah nodded, prompting him to continue.

"Benita, the cleaning lady, was in the data center when the extinguishers were triggered. We can't find any evidence of a fire, but it did extinguish Benita's life."

"How would it kill someone?" asked Leah.

Harris replied, "Asphyxiation. Halon puts fires out by removing the oxygen from the air. You can't use water or chemicals in a room full of electrical equipment, so they use halon systems instead."

"She's an illegal alien. Her husband died in a car crash yesterday morning, on the way to work. You couldn't have traced her to the tags on the vehicle because the registration was either expired or the tag was stolen, or something like that. I'm not certain which."

He looked up from the table. "How do you know that? We couldn't find any trace of her family."

"Jess came in to work yesterday talking about it. He was just behind the accident and stopped to pull Benita from the car."

"Her husband?"

"Was in the passenger's side. Apparently he didn't make it. He was in room one forty-three A in Wake Med. The vehicle was apparently struck in her husband's door."

He pulled out a small notepad. "Mind if I take notes?"

"Not at all. As long as you didn't hear any of this from me."

He smiled. "Understood. At least it gives me the information I need to start tracking some of this stuff down. You apparently work there?"

"At OptiData? Yes. I'm temping as a project manager. It's the easiest way to gather information without raising suspicions."

"I see. So you saw Mr. Wirth yesterday."

"Yes. I was there when he came in from the accident. Why did you pin the murder on him?"

"His prints are the only prints on the door handle and on the fire extinguisher activation button. Theyr'e on file from his concealed carry application, in electronic format, so it was a fast and easy match."

That *was* pretty convincing evidence. The woman had clearly been murdered in an area Jess was familiar with, and his prints were the only prints found on the scene.

"Is it possible to trigger the extinguisher system remotely? Is there a button outside the room, a number you can dial combined with a code, or anything like that?"

"There's no remote trigger capability for the system, no. We asked the fire department specifically about it, and they said these sorts of systems can only be triggered from the single control installed in the room."

"Then he didn't have anything to do with it."

"How so? I was hoping to pull him in this morning and question him, to find out if there was anyone who could vouch for his whereabouts last night. I think Sergeant Stone might have caused more trouble than he saved. I'm likely to be met by Mr. Wirth's lawyer and a rather clammed-up suspect."

"He left the office at five-oh-seven, drove to his apartment, and didn't leave there until this morning. There's no way he triggered the extinguisher system at three in the morning."

"He's being tailed?"

"We've been tailing him ever since the suicide at OptiData. We had the engineer who committed suicide fingered as our primary suspect. But, well, when he exited the picture, we assumed we'd picked up on the wrong person."

"I see. So he has a rock-solid alibi for the time of the murder. That's throws a monkey wrench into Sergeant Stone's theory."

"What is the sergeant's theory?"

"He was having an affair with Benita. A lot of his coworkers said he had a good relationship with her, that she talked to him a good bit. They had been seen, and recorded, talking in the break room during the day. She was crying. Unfortunately, the video system there doesn't record sound, so we don't know what they said. Sergeant Stone thinks he went back to work to meet her since she normally worked late, and things didn't turn out like he thought they would. So he murdered her."

Leah laughed. She crinkled the paper her biscuit had been wrapped up in and took a long drink of the coffee she had left cooling on the table between them.

"What's so funny?"

"Jess having an affair with Benita. I suppose it could look that way from the outside. Jess is twenty-eight. I figure Benita must have been around the same age, a little younger. She was certainly attractive enough, and Jess isn't a slouch, either, though he likes to think he is. But an *affair?*" She laughed again.

"Why is it so unlikely?"

"Jess hasn't even dated a girl in at least four years. At least not that anyone can find out about. His only interest in Benita was in helping her once her husband died and just a general attitude of being nice to people, even if they are just a cleaning person in the building you work at. He's about as straitlaced as they come, if you ask me, on the moral side. Not that he's not funny or laid back, but he's certainly not the type to have an affair."

"Then what makes you think he's a thief?"

"I'm not convinced he is. In fact, I'm pretty convinced he's not. But the folks I work with, well, they're pretty convinced he's the end of a long string that will lead to breaking an identity theft ring that's been plaguing us for years."

"What convinces them?"

"Well, that he's cagey. He's been hard to tail. He just bought some expensive things in cash. He's in the right position, and the data is still flowing out onto the open market. He's hiding information of some sort."

"And what convinces you?"

"He's naturally observant—or he's trained himself to be. It's not as though he's trying to hide something about his movements; he's just watchful. The data he's hiding doesn't seem to be related to the data that's being stolen."

"This really sounds interesting."

"It is. I wish I could tell you more. I could use an outside set of eyes, someone with your kind of experience, to help me sort it out."

"Would the data he's hiding have anything to do with the mole or Benita's death?"

"I don't think so."

"Then why is he hiding it?"

"He's convinced Mr. Stark didn't commit suicide."

The detective plopped his coffee cup down on the table. "I thought he might not be convinced. Why doesn't he come to the police with any information he has?"

Leah shrugged. "He doesn't seem like the trusting type. Like he'd rather have something rock-solid to produce, not just some thrown-together bits of information that might not mean anything."

"It sounds like you know a good bit about his thoughts on this suicide."

"No. I just know Jess. It's the way he works."

"And it would make him a really good data thief," said Detective Harris.

"Yes, it would. The problem is there are pieces that don't fit, even if I can't put my finger on them yet."

"So, we now have a murder and no suspect. I'm guessing the murder and the data theft are related. Coincidence isn't a kosher word."

"I'll bet they are, too," Leah said.

"Separate lines of inquiry, then."

"Until we run into each other again. I would question Jess closely. As I said, he's very observant. He might be able to lead you to the murderer. I hope, though, that it's not before he leads me to the data theft ring."

Chapter 14

Jess followed Sergeant Stone through the cell door and down a hall back towards the interview room where he had started this nightmare. He wondered if he should just admit something, anything, just to get this over with. He could understand now how the police could wear you down to the point of admitting things, no matter what the truth was.

He again settled in the chair facing the door. Sergeant Stone closed the door behind him, more gently than he had earlier. Jess soon saw the reason why Sergeant Stone had been civilized this morning; Detective Harris stepped into the room and sat opposite of Jess at the little table. Jess tried to read his face. Was it apprehension? Thoughtfulness? Or was he just tired?

Detective Harris cleared his throat before beginning. "Good morning, Jess. Sorry for your little adventure last night. We do need to chat for a few minutes before I can let you go, though."

Let him go? Of course, that wouldn't clear the charges. It could just be a matter of whether to hold him while gathering evidence, or force him to post bail to guarantee he wouldn't flee. He started thinking about where he could get the money to post bail. It would be embarrassing to call anyone in his family.

"Good morning, Detective."

"So, Jess, let's go over this again." Harris turned to the sergeant, who had stepped in to stand beside him, an angry scowl on his face. "Could you go get some coffee? Not from the machine—go get some from the coffee place around the corner. I'll start the questioning while you're gone."

Sergeant Stone turned and left the room, closing the door gently behind him again.

"I wanted to chat for a second without him here before we started recording. But I want you to tell me the entire truth. Don't leave anything out, no matter how small a detail it might seem to you." He took out a small, silver tape recorder and placed it on the table.

Jess stared at the tape recorder. He remembered being pulled into the white truck, between two officers, and sitting in this room with Sergeant Stone questioning him. But he couldn't remember there being a tape recorder anyplace or being told he was being recorded.

"Is there a recording system built into this room? A video camera, or something like that?"

"Not here. We've not budgeted for it. Why?"

"Sergeant Stone didn't record me last night."

"Did he question you? He was just supposed to bring you in for questioning this morning."

"No, he questioned me. Actually, he accused me of killing Benita."

"Hmph. I'll have to look into that later. Anyway, I wanted to get all of your movements yesterday since the beginning of the day. I need everything I can get to catch Benita's murderer."

"You don't think I murdered her?"

"I know you didn't. At this point in the case, I can't explain anything more. It's easiest if we just work through what happened, and let things sort themselves out in time. Are you ready?"

Jess wasn't feeling very ready. In fact, he was still muddled and tired, but he couldn't exactly ask them to come back later. "Sure."

"Okay, let's get started." He pressed a button on the side of the tape recorder. "Interview with Jess Wirth, concerning the murder of Benita Dias, on Friday…" Jess tuned out as his voice droned on for what seemed like forever. "Mr. Wirth, you are not under arrest, nor am I placing you under oath at this time, but I would advise you to answer each question truthfully and fully, to the best of your ability."

Taking out a small pad and a pen, he said, "Let's just start with yesterday morning. Take me through your day. Tell me who you talked to and what you talked about."

"Well, I came in later than usual and checked my voice mail…"

"Why did you come in late?"

"There was an accident on the highway on the way in to work, just a couple of cars in front of me. I stopped to help get the driver out of the car before the EMTs and police arrived."

"Can you tell me what time that was?"

"Around six forty-five."

"Can you describe the vehicles involved?"

"Yes, an older white van, not in good condition, and a white SUV."

"Did you fill out a statement, or an accident report, or anything to that effect?"

"Yes."

He made a note and continued. "Much of this should be on that report, but let's continue with the accident, just so we have a full picture. Can you tell me what happened? What caused the accident?"

"A tire blew on the van, and it slid. The other truck hit it and pushed it off the road. I stopped and cut the driver out of her seatbelt and took her to the side while awaiting the police."

"Did you call 911, or did someone else?"

"The driver of the SUV called 911."

"Did you recognize the driver, the person you took out of the van?"

"Yes, it was the cleaning lady at work, Benita."

"Was there anyone else in the van?"

"Yes, her husband. He was in the passenger's seat. The SUV had hit the van in the passenger's side door. He was taken off in an ambulance after they used some equipment to get him out of the wreckage."

"What was Benita's state?"

"She was in shock."

Sergeant Stone walked in just at that moment with three cups of coffee. He set one down in front of Detective Harris and another in front of Jess. Just the smell cleared his mind.

"Thank you, Sergeant. Could you see if there's a report on an accident at around six forty-five AM on Route Fifty-five, eastbound side?" Sergeant Stone nodded. He left the room again, carrying his coffee.

"Okay, so you came in late, and then?"

"I went up to talk to Linda. I wanted Linda, who is the general manager's secretary, to slip into his office and tell him Benita wouldn't be in that day."

"Okay. Was anyone else there?"

"In Linda's cubicle? Yes, Leah, a project manager."

"Okay, after you left Linda's cubicle, what did you do?"

"I went back down, checked my voice mail, and started my normal work. Things have been heavy, recently, since the suicide."

"Anything unusual in your voice mail?"

"No, just the usual jumble of problems that needed to be addressed."

"And then?"

"I went to the break room just before lunch to refill my bottle of water. I bumped into Benita on the way into the break room."

"Were you surprised she was at work?"

"Yes."

"What was her state at that time?"

"She was crying, very worried about her husband. According to the officer at the accident, she and her husband are illegal aliens and would probably be deported."

"Did she ask you for help or anything?"

"I offered to collect some money from around the office for her and to call my pastor to see if the church had anything in their fund for helping out in emergencies. Before the accident she told me she had seen Gerard in the building the night Carl committed suicide."

Detective Harris looked startled. "How did this come up?"

"It was a few days after Carl's death. She was in at an odd time, I asked her why, and she said because she didn't like being in the building alone. I told her that Carl's death has been ruled a suicide, there weren't any murderers around for her to worry about. Benita then told me how she had seen Gerard in his office. I asked her if she was certain, and she said she had double-checked to make certain it was him."

As Harris was making notes, Sergeant Stone walked back in the room. "What did you find?" Sergeant Stone silently laid a few sheets of paper in front of Harris. He studied them for a minute and made a few notes in his pad.

Looking back up at Jess, he said, "We found the accident report, which is good. It helps us fill in details we might not have already known. Benita's husband died, by the way, late in the afternoon."

So they were both dead. Jess set his coffee down and studied his hands. Would someone be there to take care of her children? Help them through what was bound to be a difficult time in their lives? It was something he would need to see if he could find out about.

"And then lunch?"

"Yes. Generally, I eat alone, though sometimes I do eat with Linda or Leah."

"After lunch?"

"I worked on a few more problems and some slides for some projects I'm working on. Then I decided to call it a day."

"You didn't visit the data center all day?"

"On the way out of the building, I went down there to check the extinguisher system. That's the only time I went in there."

"Tell me about the fire alarm system. What is the process for testing it?"

"There is a green button above the larger red one. You press the green button and then the red one, and then a green light comes on."

"What's the purpose of this test?"

"I suppose it's meant to check the circuitry. It's in the manual, so we make sure we do it once each month."

"And do you record these checks?"

"Yes, on a clipboard that hangs from the wall there next to the alarm button."

"Are you quite certain you marked off the inspection? And that the clipboard was there when you left the room?"

"Positive."

"Sergeant Stone, could you get the pictures taken in the data center yesterday? Just bring the whole pile." Once the sergeant had left, Detective Harris smiled at Jess. "He hates it when I send him out for errands, but it's Saturday, and there's no one else in the station to run and get things like this."

The coffee and the relief of not being charged for murder were just starting to catch up to him.

"Do the security cameras ever fail to record for short periods of time?"

"It does happen, but it's pretty unusual. Security usually opens a case when it does happen. Maybe once every six months."

"And are there any cases open on that issue right now?"

"There weren't when I left on Friday. Detective, how did Benita die?"

"You don't know?"

"No. Sergeant Stone didn't tell me. Was it like Carl, wrapped up in Ethernet cables? Maybe a rack falling over, or the halon system—"

"The halon system went off while she was in the room."

"If you are close enough to set the system off, then you should be close enough to make it out the door."

The detective was quick to answer this. "What if you weren't by the door? Could you make it all the way from the other side of the room, say, before the system went off?"

"Well, normally, there's a siren and some lights, and they should give you enough time to get out."

"If you knew what was going on."

"Yes. It's possible that someone who was unfamiliar with the system could get confused, and not get out. Or the door could be blocked from the outside."

"Well, the door wasn't blocked when we got there. That's part of the reason I wanted to pull you in today, so I could try and sort out what happened."

Sergeant Stone walked back in with a big pile of prints. He laid them on the table in front of the detective. Detective Harris flipped through them quickly, finally laying one on the table between them. He turned it so it was right-side-up from Jess's viewpoint.

"Is this what the wall in the data center looks like?"

"Yes, that's it."

"Well, I see the button by the door that activates the extinguisher system. And I see the smaller button you're talking about, but I don't see a clipboard hanging on the wall."

Jess picked the picture up and studied it carefully. There were the mouse ears, with their attendant sign, a small flashlight in a charger, an assortment of other signs, and the extinguisher activation button. But there wasn't a clipboard.

He retraced his steps in his mind, thinking through Friday afternoon. He was certain he had hung the clipboard back up on the wall just before he picked his backpack up. He remembered kicking the box out of the doorway so it would close again.

If his memory was right, where had the clipboard gone?

"Can you point out where it normally hangs?"

Jess pointed to a spot on the wall, just under the large red activator button encased in plastic. Detective Harris flipped through the pictures again, finally pulling another one from the pile. This was a close-up of the area just around the activator.

"On this hook?" Harris pointed to a small protrusion, clearly visible in the picture. Jess nodded. "Hmph. I wonder where the clipboard went. Did you call anyone while you were in the data center?"

"You've just jogged my memory. Yes, I normally call someone in to security so they can watch while I do the test. If the test goes wrong, well, I want someone to be able to get down there fast and help me. Brian answered the phone when I did the test.

"Good. We'll check with Brian and see if he remembers the call." Detective Harris made some further notes in his pad and handed the pile of pictures back to the sergeant. Stone took the pictures out of the room.

"Do you mind if I ask why Sergeant Stone thought I had murdered Benita?"

"Your prints are the only ones on the door and the activator."

"And the security tapes were erased?"

"Funny you should use that word. That, or the cameras failed to record what happened. Too convenient for my taste, though."

He studied Jess for a moment and then said, "Well, as far as this goes, you've helped me sort out what happened. I'm not any closer to understanding how it happened, but at least I can fix the sequence of events better. I think we can shut down the recording now and go out to the office." He said some official sounding phrases to close off the interview, and then he shut off the recorder.

"Am I free to go now?"

Chapter 15

Leah sat at the kitchen table, considering the possibilities. Things were getting dangerous. They needed more information, and they needed it fast. Her cell phone rang.

"Hello?"

"Leah, this is Detective Harris. I've just released Mr. Wirth."

"Thanks. Did he give you anything else?"

"Yes, a good bit more. We pulled the police report on the accident and verified what happened. We walked through the day, so I have a good sense of the sequence of events."

"Good. Any ideas on who the murderer is?"

"No. But I think Jess was set up to take the fall."

This might be information they could use. She tried to conceal the excitement in her voice. "Why?"

"Mr. Wirth tested the extinguisher system just before he left the office yesterday. That explains his prints on the doorknobs and the activator. What it doesn't explain is why the clipboard where they record these tests was missing."

"*Missing?*"

"Yes. Apparently, Mr. Wirth normally does these tests. He records them on a clipboard that usually hangs just below the actuator itself. I had Sergeant Stone pull the pictures the crime scene folks took. The hook on the wall is there, but the clipboard isn't."

"I suppose there must be a periodic inspection by the fire department."

"Good point. I'll call some people I know over there on Monday and see if they can tell me anything about the procedures they use."

"When I go in on Monday, I'll try and find the clipboard."

"Okay. Say I call you around three o'clock to exchange information?"

"Sure. On my cell phone. I'll make certain I'm outside in the back someplace, so no one will overhear me."

"Thanks." He clicked off.

As soon as she flipped the phone closed, Daniel said, "Who was that?"

"Harris."

"Calling to let you know he's let our suspect go?"

"Yes."

"Anything else interesting?"

"He thinks Jess was framed for the murder."

Daniel placed his cup of water on the table. "Why?"

"The extinguisher test signoff sheet is missing."

"Explain."

"They test the extinguisher system in the data center once a month. They sign off on the test on a sheet attached to a clipboard that hangs from the wall under the activator. The clipboard and sheet are missing."

"Interesting. That does appear to place him a little less in the crosshairs as a suspect, doesn't it?"

"I don't think he's involved with the operation we're trying to sort out."

"The evidence still points that way. This isn't becoming personal, is it?"

"No. It's just not fitting is all. Look, we traced everything we could coming into and going out of Jess's accounts. We can't find any hidden accounts. We know, on the other hand, that Carl was receiving a good bit of money from OptiData—a lot more than seems reasonable. We also know, thanks to Thuan, that this extra money was being routed through Carl's mother. It wasn't deposited directly into Carl's account. It's far too much money to pay the rent."

"Okay, that all implicates Carl. But it doesn't clear Jess. You said he's hiding some sort of information."

"He is, but I'm convinced it's not identity information."

"Why not?"

"I've seen snippets of it when I walk into his cube. One file I know he has is Carl's voice mail file. Another is his e-mail. And there appears to be a set of notes about Carl's death."

"Jess doesn't think Carl's death was a suicide."

"No."

"Interesting. It sounds like the clincher would be getting that file."

"I've been trying. No dice."

"You mean you've asked him. Why don't you just badge in and get a copy?"

"It would be hard in the middle of the day."

"It's Saturday now. No one else would be there."

"You're suggesting—"

"I'm suggesting you use your entrance privileges as an employee to get into the building and then grab a couple of files off his computer so we can try and see what he has compiled."

"Okay."

"It would prove the case against Jess one way or the other, wouldn't it? Then we would know whether to continue on this track or start looking elsewhere."

"I can get the file, but I'm certain it's encrypted. And it won't be admissible in court."

"Encryption is Thuan's department. I'm certain he can work that out. Court admission is another problem. For now, let's get the file and see what we can find. Hopefully, we'll be able to get the originals into court on our own without relying on what Jess has been collecting. What we need right now is a pointer, not court evidence."

Leah nodded. Picking up her keys, she headed out the door, leaving Daniel sitting at the kitchen table to contemplate this new turn of events.

As she waited for the soft beep indicating the door lock had opened, she decided on a story to explain her badging in over the weekend. Not that anyone was likely to ask, but if they did, she needed to have her story straight. A fast answer always quelled suspicions better than one requiring some thought.

What about that rumor aout Jess making it into the building once without being recorded by anything, to win a bet with Brian? It would be useful to know how he had done that right about now. She hoped he had stored the files on the computer at his desk rather than on his laptop.

Logging in to his computer was easy, because there wasn't a password configured. The next problem was to find the files themselves. Searching through the directories on the hard drive, she found one named "carl-loc." What could "loc" stand for? Another question for Thuan.

When she tried to open the directory, it asked her for a password. This was the harder problem. The password. She tried a few things but couldn't get into the directory. She popped a miniature USB drive into the front of the computer and copied the entire folder over.

She pulled the drive out and then pulled a small digital camera from her pocket. Thuan had asked her to take pictures of anything that might hold a hint about what his password was. She took pictures of a string of conference badges hanging from the wall, and then she turned them over and took another picture. She looked behind and into the guitar and flipped the brass prop over so she could see its back, taking pictures of everything she could.

She slid the first filing cabinet open and started looking through the papers. There was too much here to photograph or take notes about. Thuan was just going to have to do his best with the information she had. He could always ask her to look in specific places, based on the pictures she'd already taken.

At least she hoped so.

On Sunday afternoon, she called Thuan from her cell phone. "Any luck?"

"Yes and no."

"I hope more yes than no."

"There are at least two layers of encryption here. The first was pretty easy to get past. He just encrypted the entire folder using the operating system's protection. I'm past that."

"The second?"

"Well, that one is compiled from open source. Since the source code is available to everyone, everyone makes certain there aren't any back doors or some sort of master password."

"Okay. What does that mean?"

"That if he's chosen his password carefully, it's going to take a lot of horsepower and a lot of time to break the second layer. And there could be a third layer—we just don't know at this point."

"Would having someone else look at it help?"

"I doubt it. It's just a matter of trying to factor primes, at this point. It's going to be easier and faster to get his password."

"I looked everyplace I could think of."

"I'll come in with you later, and we can look again."

"That might be risky. There are cameras."

"Probably so. Ideas?"

"Let me try and get his password—or get him to give me the information outright."

"You're the boss."

"Stop saying that." But she smiled as she hung up. It was good to actually be running a case for once.

Chapter 16

Linda intercepted Jess in the parking lot on Monday morning. "Hey. Are you okay?"

"I think so. That *was* a pretty frightening experience, to be honest."

"I can imagine so. I'm surprised you didn't take the week off."

"Well, there's a lot to do, so I figured I would just come in and deal with it. They didn't charge me with anything."

"Do you think they will?"

"No. Detective Harris thinks someone was trying to frame me for Benita's murder. I expect there will probably be plenty of stuff to clean up in the data center."

"Gerard actually got a couple of folks in yesterday to clean up so it wouldn't impact business this morning. There might still be some stuff to do, but he checked what he could. I think they're coming this week to reset the extinguisher system and refill the halon."

"Well, that's good. At least I won't be completely under water."

"How can you handle the thought of going down into the basement again? Two deaths so far. When will this end?"

"Wooohooo! Whooo! There are spirits after you, *Liiindaaa."*

Linda laughed and smacked him on the shoulder. "Oh, hush, Jess. You know what I mean. Still, I'm glad you've taken it so well."

"Well, what are my options, really? I can't hide in a cave, can I?"

"You could."

"Well, maybe I already do have a cave to hide in. The basement. Only now it's a haunted cave. It would make a perfect haunted house this fall for Halloween, wouldn't it?"

Linda cut him short with a look. "No more of that nonsense. Gerard wouldn't approve of a bunch of kids with sticky fingers running around between all the servers, especially if the place is haunted. Are you still convinced Carl didn't commit suicide?"

"Now more than ever."

"Why not go to the police?"

"Because there are still gaps. At this point, I don't think anyone would believe me."

"Are you keeping notes someplace?"

"Why? In case the ghost of the data center gets me the next time I'm down there?"

She stopped him just as they started up the stairs towards the front door. "This isn't a joke, Jess. If Carl was murdered, that's two. Whoever killed them won't hesitate to kill you as well. And if they tried to frame you for murder, it sounds like they're already trying to get you out of the way."

The pressure of her fingers on his arm increased with each sentence. Jess could tell she was truly frightened.

"Yes, I know, Linda. I'm sorry for being flip, but I don't see what else I can do at this point."

"You could let it go."

"I think things have gone beyond that."

"Why?" she asked.

"Framing me for murder wasn't a warning. Someone was playing for keeps. My only way out at this point, I'm afraid, is forward."

"You could find another job, move, get out of here."

"I won't run, Linda. I've started this—"

"And you need to finish it. But if this is really dangerous, then maybe you should let it go, even if it drives you crazy. Better to be alive and crazy than dead. Curiosity killed the cat."

"But satisfaction brought him back. I don't think I can let it go now, Linda. Someone tried to frame me for murder. They've killed at least one other person, and maybe two. No, I need to do the right thing."

She nodded and climbed the stairs past Jess. She stood at the door, waiting for Jess to climb the rest of the way up. After a few moments, she said, "Aren't you going to open the door for me?"

"Oh. Sorry." He moved the rest of the way up the steps and slapped his badge against the reader.

"Any special plans for this week?"

"Nothing special, really. Just get through it, find out as much as I can, and then spend some time out on the lake this weekend."

"How's the new PWC?"

"Great,"

"Like a bicycle built for two, only with one rider, isn't it?"

He sighed as they paused together in front of the elevator. She would go up from here, and he would go on to his cubicle.

She grabbed his arm, pulling him back before he could push the button for her, and looked around furtively."Well, there is one thing you could do this week."

Caught up in the moment, Jess whispered back, "What?"

"Send Leah something for her birthday!"

"Her birthday? When is her birthday?"

"It's Thursday, but I don't want anyone else to know."

"Why not?"

"Can't have the whole place sending her stuff, can we? It's better if you're the only who knows."

"How old is she going to be?"

She huffed. "Like I'm going to tell you that."

"Okay, I'll just look it up in her personnel record."

"Jess! You're not supposed to have access to those."

"Like that's stopped me before! Besides, it's harmless!"

"Okay, I'll tell you, just to save you the trouble. She's twenty-five," said Linda.

"She's a pup!"

"Then you're a pup! She's only three years younger than you are. She actually just finished school a little less than two years ago."

"Either she started late, or she took longer than four years, then?"

Linda said, "She was getting her master's in criminal psychology."

"Okay, so how do you go from a master's to working as a project manager in a place like this?"

Linda shrugged. "Maybe she can understand geeks with that degree. You'll do something for her, won't you?"

"Yes, and I promise it won't be anything criminal. Or even embarrassing." Linda shot him a look. "Okay, I promise."

Jess dumped his laptop bag on his desk and sat down. It was time to do some sleuthing, especially since he wasn't in the mood to listen to the voice mails waiting for him. He opened the files, typing in the passwords required without thinking, and sat staring at the notes he had made. Carl's death was certainly not a suicide, and Benita's death told him the murderer was still running loose. But who could it be? The pieces didn't fit; something was still wrong.

Leah poked her head into his cube and rapped on the whiteboard. He quickly changed the screen before turning to face her.

"Heard you had an adventure this weekend."

"I suppose you could call it that. I wouldn't consider it a fun sort of adventure, though. And I missed a cowboy shoot."

"Well, you could have played the part of the jailbird in the shoot, anyway."

He laughed. "Yes, I suppose so."

"Did they at least treat you well? Is jail food good?"

"Horrid! As for treating me good, I don't know if I would say that."

"Did something happen?"

"It's odd, really. Sergeant Stone picked me up early Saturday morning and took me to the station. He was really rough. Questioned me for an hour or so before dragging me to a holding cell for the night."

"Why does that seem odd?"

"Well, I should say he accused me for about an hour, rather than questioning me."

"That *is* odd.

"Yeah, he's out to get me."

She laughed. "Don't get a persecution mania on me, okay?"

"Well, I'm not trying to, but he didn't even record the interview. Just kept saying how he knew I had killed Benita, and how it would be better if I'd just admit it."

"It is odd that he didn't record you." Leah paused for a moment before continuing. "Are you certain there wasn't a recording device in the room someplace and you just didn't see it?"

"No. I asked Detective Harris specifically, and he said there wasn't."

"That *is* odd."

"You already said that once."

She laughed. "I guess I did, didn't I?" She abruptly sat in a chair.

"Okay, what's bothering you?"

"Am I that transparent?"

"Or maybe I just know you better than you think. Criminal psychology, huh?"

"Now just who did you hear that from? Have you been snooping around in the personnel files?"

"Why is it everyone around here thinks I would do something like that? I was just talking to someone who knows."

"Linda!"

"But none of that answers my question. What's bothering you?"

"To use your words, something I'm working on just isn't elegant. The facts I have don't match reality, somehow."

Jess reached back in his memory for a favorite Sherlock Homes quote. "There is nothing more deceptive than an obvious fact."

"How often have I said to you that when you have eliminated the impossible, whatever remains, however improbable, must be the truth?"

"Touché," Jess smiled. "So you like mysteries, huh?"

"Really, who doesn't like Sherlock Holmes?"

"I prefer Miss Marple, honestly, but I do like Sherlock Holmes. I wish I had a brain like Miss Marple."

"As I recall, Miss Marple's brain was described as a steel trap. If you had a brain like her, you'd be dangerous. Or maybe you already are dangerous."

"Come on—I'm a frumpy geek. Dangerous is about the last thing anyone who saw me would think."

Leah said, "Miss Marple was pretty frumpy, too. Maybe the impression of frumpiness is just a thin veneer hiding a criminal mastermind."

He laughed. "Come on. It's not all that bad."

"For instance, why is it every time I walk in here you hide something you're looking at? It's those files about Carl, isn't it?"

"I do not!" Jess protested.

"Okay, not all the time. Look, let's find a conference room."

They walked around the floor, looking for an empty conference room they could camp in for a bit. Once inside, she continued, "Seriously, Jess, what do you know?"

He decided to equivocate. "Know about what?"

"You *know* what I mean. Someone tried to frame you for murder this weekend. What's up?"

"How do you know that?"

"Never mind how I know what I know." Leah pulled her brows together into a furrow. "Just tell me what's up."

Fear began rising in him. Who was this girl? How much more did she know? How did she know that he had been framed for murder? Or had she just sorted that out on her own?

"Nothing, seriously."

"Jess, you're in over your head."

"No. I'm fine. I can handle this."

"That's what everyone thinks until they get caught in a web they can't get out of. Friends don't let friends hide things that might be dangerous to their own health."

"You're starting to sound like my mom." She laughed. In that laugh, he found the strength to try another step towards trusting her. Really tursting her was still out of the question; it would take time to build up to that level. "How about we discuss it over dinner on Friday night?"

"You're...you're asking me out?"

"Well, why not? We've eaten lunch together. It'll just be lunch at a different time of day."

"No," Leah replied.

"That's it, just no? It's because I won't give you those precious files, isn't it? Is it *really* that important?"

"Yes, it is, honestly."

"Why?" Jess felt the hurt welling up in him. How could she turn him down flat?

"I can't tell you."

"You can't tell me, and you won't go out with me, but you expect me to trust you. Just like that."

"Yes. Just like that. You have to trust someone again some time."

"Now you *really are* starting to sound like my mother," said Jess.

She moved stiffly to the door, slinging it open in front of her. Jess mumbled under his breath, "I'm just not in her league."

She spun, her eyes an intense green, her pupils narrowed. She walked over and pulled his chair back around. Her voice was low, but he could hear her clearly. "*Daniel Jesse Wirth! If you ever say that to me again, I'm going to leave a handprint across your face to last you a whole month of Sundays! You let me be the judge of who's in my league!*" It was hard to stomp on the low carpet in the hallway, but Leah did her best to stomp loudly as she strode from the room.

Linda poked her head into the conference room. "Are you okay? I think I heard a minor explosion out here."

Jess was quiet for a moment. It was too much too fast. "Linda. Hi. How does Leah know my first and middle names?"

"Interesting question. What happened?"

"I guess I just made Leah really mad."

"I guess so. What did you say to her?"

"I asked her out on a date."

"No, I don't think that was it. What else?"

"That she sounded like my mother."

"Well, that's a pretty bad thing to tell a girl, but I don't think that was it, either."

"That she was out of my league."

Linda sighed. "Yep, that was probably it."

Chapter 17

Jess traipsed back to his cubicle, trying to get the argument with Leah off his mind. He opened the files on Carl's death again and stared at his notes. Where else could he look for information? Video recorders. Of course, the night of Carl's death, the video recorders had malfunctioned. Or at least that's what Detective Harris had told him. Getting those files would be something worth looking into.

Carl had normally worked on the video monitoring system, though, so other than replacing a couple of the cameras, Jess had no idea how it worked. Where were the video files stored? Were they encrypted? The system information documentation was the first place to start, of course, but Jess had looked there before and knew they didn't contain any useful information.

Jess opened the case tracking tool and searched for all the cases opened against the surveillance system. Most of them had been closed by replacing cameras or making some adjustment to the routers or switches the cameras were connected to. He couldn't find any passwords or any information about how the system worked. Carl's case notes had always been much less verbose than Jess's.

As he scrolled through the list to the bottom, he noticed there was an open case on the video surveillance system. Interesting. At least it was an excuse to snoop around and find out how the system worked, anyway. He wrote the case details down on a piece of paper and closed all the applications on his desktop, carefully cleaning up so the files on Carl's death weren't accessible to any prying eyes. Trudging up the stairs towards the third floor, he wondered why he had eschewed the elevator.

He made his way around the counter just behind the open security office door and stood in front of Brian, who was sitting in a comfortable looking chair, reading a comic book. He pulled a set of headphones off his ears and said, "Hey, Jess. What's up?"

"Just trying to figure out how the video surveillance system works."

Brian's face hardened. "Not looking into Carl's death on your own, are you? Gerard said something about you snooping around this morning. He wasn't happy about it." Jess held out the paper with the scribbled case number so Brian could see it. "Oh. That. Well, we have been having a problem with one of the cameras, the one just over the door down in the data center."

"I didn't really work on the system much before Carl died. Do y'all have documentation on how it works? I'd like to look at the problem before I just replace the camera, make certain something else isn't wrong."

Brian pointed to the flat screen monitors mounted above the windows. "The video is streamed onto those monitors. Right now, there's just the parking lots, but things change from time to time." As he said this, one of the monitors swapped over to a view of the break room. Jess was startled. He had been recorded while talking to Benita.

He shifted his attention to the windows below the monitors, looking out over the lake and woods in the back of the building. How did Brian convince Gerard to make this old conference room into an office for the security folks? It probably had the best view of any of the rooms in the building, being on the top floor and in a corner. Finally, he shifted back to Brian.

"There wasn't a lot of information in the case notes. What's the problem?" Jess asked.

"That camera seems to be skipping for some reason. We've lost a number of segments of video off it."

"Just video, or audio as well?"

"We don't actually record audio off most of the cameras here. Just about the only one we do record the audio off of is the one in the front lobby." Brian swiveled and clicked on a control shown on the screen of the computer in front of him. The image of the break room was replaced by an image of the front lobby.

The recording of him and Benita wouldn't have included audio, then, so no one could tell what they had said to one another. *Benita was crying during the entire conversation. It certainly would have looked incriminating.* "How many times has this happened? And at what times of the day?"

"Why would that matter?"

"The traffic level on the network varies during the day. It's possible it might relate to that or something else on the network."

Brian shrugged. "Between about midnight and early in the morning the night of Carl's death. Another one around four in the afternoon, for about fifteen minutes, a few days after. Another one at around seven in the morning, last week. And then one on Friday afternoon, around five. Does that help?"

"Seems pretty random. It's probably not network related, then."

"Didn't I say you should just replace the camera?"

"I don't like to replace hardware until I've checked everything out. Besides, I'll be working on the surveillance system a lot more now since Carl's gone, so it would be good to know how it works for the next time. Can you show me one of the skips in the recording?"

"Is it important?"

"I need to know what it looks like, yes. There must be some difference between the way a camera malfunction looks and the way a network problem looks."

"Sure, why not?" Brian opened an application on his computer and scrolled through different videos until he found the one of Friday, during the time when Benita had died. When he clicked on the video to open it, a dialog box popped up, asking for a password.

Jess shifted his gaze to the keyboard, trying to catch the password as Brian typed it in. The first three digits were *9yj*. Jess missed the rest.

Playing the tape through, he showed Jess the gap in the recording. Nothing looked different in the recording itself, but Brian pointed out how the timestamp in the corner skipped a few minutes of time.

Jess pointed at the computer. "Can I look at the application for a bit to see how it's configured? It would help a lot." Brian moved out of the chair so Jess could sit down.

Jess moved quickly through the various configuration screens. So far, he knew the recordings were encrypted and what part of the password was. Now he wanted to know if the recordings were stored locally on one of the computers in the security office, or if they were stored on a server in the data center. He found the screen with this information on it and jotted the name of the server down. It was in the data center.

He cruised through the screens a bit more, making a show of examining the rest of the configuration. "Is anything else up here acting up? Any of the computers not connecting to the network or anything like that?"

"No, not that I can recall."

Jess closed the screens and stood up.

As Jess stood, Brian moved out of his way, and asked, "Anything interesting?"

"Everything here looks normal."

"Okay. Just remember what I said about Carl. Don't get in over your head. Gerard doesn't want you poking around in that business."

He shrugged. "Whatever."

"Seriously, Jess. You already had a close call with the Benita thing this weekend. I wouldn't want you to get in over your head."

Jess walked back down the stairs to his cubicle. Going down stairs made more sense than going up since gravity was in your favor going down. Why had Brian warned him twice about looking around for clues about Carl's death? *Don't get in over my head? What does that mean?*

He could see Carl getting mixed up in something that went over his head. Carl was cocky, certain he could handle things without anyone else helping, thankyouverymuch. Gerard, too. He was bombastic and willing to stop at nothing to get what he wanted, including cutting personal attacks in very public situations. Jess had seen Gerard marshal sarcasm and anger into a fearful duo, skirting the truth and sometimes stepping over the line to get the result he thought was best for him.

Did Brian know something? Was he mixed up in this somehow? Not likely. He went to church on Sundays with his family, and he was close to his mom. While Brian was a little odd, with his fascination for all things military, something actually being in the military would probably have cured him of, he didn't seem like the type to be mixed up in anything like murder.

"The quiet ones are the most dangerous." This was something one of his shooting instructors had said, time and again. He had emphasized the importance of living in condition yellow, aware of your environment, because the most dangerous criminals always attacked when they thought they had you blind.

He settled into his chair and tapped a few keys to get his computer to wake up. His next step was to grab a copy of the video files from the times of each of the murders. He stared at the paper with the name of the server. Logging in and downloading the files would be simple enough. But if someone were really watching him, it could also be suicide.

The problem was simple. Each time someone logged into a server, the server sent a record of the login to another server. If there was an attack against the network, the records of all the logins to the servers might contain some vital clues as to how it had been done. Using another account was an option. But whose?

Carl's accounts had all been closed. Gerard and Brian were still in the building, so trying to guess their passwords, or change them, wasn't a good idea right at the moment. Linda's account wasn't authorized to connect to that server. Networks are virtual worlds, though, and in a virtual world, there's always more than one way to accomplish something.

Block the logs, of course. Blocking the server from sending information about him logging in and then erasing his login records from the server in question would cover his tracks completely.

Jess started by looking at the network diagram and determining the path of the traffic between the video recording server and where the logs were collected. All the traffic between them flowed through one router. Attaching to this router, he made a small change in the packet filters. Any packets logging events on the video server would now be thrown away.

Keeping the connection to the router open, he started a file transfer program and connected to the server where the video recordings were kept. Working quickly, he found the directory where the video recordings were kept and copied the files he wanted over to his local hard drive. Once they were copied over, he dropped his connection to the server, removed his modifications to the packet filter, and glanced down at the clock in the lower right-hand corner of his screen. He had done it in eight minutes. No one would ever notice the missing log entries.

Heaving a sigh of relief, he double-clicked on one of the files. A dialog box popped up on the screen, asking for a password. His media player wouldn't play it without the file being unencrypted first. He guessed a few times, using the three characters he already knew from watching Brian type it, and then he gave up. This was clearly a job for a program designed just to crack passwords.

Jess spent an hour surfing the Internet, finally finding a program that looked promising. After downloading and installing it, he launched the program and keyed in the first three characters in the password. Then he browsed over to the first of the files he had copied from the video recording server and started the program working on finding the password that would let him watch it.

After clearing out his inbox, Jess flipped back to the password guessing software he had left running. It had been churning through thousands of possible passwords a second, trying to find one that would decrypt the file. As the window popped up on his screen, he saw the program had quit running. There was a line of text on the screen: "9yj8th7rg."

He opened the file in the media player, holding his breath as he typed in the password. The building parking lot popped into view, a small time marker showing 22:48 in the lower right-hand corner.

He dragged the bar at the bottom of the screen to the right, browsing through the video. He stopped when Carl's car appeared. The time marker showed 06:12. He pulled the slider back to his left, backing the recording up, and he let it go so it would play normally.

Carl's car didn't drive into the lot; it just appeared, as if by magic, at 06:11. Jess backed up farther still until the time marker said 01:00. He let it go again so the file would play normally. The parking lot looked normal, just the lights illuminating empty spaces.

But there was something missing. Rain. Jess looked through several more spots on the recording and couldn't find anything that looked like rain. Was it that the cameras just didn't record rain? Even if they didn't, the asphalt should have been reflecting the lights. The night on this recording was dry. The night Carl died it had rained.

He closed the media player and opened another program. This one didn't play what was in the file; instead, it displayed the metadata, or the information about when the file had been recorded, edited, and stored. The camera itself injected this information into the file, attached to specific frames within the recording.

He pulled the slider over to the same point. The time changed smoothly. But the date wasn't the same. The recording was altered. Someone had spliced in a section of videotape, replacing the original recording. With this in mind, going through the tape again, Jess could see the splice points. It was well done. A casual observer would never notice. But it was definitely there.

Why? To cover up when Carl had actually arrived? But the badge system recorded this as well. And that data hadn't been altered. Of course, it was possible that Carl had altered the tape before committing suicide. Not likely, but possible.

There was only one other possibility. It had been done to remove evidence of someone else coming into the parking lot.

Someone had come in with Carl that night. Whoever it was had tailgated Carl, letting Carl open the door. *Whoever it was would be in the building without any record of it. He could then murder Carl without raising any suspicions. Modifying the security tapes would remove the last bit of evidence of someone being here with Carl.*

Was it coincidence Benita had seen Gerard in the building that night? The modified tape certainly corroborated Benita's story of seeing Gerard here that same night. But Gerard being here didn't prove anything other than that he was working late or that he had come by the office to pick something up. He might have murdered Carl. Or he might not have.

Everywhere he looked, the evidence was missing. Missing evidence couldn't be used to prove anything. Frustration mounting, Jess opened the next file. This one was from the same day, but from a different camera. He typed in the same password and was presented with an image of the space between rows fifty-two and fifty-three in the data center. He pulled the bar at the bottom to the right to jog his way through the video quickly.

The screen went black at 22:45. He backed the recording up and let it play through to 22:45. He could clearly see a dark object like a piece of cloth being placed over the lens. Twenty minutes later, at 23:05, the object was pulled off and replaced by the darkness of the data center with the lights shut off. Jess could make out the scattered equipment lights, but they weren't bright enough to see anything, just pinpricks in a field of dark gray. And of course this camera didn't record any sound.

Again, missing information. It was obviously intentional, but there was no telling who had put the cloth there, or who had taken it away.

He had a number of other recordings he could look at, but he was really only interested in one other one for the moment. He picked out the correct file from the ones he had copied and opened it. Once again, he had to type the password, and once again, he was presented with an image of the data center. Only this time, it was looking down on the data center from above the door. This was the camera Brian had opened a case on.

He pulled the bar at the bottom along until the time read 18:10. The fire alarm had been set off at 18:14. Releasing the bar, he let it play. There was a skip in the recording. It was very clear, not like the professional splicing that had been done in the recording of the parking lot. He pulled the slider back along the bar and advanced frame by frame until he came to the skip. The time shown in the bottom right-hand corner skipped from 18:13:22 to 18:15:54. The information was simply gone.

Who had the knowledge and the tools to modify the tapes this way? The security office certainly had a lot of editing software, but was there anyone else in the building who did? Jess shut the media player down. He encrypted the video files he had retrieved and placed them into the encrypted folder.

He searched the case database, looking for anyone who had called in with a problem for any video editing software. There weren't any hits. There was also a database of software licenses, but other than the security office, no one in the building seemed to have any.

Finally, he picked up the phone and dialed Linda.

"Linda? This might sound odd, but could you help me with a couple of questions?"

"Sure, Jess. What's up?"

"Do you know if Gerard has any video editing software on his computer?"

"He does, actually. He uses it to mess with home videos and those awful company videos he sends out every now and then."

"Okay, thanks. Second and final question. What is Leah's favorite color?"

"Blue."

"Thanks! Talk to you later."

Opening a browser, he checked the online stores of several florists. Not finding anything he really thought would work, he clicked the "contact customer service" button on one of the sites and dialed the number.

"I'd like something with pink roses, but something blue as well. Any ideas?"

"I think we could do blue and pink lilies. Would that work?"

"Can you add in any roses?"

"If you dropped the blue lilies, we could work in some roses. Red?"

"No."

"Then how about pink roses? That would work well."

"Okay. But how could we work the blue in?"

"How about we do a clear vase with pink roses, with a blue ribbon around it?"

"That would be perfect."

Chapter 18

Leah sat in Linda's cube, trying to calm down. "I really don't want to lose Jess' friendship."

"This too will pass. Give it time."

Linda can always put things in perspective. "I suppose so."

Linda sighed. "I had hoped you two would get along better than this."

"Oh, I think we get along. I'm just on edge, I think."

"Why don't you ask for help?"

Leah looked at Linda, her gray hair pulled up in a neat bun, the image of a grandmother. She couldn't imagine Linda being mixed up in this mess, and it would be good to have someone to ask advice of. But, no, she couldn't.

"It's not something I can ask for help on, I think. At least not just anyone."

"Is Jess in the could help, or couldn't help group?"

"Jess would be a great help, if he could trust me." The frustration welled up in her again. "Why won't he just trust me?" As it slipped out, she realized it probably sounded personal to Linda, even though it hadn't been intended that way.

Linda looked up from the spreadsheet she was working on. "Give him time. He might. That divorce hit him pretty hard."

But why not play along? She might discover something useful, like where Jess hid his passwords. "Did she just fall out of love with him?"

Linda laughed. "You watch too many movies. Love isn't something you fall into or out of. Worst bit of nonsense in the world, that." Leah didn't interject, so Linda continued. "It's something you decide. And not just once, but a thousand times a day, seven days a week, fifty-two weeks a year. You get up and love every day, not because you have some warm fuzzy feeling, but because you know it's the right thing to do."

"Sounds kind of dreary or old-fashioned."

"Like you'd expect anything other than old-fashioned out of me? As for dreary, no, it's not. Dreary is trying to chase a feeling all over the place. Chasing a feeling is like nailing gelatin to a wall." Linda looked stern, peering over her glasses. "You remember that, Leah."

"I think I'm going to head home early."

"It's been a rough day, hasn't it?"

That afternoon, Leah sat at her table. Daniel faced her, and Thuan sat to one side. "Any luck?"

Thuan glanced up from his laptop. "No. I know what he encrypted it with, but breaking it is going to take more processors than we have access to right now. It would take a week or two, even if we had enough processing power."

Daniel said, "We don't have a week or two, unfortunately. People's identities are being stolen, hundreds by the day."

Leah drummed her fingers. "Well, we've had him tailed as closely as we dare. No one has seen him drop a single thing anyplace. Has anything changed on the network side?"

Thuan glanced up again. "No, nothing I can see. All their traffic looks normal to me and to all the network folks who've looked at it."

Leah turned to Daniel. "You're still convinced he's the one stealing the data?"

"I don't know. He's still the best lead we have, though. The only way we can know for certain is to break into those files. If they are identities, then we have the tail of the network, and we can follow it up."

"And what if Jess's files don't contain the information we need?" *Or what if we get more than we bargained for?* Leah was disturbed that Daniel seemed to be focusing on Jess as being involved in the identity thefts.

"Then we're back to square one."

Thuan glanced up for a moment before burying his head in the laptop again. "It's pretty useless to speculate as long as we don't have a password to get into those files."

Leah sighed. "Well, I've tried, but I can't get him to show me anything, and I can't find any hint of his passwords anywhere."

"Cagey," Daniel said.

"I know."

"Well, let's just get a warrant. We serve it at his house and compel him to open those files for us."

Sure, well just sweep in there and force him to give us the password to these files. That'll work. Leah knew Jess well enough to guess he'd refuse just on principle. "And if he's the tail of the network, then we've lost our chance to find out who's at the top,"

"That's a risk we're going to have to take. What's your take on it, Thuan?"

"I'd say it's fifty-fifty he's our guy. But Leah should know better than either of us; she's had more contact with him."

"Maybe too much."

Maybe Daniel was getting a little jealous? What of, I've never agreed to go out with him. "Hey, now wait! I've been very professional here. I'm not involved with him in any way."

"I heard you two had a row today, though. The folks at the office say it was a lover's spat."

Leah laughed, trying to calm Daniels' fears. He was in line for a promotion, there was no reason to push someone who was likely to become your boss in the future. "Hardly. It was over those stinking files, actually."

"Okay, well, it's your call. How should we handle Jess?"

"It's Tuesday. Let's give it 'til the end of the week. If we can't make progress by Monday, we go for a warrant," she said.

She looked around the table, measuring the reactions of the other two. Daniel nodded firmly. Thuan didn't glanced up from his computer screen, but he did nod, if just barely.

Chapter 19

Jess sat in his truck, his irritation growing at the slow pace of the traffic. Normally it wasn't like this on a Wednesday morning. *It's like swimming in molasses. It's what I get for leaving home so late this morning. Silly alarm clock.*

He'd have to double-check his alarm clock tonight because he couldn't be late tomorrow morning. Leah would get the flowers he'd sent her for her birthday tomorrow morning. He wanted to be there before the florist arrived so he could check them before Leah got in. It gave him a chance to change his mind, to pull them out of her cubicle if he got cold feet.

She seemed to be under a lot of stress, but Jess couldn't figure out what it was. She hadn't talked to him since the argument. He'd checked out her project files, and they didn't seem like anything out of the ordinary. In fact, he considered the project she was on pretty simple, something Gerard had given her as a first test or a way to get her feet wet before moving on to something larger.

The traffic light far out in front of him turned. He crept forward a few car lengths and then stopped again. The signal flipped to red again, leaving him stuck not far from where he had started. Frustrated, he worked the clutch and brought the truck to a stop.

And what about Carl's death? It was about time to take action on that front. There had to be some way to break out of these persistent dead ends. A convenient lack of information about anything dealing with Carl's death hung like smoke over his work. Altered video recordings, erased e-mails, and missing voice mails. With so much smoke, there had to be a fire. But *where?*

And even if he found the fire, what was he going to do with it? How can you play with fire, and not get burned? Turning the information over to Detective Harris was on option.

Leah was another. His hands dug into the steering wheel. Why had he thought of Leah? She was interested in what he was doing. And she was really upset when he wouldn't explain or show her. But why would a project manager want this sort of information? Was she just fascinated with this sort of thing?

For now, it didn't matter. He had trusted before and been burned. This time, he would be certain before he trusted. The light turned green. He turned his attention to his driving again.

His morning followed the normal routine, even if it started later than normal. There was nothing unusual in either his voice mail or e-mail. The office felt cold against the heat of the day as he sat nursing his cup of coffee, staring at the file of notes he'd made on Carl's death. There had to be a connection someplace.

Carl had been killed in the data center, strung up from a server on row fifty-three. His cell phone hadn't broken against the floor—it had been intentionally crushed. A large number of floor tiles had been pulled up, which obviously meant he had been looking for something. But what? A cable, maybe.

Chasing a cable through the data center would be like trying to find a needle in a haystack. Miles and miles of cable inhabited the space under the floors, neatly wrapped in bundles, all with precisely the same markings, in precisely the same colors. Chasing cables wasn't his favorite sport, not since he'd spent a year finding and clearing out those ancient paper-wrapped cables while replacing the telephone switch in the U.S. Air Force.

But Carl had been killed. So there must be something there to find. And if Carl had found it, there wasn't any reason Jess couldn't find it. Maybe the answer was down there, in the basement. There wasn't much to lose, other than lost time.

He watched the digital readout above the elevator door, waiting for it to change from two to one. As it switched, he glanced down, catching his distorted reflection in the polished surface of the doors. He was wearing the same shorts and shirt he had been the morning he'd found Carl's body. Was this a good sign, or a bad one?

Leaving the elevator, he hurried up the ramp amid the clutter of boxes along the corridor leading up the ramp to the doors. Maybe the new cleaning contractor would clear them out once Gerard sorted out who to hire. The lights lit up the room as he passed through the doors.

He moved down row fifty-three, positioning himself in front of the rack where he'd found Carl. This was the place to start, where it all began. He looked at each server in the rack carefully. Every server was identical. The nameplates carried the same brand name, the power cables neatly wrapped and pulled down tight, the little inventory bar code stickers were all in the same place, and two yellow Ethernet cables plugged into the same places.

Each server had two connections for multiple reasons. The first, and most obvious, was to allow the server to continue operating even if one of the interfaces failed or if part of the network failed. There was also the issue of trying to push too much data down a single cable if the load on a specific server peaked, although Jess had never seen that happen before.

He moved one rack to his right. Each server here was identical as well, each yellow cable pulled neatly into the cable management system at the top of the rack. Nothing was out of place. There had to be *something.* What if all the servers in all the racks were actually identical? What had Carl seen that Jess didn't see?

He sighed and moved two racks to the left. Again, all the servers were identical. He squatted down to look at the bottom row of servers more closely. Everything looked the same. As he stood up again, something caught his eye.

One of the servers along the top looked wrong. One of the cables was plugged into a different place than the others. It was hard to see, though. Jess parted the curtain of cables pulled tight in front of the server, the gesture reminding him of pulling open a bundle of grape vines on his grandfather's farm. The server at the top of the rack had three connections.

His hands shook as he began to trace this odd connection. Here, at last, there was something to chase down and discover rather than something missing.

Tracing cables among huge bundles of identically marked and colored cables was a simple if tedious affair. He grabbed the cable with one hand, alternately tugging and pushing the cable gently. His other hand felt among the bundles above the server, trying to feel the cable's movement. It only took a few minutes to find the cable as it entered the trough hanging above the row of racks. He marked it with a small dot from a permanent marker, something small enough few other people would notice it, but it would enable him to find it again, knowing where to look.

There was no way to trace the cable along the long steel cable holders without using a ladder to climb up and look down into the gray trough itself. He glanced down the row of racks at the security camera.

At this point, he could simply erase the data he'd recorded and pretend none of this had happened. He could walk away. Once he pulled the ladder over and started tracing this cable down, it would be much harder to deny what he was up to. He could make something up, of course, as an excuse, but if the killer saw him doing this…

He sat heavily on the floor, his back against the coldness of the equipment across from the fatal rack, considering what to do. A vision of himself, strung up in the same place as Carl, sprung unbidden into his head. He shook it off and got up. There was nothing to do at this point but to go forward.

He moved quickly down to the door, picked up a short ladder, and brought it back down to row fifty-three. The gray walls of the server room felt oppressive as he climbed up on the short ladder and started tracing the cable down the trough. He knew the cameras were recording this, but short of establishing his guilt beyond the shadow of a doubt by covering them or breaking their connection to the server, there was little he could do.

It took some time, but he finally traced the cable down into the first rack on the row and into the patch panel. He took out a small slip of paper and noted down the number of the jack the cable was plugged into. This was the first piece of information he needed to figure out where that third connection ended up.

There was no time to run back up to his desk, at this point, to check out the wiring diagrams. Moving down two rows, he found a monitor and keyboard mounted to one of the racks. He slid the top drawer out and flipped up the flat panel display hidden there. He slid the next drawer down open, revealing a keyboard.

He tapped furiously on the keyboard as the monitor sprang to life. He connected to a server and quickly navigated through several directories until he reached the one with the wiring diagrams.

He opened a spreadsheet. There was one tab for each row of racks in the data center, each column within a tab matching a rack. Each row matched a piece of equipment; the cells contained the jack number the cable running from that piece of equipment was plugged into. The bottom row listed each jack in the patch panel at the end of the row, which was matched to a letter indicating a bundle of cable and a number indicating the cable number within that bundle.

Running his finger down the columns, Jess found the server with three yellow Ethernet cables attached. The spreadsheet only showed two cables attached to it. He then checked the jack number along the bottom row. There wasn't an entry for the jack number in question. He double-checked the sheet of paper and looked again. No, there wasn't supposed to be anything plugged into that jack. He'd have to chase the cable manually.

Tilting the monitor to its normal horizontal position, he pushed it back into the slot in the rack, and then he slid the keyboard in behind it. He went back to the server and rechecked his trace. The mark was on the right cable, and the cable traced the rest of the way back to the same jack.

Moving to the back of the patch panel, he examined the cables going between the jacks and the data center floor. All of these cables were white instead of yellow, but again, they were all identical. Each one had the type of cable and the manufacturer imprinted along the cable, along with a marker showing where the cable had been cut off the roll.

He moved the bundles of cables around so he could see the jack the extra connection was plugged into. The cable was newer. Looking closer, he could see the manufacturer was different. This cable had been added recently.

He carried the ladder back over to the wall, carefully hanging it up on the hook. Was Carl tracing this cable, or was he installing it? Was he involved in what was going on, or did he stumble on it? There was one way to tell—looking at all the cases Carl had solved in the last few months to see if there was anything there that would have brought him down to that row.

He grabbed the mouse ears and headed back down the rows. The tile beneath the patch panel slid up, the cables below coming into view. The newer cable sat on top of one of the bundles. It must have been done in a hurry. Otherwise, whoever put it there would have tried to bury the cable in the center of the bunch to make it harder to find. Or the person who did it just assumed no one would ever notice.

Each set of cables was pulled into a bundle with a long, white tie wrap. A tag was tied to the tie wrap as well, a bundle number noted on one side. He noted this down on the sheet of paper next to the jack number and other information. He gently reset the tile into place, hung the mouse ears back up, and headed back to his cubicle. Enough risk for one day.

Jess slouched into his chair, making it bounce a little. He opened the encrypted files and spent some time typing the information from the pieces of paper he'd brought up from the data center into the file of notes.

Ding! An instant messaging window opened up. Linda's name was in the title bar, the background filled with flowers.

"You'd better get up here."

He typed back, "Uh oh."

"He's steamed. Wants you in his office now."

"Any idea what it's about?"

"Tiles in the data center."

His heart sank. How had Gerard seen the recording already? "Okay, be there in a minute."

He closed down the instant messenger window and encrypted the files once again. Leah didn't say anything as he passed her cube on the way to the elevators.

"I don't know *what* you've done," Linda said as he stepped up to the counter in front of her cubicle, "but he's really steamed. I've seen him get mad at other people like this, but never at you. I don't know, Jess, I'm worried."

"What's the worst he can do, fire me?"

"Don't be flippant."

"I suppose you're right. But just in case, could you give this to Leah for me?" He picked up a pink sticky note from her desk and wrote his cell phone number on it. Her purse was sitting on the desk, a field of black leather that needed some pink. He stuck the note to the purse. "Thanks."

He stepped into Gerard's office.

"Close the door behind you." Jess gently closed the door and turned to face him.

"What were you doing down in the data center?"

"Just chasing a problem with one of the cameras."

"Why would you be chasing a problem with a camera down on row fifty-three? I saw you from the security office, pulling up floor tiles, so there's no point in trying to hide behind the camera story."

"I just noticed a couple of cables that didn't seem right, so I was checking them."

"What sort of cables?"

"Oh, nothing, really. One of the cables down by the camera wasn't bundled correctly, so I was just redoing the tie wraps back to the patch panel."

"We don't pay you to chase random cables. If there's a problem with the cabling, we call the contractors that do that stuff. You don't mess with the cables." His voice rose as he continued, his last sentence coming out as a suppressed shout. "Do you understand?"

Bad memories of drill sergeants flooded into his mind. He shot back, "There is nothing to get upset about."

"You don't tell me when to be upset or what to be upset about. Do you understand? You're just an engineer." He picked up a pile of papers, waved it around, and slammed it back onto his desk. "I have a dozen résumés better than yours in this pile who'd dearly love to replace you. So don't get cocky with me."

Jess kept his voice down, trying to retain his calm. "Gerard, I'm just trying to figure something out that doesn't match the network diagram. You know I'm a stickler about the documentation."

"I'll tell you when to update the network diagrams. It's *my* data center, and I'll tell you when you can pull tiles up and when you can't. I'll tell you what this is about. You still have some theory about Carl, and you're trying to prove something, like you're some detective in a dime-store novel. Now *stop it*, and *get back to work*."

Jess let out a short, nervous laugh. "I think your imagination is running overtime, Gerard. This has nothing to do with Carl. Unless someone's hiding something in the cabling under the floors, I don't see why it's a big deal for me to straighten out some cable ties."

Gerard wheeled, his back to Jess, and remained silent. *There must be a raw nerve here someplace for Gerard to get this upset about floor tiles being pulled up around that server. Maybe Gerard is involved somehow?* Jess noticed, for the first time, how barren Gerard's office was. There were no books, only pictures of pretty girls with cars and a single forlorn college diploma.

Either he was getting up a head of steam, or he was done. Jess broke the silence. "Is that all?"

"No, that is not all! Your problem is you have no social life and no sex life. You need to get a life rather than spending so much time sticking that nose of yours into other people's business."

Jess took a deep breath and let it out slowly. Gerard was just building up a head of steam. Jess spoke to Gerard's back. "I don't think my social life or my sex life is any of your concern."

"Someone needs to be concerned about it. You're too good to come to the company party, aren't you, and have a little fun. Trying to show the rest of us how to live, shove your morals down our throats?" Gerard spun again, an impish, sardonic smile spread across his face. "Why don't you go get that little hussy you're so fond of in bed before someone else does and breaks your heart?"

The blood drained from Jess's face. "Gerard, this is between the two of us. Don't bring Leah into this."

Jess struggled to control his anger. A verse he'd memorized years before popped into his mind: "Whoever is slow to anger is better than the mighty, and he who rules his spirit than he who takes a city." Slow down. Think. Get the conversation back under control.

"Gerard," he said in a less threatening tone, "you have no right to pry into my relationship with Leah or into Leah's life. She's an employee here, not a treat to be passed around to everyone in the department at your whim. Leave Leah out of this."

"It's too late, isn't it? Leah is already in this because both of you are just alike, both too good for the rest of us. Just wait until tomorrow, and then you'll understand. The guys in the office are having a little contest to see who can send her the most and biggest flowers on her birthday. Each one is attaching a card to thank her for her 'favors.' That'll be fun to watch, to see how she handles it. She'll probably run out of the building, crying, and never come back. If you're smart, Jess, you'd come to me and ask *me* how to get a woman." Gerard laughed, a mean, short burst of angry venom.

The tension flowed out like a wave as this last bit brought Jess back to his senses. Of course Gerard was trying to get under his skin, but there was no reason to give in to this. The best thing to do was to let Gerard wind down to quit feeding him, so Jess just remained silent.

After a few moments, Gerard's eyes narrowed. He obviously didn't like this new tactic. "I'd be careful if I were you. Like I said before, you can be replaced." Gerard put his hand on the stack of papers on his desk. It didn't bother Jess any longer; he'd seen all those résumés, and it would be Gerard's loss, not his, if he left.

Gerard continued, "If you continue down this path, I can only say I hope you don't wind up like Carl. Don't open this can of worms. Now get out of here."

Gerard's door clicked as Jess pulled it firmly closed behind him. He had definitely hit a raw nerve. What was the next step?

Two options were apparent. The first was to continue and risk losing his job. Maybe it was time for a change, anyway. Finding a new job probably wouldn't be all that hard, given the certifications Jess had hanging from his cubicle wall. He would miss Linda, of course, but he would find new friends wherever he went.

The end of the conversation, though, had truly bothered him. Losing his job was one thing. A direct threat against his life was another. But that threat also implied there was something deeper involved, something Gerard was involved in. It indicated his work, in fact, might be contributing to something criminal, something he didn't want to be mixed up in.

This conversation had certainly sped things up. He now had the choice to either act fast, before what he'd found could be covered up, or he needed to let it go. Either risk getting fired and losing his life, or quit and find someplace else to work.

Two people had already been murdered, at least one of them unaware of any deeper meaning to her death. Jess couldn't let that stand. It was time to find the fire.

The first order of business was to finish tracing that cable. That was a project for tomorrow morning. The case opened on the camera above the door would provide cover for that much, at least. For the rest, he would have to follow the cable's lead.

As he wheeled into his cubicle, he ran directly into Linda. "Sorry, Linda, I was—"

"Not paying attention to where you were going. I can see that."

"Sorry."

She smiled. "It's okay, I can understand after that discussion with Gerard. Do you still work here?"

"For now."

"Are you going to let this go now?"

"How can I?"

"You just quit thinking about it is all. What happened to Carl is done, and it's in the past."

"And Benita, right?"

She was quiet for a minute. "I see. You think the two are related."

"I'm certain. And I'm certain Carl was murdered."

"Why?"

"Gerard threatened my life."

She gasped. "Jess, it's time to stop this. Go to the police."

"There's nothing to take to the police. All I have is a hunch and a bunch of missing information. Besides, you think I'm going to be better off if a bunch of cops come in here questioning Gerard? Don't you think he'll know who talked to them?"

She slumped in the chair. "I guess you're right. But it's not worth risking your life."

"Two people have already died. Him insulting Leah is just icing on the cake."

She looked up again. "He insulted Leah?"

"Called her names. They're going to try and embarrass her with flowers tomorrow."

"What?"

"The guys in the office are having a contest to see who can send her the biggest and most impressive bouquet tomorrow with insulting notes on them. He wants to see her run out of the office crying."

"That's *horrible!* Why?"

"Because it's her birthday, of course. And because she's not slept with any of the guys she's dated in the office. It's like people get so *mad* when you try and live a moral life. Is it really that offensive when people try to live up to their own standards?"

"This fellow came here to live among us, and now he is judging us. Isn't that the way it always is?"

"Huh?"

"That's what the men of Sodom said about Lot. Things haven't changed a lot, Jess, in the last four thousand years."

"But what can we do about Leah?"

"I'll warn her. That's all we can do. She has a good head on her shoulders; she'll sort it out. But you, what are we going to do about you?"

"Why?"

"You're going to end up losing your job over this. This place won't be the same without you, Jess. Are you certain you can find something else?"

"I'll find something, Linda. And I'll look for a job for you, too, or at least meet you out for lunch every now and again."

"You could still try to wait out the storm."

"If Gerard is hiding something, how long before it comes out, anyway? What's the point of working someplace when you know, at any moment, the entire thing could blow up around you? How can this place survive if it's built on a lie?"

She laid the slip of paper with his cell phone number on his desk. "You have a reprieve. I think you should give this to her yourself."

"She's still mad at me."

"It will pass, Jess. I know it will. Just give it time. Anyway, I need to go talk to Leah to make certain we handle this flower nonsense somehow."

"Okay."

"Remember Lot."

"When you have a guilty conscious, I guess everything looks like a judgment, doesn't it?"

After she left the cube, Jess put his head on his desk and thought. He did more than think; he poured his heart out to God in prayer. He had to find a way to sort this out. He was convinced now that Gerard was hiding something; his reaction had been far too strong for it to be otherwise.

He didn't care about his job any longer. He just prayed he would get through this mess alive.

Chapter 20

Jess picked his cell phone up off the seat next to him, glancing at the time before shoving it into his pocket. Six in the morning. He would have at least an hour before Gerard or anyone else came in. He would trace the cable for forty minutes, giving himself a fifteen-minute cushion for his normal morning routine. Everything had to look normal before Gerard came in, around seven.

He badged into the first set of doors at the top of the stairs and hurried across the polished concrete lobby floor to the second set. Badging in through these let him into the carpeted hallway.

He dumped his laptop case onto his desk, settled in his chair, and hit the space bar on his computer. Impatient, he rolled the mouse around on its little pad while he sipped coffee from the foam cup with his other, waiting for the dark gray screen in front of him to come to life.

The whirring noise of the hard drive in his desktop computer protested at being awakened so early as the screen came into color and then focused and auto-adjusted to the proper size.

He quickly opened the help desk software and opened the trouble ticket on the data center camera so it sat in the center of the screen. It was important to give the impression he was working on an open ticket if someone wandered by his cubicle before he got back.

He picked up the phone and dialed the number for the security office. When it was answered, he said, "Hey, this is Jess. I'm going to be unplugging one of the cameras down in the data center for a bit, the one right by the door, so I can look at it and see what's going on."

"Is there a case open on it?"

"Sure." Jess read him the case number.

"Okay. Thanks for letting me know."

Jess dropped the receiver back on the phone and headed out of his cube. *I'm lucky Brian didn't come in early today.*

He badged through the data center doors, picked up a short ladder, and positioned it so it would interfere with the doors if they opened. Noise was always useful when you didn't want to be discovered. He made a big show of cleaning the lens with a bottle of cleaner and a soft cloth from the ladder. Then he reached under the camera and unplugged it.

Reaching into his backpack, he pulled his laptop out, set it on the floor, and plugged the camera into it. He opened an application that would show what the camera was seeing. He left this running and plugged a cable tester into the wall jack he'd removed the camera's cable from, hanging this from the camera's wall mount. He left it there with the little lights blinking, thinking this little display should be convincing enough should someone walk in.

He pressed a button on his cell phone to reveal the time. 6:15. The screen indicated an alarm was set for 6:45. Just in case he got so wrapped up chasing cables that he lost track of time. Time to find where that mysterious cable ran to.

Hoping the new cable followed the same bundle all the way to the patch panels on the first row of racks, he pulled up the floor tile directly in front of the disabled camera. Squatting, he examined the bundles of cable. It was there, on top of the same beam. Kneeling down so he could see better, he used a small flashlight to illuminate the space between the raised tiles and the concrete underneath to see where the bundle of cables went.

He wasn't far from the first row of racks. It turned up into the first patch panel on that row, at the end closest to the door. He quickly stood up and put the tile back into place, hanging the mouse ears back in their place when he was done.

The first rack on the first row was stuffed with patch panels. Most of the cables in the data center came up into one of the end patch panels, where the circuits were carried into switches or routers among the racks. He opened the door on the back of the rack and used his flashlight to examine the back of the patch panels. It was a forest of cables.

Sighing, he began to pull and prod the different bundles of cable, getting as close to the bottom of the rack as possible. As he checked a bundle, he marked it with a red cable wrap. There wasn't any time to waste rechecking bundles he'd already checked.

There was the bundle, the cable running just along the outside. He marked this bundle with a red tie and cut off the rest of the red ties he'd put on bundles.

Looking behind the patch panel the bundle of cables ran to, he could see where the cable was plugged into a jack. One, two, three...the jacks passed under his fingers as he counted until he reached the cable he was looking for.

Moving to the other side, he counted the same number of jacks and tied a yellow bag tie around the yellow cable issuing forth on the front of the patch panel. The color matched almost perfectly; unless you were looking for it, you would never notice. He moved back to the back of the rack, cut off the red cable tie, and closed the door. Everything looked normal.

He pushed a button on his cell phone. Twelve minutes left.

Quickly, his hands shaking, he began tracing the cable from the bottom patch panel. Up. Into the cable trough. There was no time for a ladder now; he would either have to wait or find it now. He jerked the cable hard and was rewarded with a movement in the mass of cables coming down into the fourth rack.

He stared hard at the equipment in the fourth rack. There must be something different here. He had to find it fast. There it was. A box that looked like the others, yet different. It was a firewall, an older model they had replaced last year. The inventory tag was new, but the number was wrong. It was fake.

Examining the device, he saw there was another cable coming out of it, heading up the rack to one of the overhead troughs. How much time? He glanced at his cell phone. Five minutes. He could probably run a little over, but he didn't want to take too much of a risk.

He tugged at one of the two cables and was again relieved to see the cables down at the patch panel to his right move. He had already traced this one; he needed the other one. Again, it went up, into the trough, and there wasn't much time. He tied a red cable wrap around it just where it went into the trough, and then he moved to his left, pulling on cables as he went.

It moved. He tugged again, and the red cable tie moved again. He looked down at the place where the cable connected to the patch panel, and he let out a low whistle. The patch panel that connects to the inside of the Internet router. Anything connected at this point in the network would have access to the Internet without passing through any of the firewalls or other security devices. Traffic running along this path would be invisible to the traffic monitoring equipment they had installed on their network, as well.

Jess stared at it for a moment without realizing time was passing while he thought. His cell phone rang. He picked it up to answer it and then realized it was just the alarm going off. He had run out of time. Just as he pulled the red marker off the cable, the door leading into the data center clicked. Someone was badging in.

Jess walked, as casually as he could, over to the camera. The door hit the ladder.

"Hey! Hang on a second, would you? I need to move this ladder out of the way."

The door swung open, and Brian stepped in.

"You came down here to work on this camera first thing?"

"Well, it's been in the list for a while, and it seemed important to keep the security systems up to snuff, what with all the problems we've been having."

Brian looked at the cable tester hanging from the camera mount. "How do they look?"

"The cables seem to be fine. I've been watching the output from the camera, too."

"Is the camera okay, too?"

"There have been some funny looking lines running across it. I didn't see it go blank or anything, but it's probably best to replace it. The problem's there, if it's anyplace."

Jess moved the ladder back into place, removed the tester, and plugged the camera back in.

"Okay. What's the next step?"

"I'll replace the camera tomorrow morning."

"Why not replace it today?"

"I don't have one. I'll have to call the security folks and get them to run one over. They normally have them in stock, so it'll probably be here this afternoon. I'll replace it first thing in the morning."

Brian considered this for a moment. "Okay, that's sounds fine. Don't kill yourself, Jess; it's just a camera." Jess started. "Sorry, Jess, I didn't mean to say it like that."

"No problem. I'll just clean this mess up. Thanks for running by to check on me, though."

"Okay, see you upstairs."

When the elevator doors opened, he walked out onto the first floor and around so he could see what was going on at Leah's cubicle. A florist was there, unloading vases full of roses from a cart. Jess waited, not certain what to do.

When the florist finished, Brian escorted him to the door. Jess moved to the door of her cubicle and stared in. What a childish thing to do, sending her all these flowers on her birthday just to embarrass her. He felt compelled to do something, but he was frozen in indecision. Would it be rude to stop them or to use another cart to clear the mess out, carrying it all out to the dumpster?

Hearing footsteps, he ducked down into the cubicle across the hallway. Brian and Gerard came down the hallway and stopped in front of Leah's cubicle. Gerard said, "Well, that will get her goat. I'm certain she'll be completely embarrassed when she sees this mess. It'll teach her to be so judgmental of people. Stay here and tell me how she reacts when she comes in."

"Sure, I don't mind. I'll have to control myself so I don't laugh at her outright, though." Brian remained where he could see what happened as Gerard snickered and moved towards the elevators.

There was no way to get out of the cubicle he'd hidden in without Brian seeing him, so Jess settled in to wait until Leah came in. He was afraid it would be a long wait. Leah didn't normally come in before eight, and it wasn't yet seven thirty.

The wait wasn't a long as he thought it would be, though. In just a few minutes, he heard the doors leading into the lobby open again and the sound of footsteps treading down the carpeted hallway. Wriggling around as quietly as possible, he positioned himself so he could see through a crack in the corner where the cubicle walls joined.

Leah stepped up to the cubicle entrance, watching Brian warily. She looked in for a moment and then looked towards Brian, leaning against the wall.

"Brian, go make up some story to make Gerard's day. I don't care what it is—just leave. *Now!*" Jess could see Brian move past. *I could just reach out and wipe that smirk off his face for him.* But he didn't, he waited, allowing the anger to flood over him.

After a few moments, Leah walked off as well, leaving Jess hidden in the cubicle by himself. He took the chance to scoot out, around a corner, and finally to the break room to make a pot of coffee.

He ambled back towards his cube, going around the perimeter of the building to see how the little drama at Leah's cube had developed. No one appeared to be around when he looked down the hallway, so he decided to go by her cube and see what she had done. He stopped in front of her doorway and looked in. Her cubicle was empty. There wasn't a single vase, flower, or note remaining.

Well, at least she'd handled it. He wished she hadn't thrown his flowers away with the rest, but there was nothing he could do about it now. She probably hadn't even read the tags.

Back in his cubicle, Jess stared at his computer, trying to get his mind off the flowers. He decrypted the files, carefully noting the point where the cable ended, the rack and position of the firewall that shouldn't have been there, and the connection between the firewall and the Internet.

He could stop here and turn what he had over to the police. They would probably get a search warrant, investigate the data center, and find out as much as they could. There were two reasons not to do this, though. First, any information being pulled from the data center wasn't stored locally—it was being carried through the Internet to some other server. Second, there was probably a simple and fast way to tear down whatever was going on, leaving just the cable and no data and no indication about what was being stolen.

The police, then, would find the cable and nothing else. He had to gather more information before he could go to the police. But what if whoever it was who was using this connection discovered he had found it and closed it all down before he could gather anything else? No point in being like Gideon, refusing to fight until you have proof you'll win.

He sipped a bit more from his coffee mug. What sort of information would someone kill for, anyway? There was one way to find out. He logged into the router that connected their network to the Internet. He typed in a command, and a list of the devices connected to the router scrolled onto the screen. Each one had two addresses, an IP address and an Ethernet address. Looking down the list of devices, he quickly found what he was looking for. The older firewall's Ethernet address had a different manufacturer code.

He noted down the IP address for the rogue and configured the router to show him the address of every packet being transmitted by that device. As the information about the packets scrolled by on the screen, he noted the destinations down on the piece of paper. Finally, he removed the configuration.

Next, he configured the router differently so he could see some of the packets actually being switched through the router to one of the destinations. After he had captured a couple of them into a file, he cleared his configurations out and closed the connection to the router.

Now that he had some of the packets being transmitted along that link, he needed to figure out what the packets contained. He started a network analysis program and copied the captured packets into them.

They were encrypted. Well, he should have known that before he went to all the trouble. If data was worth killing for, it was certainly worth encrypting. Sighing, he saved the captured packets along with their analysis, encrypted the file, and copied it into the encrypted directory.

There was one more thing he could do. Opening a Web browser, he entered the address of a reverse lookup service and entered the IP addresses in, one at a time. Each of them mapped to a domain name, the part of a Web address that tells you what company you're connecting to. Jess wrote each one down.

Then he opened another page in the Web browser and looked up each of these domain names. In each case, the domain's owner was displayed, and in each case, it was the same name. Sylvia Hartwell. Who was Sylvia Hartwell? Well, if there was one person in the building who knew just about everyone, it was Linda.

He glanced at the clock on his screen. 8:22. She would be in already, so he opened his instant messaging program and double-clicked on her name.

"What's up, Jess?"

"Do you know anyone named Sylvia Hartwell?"

"Hmmm...Brian's mother's name is Sylvia, but I don't know her last name. There are some other Sylvias I know at church, but no one whose last name is Hartwell."

"Thanks. TTYL."

The packets were encrypted. He needed a way to get the data before it was encrypted, which meant before the rogue firewall he'd discovered in the data center. But how was he going to monitor and record this data when it didn't pass through any of the equipment he had access to?

He could break into one of those pieces of equipment and monitor the information directly from there. A good network engineer would have things set up so anyone logging in to a piece of equipment would be recorded someplace. Once he had been discovered, the connection would be shut down, leaving him with nothing.

The only other option was to redirect the traffic through another piece of equipment so he could monitor the data passing through the link without the people who'd set it up knowing.

It would be hard to do without being detected, but it was possible as long as he was clever about the way he ran the cables.

He typed the information about the IP addresses, domain names, and the domain name's owner into his notes, closed the file, and stored everything away again.

Where could he break into that circuit? He opened the physical wiring diagrams on his screen and compared them to the rack layout diagrams. There was a switch on that corner he might be able to run the data through, in between the server and the firewall. The key was hiding the cables. He would have to do a better job than whoever had set the original cable.

Hearing soft footsteps coming down the hall, he quickly switched to the help desk application and started making notes in the case he had opened earlier in the morning. "Need to replace the camera," he typed before saving it.

"Glad to see you're working on real work, Jess." Sarcasm laced Gerard's voice.

"Good morning, Gerard."

"And what have you been up to?"

"I ran down and checked out the cables running to that camera that's been acting up in the data center. It looks like they're all fine, but the camera is acting up a little. I was just about to call the security vendor and get them to run another camera down here."

"Why not just let them replace it?"

"Are you authorizing the bill?" The look on Gerard's face told him all he needed to know. "No, I didn't think so. It doesn't take but a minute to replace it, anyway. I'll do it first thing in the morning."

"Well, it certainly is a good morning."

"All mornings are good, Gerard."

"Well, this one is especially so."

The anger built in Jess again. "And why is that?" asked Jess.

"Have you checked out your girlfriend's cubicle?" He smiled like the Grinch stealing candy out of Cindy Lou Who's hands.

"Gerard, she's my friend."

"Then maybe you sent her the pink roses. Pink roses are stupid, really. Girls don't want pink—they want red."

"Maybe there are girls in the world who like having a friend, rather than someone chasing them."

"I've never met a girl that didn't like to be chased." Gerard was obviously enjoying himself far too much.

"Maybe you've just never paid attention long enough to find out."

"I think I'll walk back by there, just to see how she's doing and to congratulate her on all the pretty flowers. Nothing like seeing a prude squirm."

"You're sick, Gerard."

"And I hope your morning is as good as mine is going to be when I walk by there to see how upset she is."

Jess returned to his computer, looking up the number of the security company. Just as he picked up the phone, Gerard stormed down the hallway, stopping at his cubicle. "Did you help your friend carry all those flowers out to the dumpster?"

"What are you talking about?"

"The flowers. They're gone. She apparently took them all out to the dumpster and threw them away."

"I know that. But I didn't help her."

"What a waste of good flowers."

"Actually, sending her the flowers was the waste. Her throwing them away was just justice."

Gerard turned and headed for the elevators, stomping and huffing. Jess finished making his call to the security company. He made a special point of asking them to get the camera there that afternoon, even if it would cost a bit more. He needed the camera to finish up his plan for monitoring that data. After making a few more notes in the case, he saved the case and moved the help desk application off his desktop.

Linda popped into his cube a bit later, sitting down on the spare seat he always kept sitting just inside the door. "Did you see her cubicle?"

"Yes. It was ridiculous."

"She threw them all away."

"Yeah, I saw that, too. I walked by there afterwards. There wasn't anything left."

"Do you think she did the right thing?"

"Of course. It certainly made Gerard madder. Maybe they'll leave her alone now."

"I doubt it. You know Gerard—he won't let her get away with it. He'll have to get back at her somehow."

"Why doesn't he Gerard just fire Leah if he feels this way?"

"For what reason?"

"She's a temp; he could get rid of her anytime he wants."

"I don't think it's that easy. Besides, if he fired her, who else would he try to embarrass?"

"Well, me. I just wish he'd leave Leah alone."

"Yes, well, at least she's sharing the load, for now." Linda got up, winked at Jess, and headed back to her cubicle.

At noon, Jess took his guitar and lunch bag out through the back door. Sitting on the picnic table by the lake, he started strumming a few songs he knew by heart. He switched to picking, moving through "Amazing Grace." He'd left the tabs sitting on his desk, and he couldn't remember the notes to anything else to pick through.

He got up, stuffing the garbage back into his lunch bag, and slung the guitar over his shoulder. As he turned to walk back towards the building, he saw Leah, standing a few yards off. Close enough to have heard him playing.

"Going back to the building?" she asked.

"Yeah, I'm done with lunch; I figured I'd better get back to work. I should get as much done as I can this afternoon so I can leave around lunch tomorrow."

"Someplace special to go?"

I wonder why she cares? She has to know I don't have any plans this weekend. "No, not really. Maybe just a run on the lake. It's just been a long week, and I've had enough."

"I know how you feel. This morning was a mess. All those flowers in my cubical—"

"It was intended to be, from what I gather."

"Why do you think they attacked me like that?"

"Because they think you're a prude."

"And what do you think? Do you think Gerard is right?

"I think you're just a nice girl, Leah. And the world doesn't really appreciate nice girls any longer." She didn't answer, so he continued. "I thought you were still mad at me."

"I was. But Linda told me you stood up for me."

"Oh, Gerard. His bark is bad, but his bite is pretty feeble, if you want to know the truth."

"Thanks for warning me about the flowers, too."

"You're welcome. Coming in early to throw them away was brilliant."

"Thanks. How's it going with Carl?"

"Why do you think I've been looking into Carl's death?"

"I just do." She smirked. "You didn't think you could hide it from me, did you? Gerard, maybe, and other folks, but not from me. Maybe you're so interested because you murdered him!"

Jess was taken aback. "What makes you think I murdered him? You could be next on my list, after all."

She laughed. "I had considered the possibility, but it doesn't seem like a reasonable explanation. If you were trying to cover something up, you'd be hiding information you already have, rather than stuff you were trying to dig up."

Jess sighed. "I don't think I've hidden it from Gerard well, either. He called me into his office to yell about it."

"And will you know the answer when you're done?"

"I don't know. But I'll know more than I know now."

"What will you do with the information you find?"

"I don't know yet. I suppose it depends on what I find."

"Why not tell me what you have?"

"Please, can we avoid this subject? I don't want to get into another argument." The look in her eyes indicated she wouldn't press the point, but it was still important to her to see what he had gathered.

"Tell me, what do you think the word faith means?"

What is her game? What does this have to do with those files? What is she driving at?"Faith is the belief that someone will keep their promises to you."

"But how can you have faith in someone?" she asked.

"Because they always *have* kept their promises to you. It's like God. I don't have faith in God just because. I can see God has kept his promises in the past, so He'll keep them in the future."

"And if He doesn't do something you've asked Him to?"

"Well, what I ask for might not be the best for me... besides, what I ask for isn't what He's promised. Faith is based on promises kept, not requests kept."

"Why do people struggle with having faith in God, do you think?"

"Because they either don't think what God wants is best for them or what they want, or because they've been hurt in some way that makes trusting hard."

"I'm not the one who hurt you, Jess."

"I know, Leah."

"And I've never made a promise I've not kept, right?"

"I suppose that's true." He could see what she was driving at now, but it wasn't going to be that easy.

"Then trust me, Jess."

"When I'm done, Leah. I don't really want to talk about it anymore."

"I know. But I wanted to make one last pitch."

"I'll have to admit it was a good pitch," Jess said.

"Do you know Carl was murdered?"

"I'm certain of it."

"And Benita was murdered."

"Yes."

Her eyes softened. "Remember, if you get in over your head, you can trust me."

"Yeah, sure. Thanks." He turned towards the lake, looking over the water towards the buildings on the other side. Water had always given him peace, and he needed peace right at this moment.

"I'll see you in church on Sunday."

"You're going to be coming? What made you decide to try my church?"

"I figured there's no harm in it, really. Someone has to watch over you, after all," said Leah.

"I have angels already."

"Another one wouldn't hurt." She smiled as she turned and walked back towards the building.

When he walked back into the building, Jess was gratified to see a cardboard box sitting on his desk. He cut it open with his pocketknife and pulled out the new camera. Digging through his desk drawers, he found a few cables of the same yellow cable as those in the data center. He checked the wiring diagrams again and noted down the port numbers on a switch on the first row he thought he could pass the data through without anyone noticing.

He was set for the final act, tomorrow morning.

Chapter 21

"Don't bug me about the flowers. He's just a friend." Leah walked into the kitchen where Daniel and Thuan sat at the table, waiting for her. She set the vase with pink roses and a blue ribbon on the counter.

Daniel's face was a sneer. "Are you sure?"

"Yes, they're pink. They were in a sea of red, so I think that says it all."

Thuan glanced up. "A sea of red?"

"Roses. All the guys I've dated there in an attempt to pull information out of the woodwork sent me flowers." Leah sighed. "Red roses. With nasty notes."

Daniel laughed. "The travails of being a cop, I suppose."

"Well, I suppose it could be worse, yes, but it didn't seem very funny at the time. Linda helped me clean them all up; we pulled in a cart and dragged them all to the dumpster. Glad I'm a temp there and don't have career plans."

Daniel's sneer turned to concern. "That bad, huh? It won't impact the investigation, will it? Think you can hold out for a while longer?"

"Gerard Mattingly sent me flowers, too."

"Oh. That is bad. So you're on his bad side now?"

"Who isn't?" Leah leaned back against the counter, considering the vase of flowers.

"Why did Wirth send you flowers? Was he in on the joke?"

"No. Read the tag." She pulled the flowers off the counter and set them in front of Daniel. He spent a few moments reading the tag.

"Had a blowup, huh?" He smiled. "Trying to put the pressure on. Did it help?"

"No. He won't budge. I can't explain why I want a look at the files, and he won't budge without one."

"It's Thursday."

"I can read a calendar as well as you can, Daniel."

"On Monday we need to start the process to subpoena the records on his hard drive. That's only one more work day to try and convince him."

"I know. I don't think he's going to budge, though. I'm probably going to have to tell him the truth to get those files. Is there any way to do this without exciting any suspicion?"

Daniel considered this for a moment. "It would be hard. Is it possible to serve the subpoena at his apartment and tell him not to tell anyone else about it?"

"I wonder if Detective Harris could serve the warrant for us, just to keep the jurisdictional matters straight?"

"You're assuming your family friend hasn't changed in all these years, Leah. Maybe we should just serve it directly."

"What if his landlady calls the police? Then we'd have a mess. I don't think we can risk having the local department coming in while we're searching through his apartment, can we?"

Now it was Daniel's turn to sigh. "No, not really."

"Okay, let's go that way with it." Leah turned to Thuan. "Get the subpoena under way. I'll try to get the information one more time tomorrow. If that doesn't work, we'll get Detective Harris, by himself, to get involved and help us sort out how to serve it and get the information without anyone else finding out."

"And what if he runs? We'll need a net." Daniel was in operational mode now, making assumptions Leah wasn't really comfortable with. "Don't *you* think Wirth is our man?"

"No, Daniel, I'm not convinced. In fact, the longer this goes on, the more I'm convinced he's not the bottom rung of the identity theft ring."*But who else knew the data center like he did? Who else would be able to spirit away data other than someone who had access to virtually every computer in the entire company?* "Thuan, thoughts?"

"I don't have enough information. He certainly has the skills and access to be stealing the data. The problem is that just because he's the one who obviously has the skills doesn't mean he's the only one with the skills. There could be a hidden actor in here we don't know about yet."

Daniel said, "We've run backgrounds on everyone else, and there isn't anyone else with his technical skills, that's for certain."

Thuan ducked behind his computer monitor. "What about Gerard Mattingly?"

"Mattingly isn't an obvious choice, either. He's not worked on the network in several years, so he probably doesn't know his way around as well as Wirth does."

Leah thought about the options as she listened to the exchange between Daniel and Thuan. Gerard *is* sharp, but would he know the network good enough to pull off stealing this data? He certainly had access to the same accounts as Jess, and probably more. "There could be more than one person involved within the company, too, you know."

Daniel looked at her. "Of course. We've assumed it's a single actor, but it could be multiples. It could be Wirth and someone else."

The wheels in her head were spinning now. "Or it could be Gerard and someone else."

"What do you mean?" asked Daniel.

"Well, they have contractors in all the time. I suppose you could pass the data out when the backups are taken to storage, couldn't you?"

Thuan looked up from his computer, startled. "Why didn't we think of that before? We need to set a tail on the backup, follow it after it's taken out of the building. I'll need to do some checking on their storage company, the security there, and when the next time they're going to pull a copy is."

"Okay, that would be a good line of investigation. There are also contractors who come in and run cables through the building, that sort of thing. Today someone from the security company ran by and left a camera at the front desk, too."

Thuan was typing on the keyboard. *Probably trying to dig up a list of contractors OptiData uses.* "Did they pick anything up?"

"No, not that I saw, but it's yet another place to check."

Thuan stopped typing for a moment, looking at something on his computer screen. "These technical companies, they're like a sieve. There are so many places data could be leaking out of that building, actually."

"Yep. We'll need to start checking on all the ways we can think of."

Daniel broke into the exchange. "Okay, so what about this weekend? We still need to tail Wirth, I think."

Leah said, "He's going out on the lake on Saturday. I'll tail him there."

Daniel asked, "Should two of us go so we can make certain we don't lose him, or in case—"

"He's attacked or something? No, I can handle it," Leah replied.

Thuan said, "Then I'll take Friday night. I'll call you on Saturday morning and let you know if I see anything suspicious."

Before Daniel could break in, Leah said, "I'll take Sunday morning, too. Daniel, you can follow him after church and take the rest of the day, but I feel like if I show up in church, it might make him more willing to pass the information over."

There was silence for a moment. Daniel was the first to speak. "Why not serve the subpoena after the services? We could catch him coming out of the building and just gather around like friends, explain the situation, and see if he cooperates. He's not likely to run from there, and it's fairly neutral territory."

Leah considered this. It *was* neutral territory. He would probably be less defensive there than in his apartment. They could just make it look like a group of friends going out to lunch together. "Sure, why not? I'll just tell him I have some folks I want him to meet after the service. We can hang out and explain that we have a subpoena in progress, and it would be simpler, and better, if he just gives us what he has before it blows up. Even if he's the bottom rung in the organization, we might be able to convince him there."

"Anyone else go to church with him?" Daniel was obviously in operation mode, thinking of the best way to apprehend a suspect, rather than how to deal with getting information they needed to close a case.

"No. Linda goes to the big place on the corner downtown. I don't remember seeing anyone else from OptiData there the last time I visited."

"And ran out of the church to keep from being caught." Thuan laughed at Daniel's statement, and Leah shot him a look. "Okay, that settles it. Thuan, Friday night. Leah, Saturday and Sunday morning. We'll meet you after the service and see if we can all talk him out of the information."

Leah walked them to the door. On returning to the table, she opened her laptop and started filling out various reports and putting her current thoughts about the case into writing. This job certainly had a lot of paperwork. Was the paperwork more irritating, or the roses?

Finally, giving up, she grabbed a book and stretched out on the couch to read until she was tired enough to sleep.

Chapter 22

Jess settled the cup of coffee on his desk and at the computer screen. This trouble ticket really needed to be dealt with. *It's pointless. I just can't focus on this.* He picked up his headset and settled it on his head, the soft foam pressing against one ear. He dialed Linda.

"I didn't see you in the parking lot this morning."

"Sorry, I was a little later than usual." He didn't want to tell her he had been trapped in traffic again because he'd left his place too late. That he didn't even really feel like coming in to work in the first place.

"You've been later than usual for the last few days. Is everything okay?" Linda could always tell when something was wrong, anyway. *Time to change the subject, before she digs too deep.*

"Yeah, sure, just not as much energy in the mornings, I guess. Hey, could you leave a note on Gerard's desk for me?"

"He's not in there right this second. You could leave him a voice mail without risking him picking up."

"I'd rather he not get the message until later this afternoon—"

"Oh." There was silence for a moment, and then Linda continued. "I see. You want me to bury the note, not leave it on his desk.

"That's about the size of it. Someplace where he'll see it before he leaves, but not until around three or four, if possible."

"In other words, you don't want him to come by and see you before you leave. And what should this note say?"

"That I'm leaving for the day around two in the afternoon."

"That's it? He's never yelled at you for leaving early before, so what's the big deal?"

"I'd just rather he didn't know until long after I'm gone."

"What *are* you up to? Are you *still* poking at Carl's death?"

Jess couldn't let her know she was on to what he was planning on working on today. "I'd rather not say, to be honest."

Linda's sigh came through the phone as a burst of white noise. "Okay, I'll leave a note on his desk, placing it so he'll find it as late as possible in the day, but before he goes home. Is there a reason I should give for you going home early."

"No, not really. I'm just tired, and I can't focus on anything. Time to take a break."

"It's not very convincing."

"Well, I am going to the pastor's house a bit later—"

"Great, I'll tell him you have a date. That should set him off."

Jess laughed. "Good idea. Thanks, Linda."

"Anything else going on over the weekend?"

"Just hitting the lake for a while on Saturday and then church on Sunday, but nothing else special."

"Okay. See you on Monday."

"Yep."

Jess picked his guitar up and headed out to the picnic table by the little lake behind the building. It would be easier to think there, outside, watching over the lake, doing something with his hands rather than sitting in his cubicle.

Sitting on the table, his feet up on one of the two benches meant for seats along the side, he cut each string off his guitar, replacing each one with a new black string. It took some concentration to pull each of the new strings through the machine head carefully so the black coating would remain intact.

He pulled a tuning fork from his pocket, popped it against the tabletop, and held it to the guitar. If whoever had run that circuit discovered what he was doing this afternoon, he would be in real danger. As if he wasn't already. Carl had certainly been killed, and whoever had killed Carl wouldn't stop at murdering Jess, either. It was a new sensation, being scared, literally, for his life.

He turned the machine head, adjusting the tension of the string so it slowly came into resonance with the tuning fork. It was time to make a copy of the information he had and give it to someone. If anything happened, he would at least know whoever was behind this would be brought to justice.

Setting the tuning fork down, he fingered the top string in the fifth fret and adjusted the second string so the two strings intoned the same note. Whom could he trust with the information, though? Detective Harris, somber and old-fashioned? He didn't know these people and probably wouldn't understand the technical details of what Jess had collected. Nor would he know how to go about getting the information Jess was about to collect. Someone in the detective's office could certainly be roped into doing it, but how long would that take, and what would happen in the meantime?

He moved his finger to the second string, on the same fret, and started slowly turning the machine head on the third string, making the two strings play the same note again, this time a D. Sergeant Stone? No. His eyes, squinted and beady, full of malicious anger, gave him away. Although there was no knowing why, the sergeant wasn't happy with Jess and couldn't be trusted with this information.

The third string, fifth fret, was a G. Jess tuned the fourth string to this G so the two sounded like one string when he picked them at the same time. What about Gerard or Brian? The problem there was while there was no evidence either of them was involved, there was no reason to think they weren't involved. Neither of them would work, either.

Fingering the fourth fret on the fourth string, Jess started tuning the fifth string to B. What about Linda? But what would she do with this sort of information?

Finally, he fingered the fifth fret on the fifth string and tuned the last string. He strummed a couple of chords and then picked out "Amazing Grace" again, a good song to check out the new strings since it was played with mostly open strings.

Linda would give the information to Leah. He couldn't sort out why he knew that, but he did know it. He could easily tell their relationship was one of trust and respect by the way they talked together in Linda's cube and by the amount of common knowledge they obviously shared. So then why not give the information to Leah directly?

Jess set his guitar down on the table and tapped on the front of the body. The tapping started the string resonating, a low hum in the quiet of the late morning air. Could he trust Leah? She had asked him about the information a number of times, and she had said that if he was in over his head, she would help. But she was just a temp, doing project management work. What could she do?

On the other hand, he was starting to feel like he was in over his head. Someone had killed Carl. Someone had killed Benita. Someone had tried to frame him for Benita's death. Whoever it was, he or she would certainly try to kill him if what he was about to do was discovered.

He decided. He grabbed the guitar by its neck, the strings squealing as if in protest as his fingers slid from the body to the head. He would trust Leah, no matter how uncomfortable it made him or how little sense it made to do so. It was just a matter of setting things up so she would get a copy of the data if something happened to him.

Back at his desk, he tapped out commands on the keyboard at top speed, his fingers flying through the commands as quickly as his mind could work. Now that he'd decided his course of action, there was no room for hesitation. Digging through the drawers of his desk, he found a portable USB thumb drive and inserted it into his desktop computer. He then copied the information he'd collected on Carl's death, still encrypted, onto the thumb drive.

While the files were being copied to the USB drive, he logged into his laptop, opened a file transfer program, and copied the information he'd collected on Carl's death there, as well. Once they had all been copied, he used a special piece of software to erase the files so they couldn't be recovered by someone with access to his desktop computer.

Digging through the papers on his desk, he found an old notepad, from which he ripped a sheet of paper. He then ripped the page into quarters and folded one quarter in half. On this slip of paper, he recorded the password for each file he'd copied into the USB drive. On the back, he wrote down every phone number he could think of where Leah could possibly reach him and all his e-mail addresses.

He dug around on his desk again and found an old, used envelope that had originally enclosed an offer for some sort of networking magazine. Stuffing the paper and the USB drive into this envelope, he sealed it closed with a piece of tape. He dropped the envelope into the back pocket of his laptop bag and zipped it closed.

The data, at least, was ready to hand over to Leah, if events warranted. Now, to set things up so he could get a copy of the data being sent out of the network before it was encrypted.

The first step was to build a hole into which to stuff the data as he collected it. This needed to be double-blind. If they found his collection of their data, he wanted to convince them they had found all of it, whether or not they had. If they were convinced they had found it all, they would stop looking for more.

Three boxes. One that was obvious and easy to find. One that wasn't obvious, but with clues left to lead them to it. This would be the honeypot, the place where they would get bogged down and stuck. A third copy in a normally obvious place, but with no trail to find it.

He took one of the other quarters of the sheet he'd ripped up before and sketched out several possibilities. Settling on one, he turned again to the computer, his fingers flying over the keyboard.

Jess connected to one of the servers in the data center and created two new accounts, "databox" and "smith-w." He set the passwords to long, convoluted strings of letters, numbers, and other characters, carefully noting each password in a text file. The passwords wouldn't really matter in the end; anyone with administrator privileges on this server could reset them. And whoever was involved here certainly had administrator privileges.

The next step was to build the honeypot. He modified the smith-w account so it had access to all the files the databox user account had stored on the server, and he set up a backup job on his local desktop, using the smith-w account to copy all the files from the databox user directory to a local, encrypted directory. This would seem clever without really being clever—easy enough to find, but hopefully convincing enough for anyone searching to stop on his desktop machine.

Now to find someplace no one would think to look. He opened the log files, scanning them to find an account that was used all the time and logged in from a wide variety of places. The name of one of the sales engineers showed up regularly, logging in from all sorts of remote locations. Switching to the trouble ticket software, he searched on the username. Certainly enough, there was a ticket within the last week, and it included a note containing the person's password.

Switching back, he modified the account so it had access to the files in the databox user directory. He then connected to a server that was sitting on a shelf at his apartment. He set it up so it would log into the compromised user account and copy everything from the databox directory into a working directory, encrypt it in a single file, rename the file so it appeared to be a picture, and then move it to a folder with a lot of other pictures in it.

The collection boxes were all set. Now all he needed was some data to put in them.

First, he had to get the information off the network and into the databox account. Connecting to the switch he'd already identified as the best place to run the cables through, he configured one port so any received data would be copied to a running log file in the databox user directory. He noted the port number on the sheet of paper he'd done the sketches on earlier, and then he shut down all the connections.

The chair squeaked as he leaned back. Now for the dangerous part. Logging out of his desktop computer, he slid his laptop into his backpack and gathered up all the other stuff lying on his desk. He took one last look around to make certain he hadn't left anything in view that would give away what he was doing; he also was not certain if he'd see this cubicle again. Finally, he picked up the new camera the security folks had dropped off the day before and headed down to the data center.

He badged in through the data center doors, hung his laptop case on a hook next to the corral of cable hooks in the corner of the room, and glanced over at the colorless gray clock hanging on the wall, noting the time he started.

He climbed to the top step of a stool he dragged over in front of the camera, snapped the plastic retainer down, and pulled the cable from its socket on the wall. He covered the three steps down in a single motion and slid a heavy cardboard box over in front of the door, making certain no one would intrude while he was working. There was still the glass in the doors, but that was a risk he was going to have to live with for the moment.

At the first rack on the first row, he quickly located the cable. Pulling the cable from the patch panel, he plugged it into one of the two switch ports he had reconfigured earlier, and he ran a short patch cable between the other port and the patch panel so the link would come back up and traffic would start flowing. Hopefully, they weren't watching the interfaces on the server constantly, so it would take them a while to find the cable rerouting.

To hide the new cable route as much as possible, he cut some nearby bundles open and rewrapped them with the cables he'd just modified in their centers. Stepping away, he examined his handiwork. It would take more than a simple glance at the cables to see that something had changed, and it would take a real effort at tracing the cables all the way through to actually find out what the change was.

Back to the camera. He pushed the box back to where he had moved it from and bounded back up the stepladder. The old camera came off easily, but getting the screws back into place while holding the new one was harder. Between his hands shaking and trying to hold the camera steady while starting the screws, it was a harder job than he anticipated.

Once everything was mounted, he plugged the camera into his laptop and started up the software that allowed him to monitor its output. It looked just like the output from the old camera. But anything that helped him figure out why Carl was killed, and by whom, wasn't a waste of time.

Chapter 23

Brian checked the cameras again. Jess's truck was still in the parking lot. It would be a while before Jess left for the afternoon, anyway. He turned back to his paper and read a few more paragraphs about the games coming up over the weekend. The corner of his eye caught some movement; he glanced up. Jess was just pulling out. Good luck. Jess had left early. Setting the paper down, he pushed himself roughly from the chair and strode towards the elevators.

Jess's computer was password protected, of course, but being in charge of security had its advantages. He had a back-door account on every computer in the building. There was no way Jess was going to be hiding anything from him. These last few days he'd been very suspicious about how Jess had handled the entire problem with the camera down in the data center. What was he up to?

Although he didn't know computers too well, he knew a few places to check. There was a packet collector running on Jess's computer. Why would he leave that running over the weekend? He checked the address from which the packets were being collected and recognized it as being someplace in the data center.

He picked up the phone and punched out Gerard's number.

"I thought you'd gone home early. Nice how you had Linda bury that note so I wouldn't find it until—"

"Gerard, it's Brian, not Jess. Don't be so gruff, would you? I'm sitting at Jess's desk, and I think there's something you need to see."

"What is it?"

"I don't really understand what he's doing. It's better if you come down here."

"Sure, be there in a minute."

Gerard's footsteps were heavy once he left the elevator. Even on the carpet, it was obvious he was storming through the building. At some point, his temper was going to get him into a mess he couldn't get out of. Brian pushed himself from Jess's chair, indicating Gerard should sit down in his place.

Gerard typed quickly, moving through the information on the screen so quickly Brian couldn't keep up. Finally, he let out a low whistle. "We'll need to deal with this. Give me a few minutes; I'll clean this up." Brian sat in the visitor's chair while Gerard continued to type, his hands flying over the keyboard. Brian caught parts of the process, stopping the script, deleting a large number of files.

"He has it copying the data to another server. I'll have to clear that up too." Gerard set off again on the keyboard. Brian watched him with intense interest, wondering how computer geeks could be seemingly slow in real life, and yet move this quickly on a computer. "Okay, I've killed the other account and all the information in it. It doesn't look like he's stored anything anyplace else. Let's go down to the data center and see what he's been doing down there." He turned and pushed himself up, rushing out of the opening between the cubical walls so quickly Brian could barely keep up with him.

Brian followed Gerard as he flung open the doors to the data center. "I wondered what he was doing down here all that time."

"That stupid case on the video camera. He's used it to cover what he was doing down here."

"I should have insisted on having the security folks come in rather than letting him replace it."

"Well, it's lucky I checked up after he left."

"It was clever of him having Linda bury that note in the pile so I wouldn't find it until after he left."

The doors closed smoothly behind them. As the lock clicked, Brian looked over his shoulder, distracted by the sound. The clock read 3:48. It was late in the afternoon, and he had things to do tonight. "I hope this doesn't take too long."

Gerard's eyes pierced him. "Don't worry, it shouldn't." Gerard moved to the rack on the corner of the first row and examined it closely.

"What are you looking for?"

"He must have modified the cabling, but I don't know where or how."

"Why does it matter?" asked Brian.

"Because we should undo it," Gerard replied.

"What if he logs in and finds out someone has shut down his script?"

"I've taken care of that; his accounts are disabled. If we can clear this up over the weekend, we can just re-enable them on Monday morning."

"Okay. So what next?"

"We try and figure out where he modified the cabling. Get the mouse ears off the wall and help me start tracing the cables out so we can find it."

"Shouldn't we call someone—"

"Call someone? No. The last thing we want is to have anyone find out what is going on here. It would ruin us, the company, and the entire situation. No, we don't call anyone, yet. Not until we find out what's going on."

Brian's chest constricted, making it hard to breathe. The whirring of all the fans in the computers drilled into his brain, the impassive gray walls of the data center hemming him in.

"What are you doing standing there? Help me find out if Jess has done anything down here!" Gerard's hands were on his chest, his arms pushing him back roughly into the space between the wall and the first row of equipment.

"If you don't get the mouse ears, I'll do it. Feel free to stand there while I do all the work." Gerard spat the words out as he moved past Brian, rounding the corner into the space between the first and second rows of equipment.

Brian's knees wouldn't cooperate. Losing his balance, he began to fall, heavily, accelerating. He reached out and felt steel. The edges of a rack, the last rack in the row. Equipment filled his eyes, and the rack felt like it was moving. He gripped the sides more tightly and pushed, trying to right himself, to regain his balance. The top of the rack moved further away from him. He pushed harder and let go, the final push getting him back on his feet.

In slow motion, he watched the top of the rack as it kept moving. It moved out past the wheels, locked into place; gravity had taken over, pulling the top of the rack towards the floor. There weren't any cables along the top, nothing to keep the thousands of pounds of equipment from continuing their drop to the floor.

Gerard voice broke over the hum of the equipment, "*Help!*"

Brain moved around to the end of the row. Gerard was standing, his arms bulging as he pushed against the rack. Brian tried to move in, but what could he do? Gerard's foot slipped, and the rack slid downwards with his motion. His hands released the rack, instinct taking over as he grabbed for the floor.

The gray steel gained speed, pinned Gerard's body between the floor and the equipment, and then rolled, hitting his head, crushing his life out on the data center floor.

Brian's stomach revolted, but he held it in until he could make it up the steps and out into the fresh air. This was how Jess must have felt on finding Carl's body. He settled himself and moved back inside towards his desk. He needed to think about what to do next.

He could call the police, of course. He *should* call the police, in fact. But that would be a mess. There would be a lot of questions, and while it had been an accident, it would be hard to explain what they had been doing in the data center together, especially once Jess figured out his account had been disabled. That would generate a lot of publicity, and that was the last thing they would need about now.

So far, the police hadn't solved the other deaths in the data center, so why should they solve this one? There were his fingerprints on the rack, but his fingerprints were probably on all the racks since he was down there checking things out on a regular basis. Gerard had badged in to the data center, so there was no record, other than the video recording, that Brian had even been there at all.

The video recording. Of course, that needed to be taken care of. He swiveled in his chair and brought the computer in front of him to life with a few taps on the space bar. Opening the video recorded by the camera by the data room door, he marked off two points, one before Gerard had walked into the data center, the other after, and he pressed the erase button on the side of the screen.

It didn't seem like Jess had fixed that problem with the video camera over the door after all. Gathering his laptop case and lunchbox, he headed out of the building.

Chapter 24

Jess climbed up the steps of Pastor David's house, stepping up onto the low-ceilinged porch between the squat columns. The leaded cut glass in the windows on either side of the door drew his attention as he approached the door. Their passion for the Arts and Craft style was one of the many things he and the pastor had in common.

He knocked gently on the door.

"Jess," Mary whispered as she swung the heavy wooden door open. Their grandkids must be in the house, napping while they waited for their mom to come by and get them. It was good he hadn't knocked louder. "Why don't you come in?"

"Thanks," Jess whispered back. He crept through the door and gently laid his backpack in the hallway. After retrieving the envelope, he laid his shoes next to the backpack. He glanced up, admiring the leaded cut glass chandelier hanging in the hallway. This was a new addition, a perfect piece from the time. Although it wasn't quite the right style, it was very common in those times for people to mix similar leaded glass pieces from the various styles.

"Pretty, isn't it? David just found it a couple of weeks ago in an online salvage sale. It's from a house built in the 1920s in High Bridge, New Jersey. Someone was redoing the original lighting in some old duplexes there and decided to get rid of these. It was a steal."

"That really is a rare find."

"Yes, isn't it? So, are you staying for dinner? It's not for another hour or so, but you could hang out 'til then if you want."

"I was just hoping I could talk to Pastor David for a few minutes before y'all ate."

"You have plenty of time to talk before we eat."

"I couldn't stay—"

"Too late." She swung the front door closed behind him with finality. "You're in the house. The grandkids won't forgive me if you come by and aren't here for dinner."

"But—"

"There's plenty to eat." She turned and led the way to the pastor's study. "He's been working on something all day long. It'll do him good to get his nose out of the computer and talk to someone." She opened the door to his study and winked as she motioned him in. "Besides, it might be nice to hear how you and that girl you were chasing in church are getting on." She didn't wait for him to answer.

He stepped into the study. It wasn't really a study, more of a parlor where two or three ladies might gather on a spring afternoon while getting ready to go out and sit with the gentlemen on the porch. The walls wore wainscot, beaten up from years of chairs being slid into the soft wood.

"Hey, Jess." Pastor David stood up as he walked in.

"Hey, Pastor. Nice piece of glass out there in the hall."

"Really fits with the rest of the house, doesn't it? It's hard to find stuff that's original to the period. Took some work to rewire it, too."

"I'll bet. Mind if I close the door?" asked Jess.

"That serious, huh? It might get stuffy in here."

"It's okay if it gets a little stuffy."

Jess closed the door and pulled a chair out of the corner of the room. The desk was arranged so it faced into the bookshelves along the wall, so he set it facing the pastor's chair directly. The floorboards creaked as he sat.

"Is this a girl problem?"

"Noooo..." Jess Laughed.

"Well, Mary will be disappointed. She fussed at me for getting in between you and that girl at church the other day."

Jess handed the envelope to him.

He turned it over in his hands, considering the address and the business reply mail stamp in the corner. "You want me to subscribe to a networking magazine?"

Jess laughed. "No, that's not it either."

"A confession? You're not in some sort of trouble, are you? Should we expect the police any second? I hope not; Mary's probably already put an extra plate down for dinner."

"No, it's not a confession. It's just some information I want you to keep for a while."

"Is it something you're trying to hide?"

"Yes. Well, it's not like that, anyway. It's not anything that I would get in trouble for having. At least not in trouble with the police or anything."

"Okay, how about this. Let's start from the beginning."

He hadn't expected the pastor to ask what the information was about. It was probably natural, though, but did he want to draw the pastor into this mess? If his life was really in danger, was it really right to pull someone else in, too?

"Jess, if it's something bad, really, we've been through all of this before. I'm certain we can come through this one as well."

"It's not like that."

"Then why don't you explain it?"

On the other hand, hadn't he already brought the pastor into it, just by being here? Just by handing that envelope to him? If he were being watched, wouldn't they come here, too, trying to find out what he knew and how much he had told someone else? Since he had already brought the pastor into it, he should at least tell him the truth.

"Does the name Carl Starks mean anything to you?"

"He committed suicide recently. There wasn't a big story on it in the papers, but I always remember a suicide."

"Yes, Carl worked with me—in the same department, in fact, doing pretty much the same job."

"So you knew him well?"

"We were acquainted. We didn't share the same taste in lifestyles, you might say."

"Oh, I understand how that goes."

"Yeah, he was something of a party animal, really. Fast cars, fast girls, and all the rest."

"So what about Carl?"

"He didn't commit suicide." The only sound was the whirring of the short-bladed ceiling fan overhead. "At least, I don't think he committed suicide." It didn't sound so convincing now that he said it. Was this all just a mistake? But no, being framed for Benita's murder, and Benita's murder itself, those were not a figment of his imagination.

"Are you certain? You sounded certain at first, but now not so much."

"I'm certain. It just sounds crazy when you say it out loud."

"And this," the pastor said, lifting the envelope up a bit, "is the evidence?"

"I don't know. I'm not a good judge of how much evidence is enough."

"Why not go to the police?"

"The evidence I have is mostly missing evidence—video recordings that have been erased, missing e-mails, missing voice mails, things like that."

"Then why do you think he was murdered?"

"Do you remember I was arrested a few days ago and held overnight?" asked Jess.

"Yes, you said they thought you had done something, but new evidence turned up that proved you were innocent."

"Did you see any stories about the murder of an illegal immigrant last week?"

"Yes. You were arrested for *that*?" asked Pastor David.

"Yes."

"That happened where you work, too?"

"Yes."

"And that was definitely murder. And they arrested you for it."

"I was framed for it, actually."

The pastor looked up from the envelope. "How do you know that?"

Jess sighed. "I'm just certain I was. And the same things happened around Benita's death."

"What do you mean?"

"Missing video recordings, things like that."

"If you think you were framed, then you really should go to the police," said the pastor.

"I'm still collecting evidence," Jess replied.

"Don't you think you should let them do that?"

"I don't think they could, in this case. It's technical."

"Oh, I see. But why bring it here for me to keep?"

"I was framed for Benita's murder."

"And you're convinced someone might try something else?"

"It's possible. You don't have to keep it. If having this information endangers my life, it could endanger yours as well."

The pastor looked in his eyes. "I think you already know the answer to that one, Jess. So tell me what's in the envelope."

"The recordings with the missing information. Carl's e-mail files. Carl's voice mail files. Information on some cables that shouldn't be there, and other things in the data center. Some notes on things Benita told me before she died."

"It sounds like an odd collection of clues. Okay, so how did you think this would work? What did you think I could do with this information?" asked the pastor.

"Just hold onto it. I should have what information I can gather by tomorrow afternoon. If I don't show up for church on Sunday, I have someone I want you to give it to."

"Not the police?"

"No, not yet," Jess replied.

"Who?"

"Someone I work with. Her name is Leah."

"So there is a girl involved."

Jess laughed. "I wish, but it's not like that."

"What makes you think Leah can do anything more than the police with this information?"

"I don't know. Call it intuition, or a guess. She's asked me about it several times, to the point of getting into an argument with me over it."

"And why not your boss or one of the security people at the company?"

"Because it's an inside job. Someone inside the company is involved—they have to be. Someone erased those recordings, e-mails, and voice mails. Not many people have access to all three sets of accounts."

"Okay. You certainly do get yourself into some messes, Jess. You might be in over your head here."

Jess smiled. "And how would that be different from usual?"

Just then, someone knocked gently on the study door. Opening it, Jess saw Mary standing there, holding to two tall glasses of iced tea. "Enough of this talk, you two; now come out and talk to the kids and me for a while. Our daughter's here to pick up our grandkids, too. We're all feeling left out." She smiled as she waited for them to come out of the little office and into the fresh air of the hallway.

Jess turned into the gravel drive leading to the back of the house, his headlights splashing on the trees and bushes lining the yard. The stopover at the pastor's house had certainly lasted longer than he expected. Mary had finally satisfied herself that he and Leah really weren't anything more than friends, much to her chagrin, and let him find his way to his apartment.

It was late enough that Ms. Parker would already be asleep, and he didn't want to wake her, if possible. He turned into the tan metal carport along the side of the fence, his headlights washing over the PWC parked there. After shutting off the engine, he set the parking brake, pulled the shifter into second gear, and released the clutch. He got out and checked the cover on the PWC, making certain it was still pulled down tightly, grabbed his laptop bag, and headed to the back porch of the house and the door there, which entered into the small set of rooms partitioned off to make an apartment.

Something definitely wasn't right. His front door was open. He rewound his day. He had definitely closed it when he left this morning. Someone must have broken into his apartment. They could still be there. Call the police? No, there wasn't any point in that. It would just start a chain of traipsing through evidence they would dismiss as not related to someone breaking into his apartment. He settled his backpack on the bottom step, leaning it against the shiny white paint of the bottom post, and quietly pulled out a small flashlight.

Turning to the yard, he swept the beam around, looking for anything suspicious. No other cars were parked in the yard. He headed back to his truck, searching the street for cars that didn't belong. Nothing seemed out of place.

At his truck, he reached under the seat and withdrew a padded case from a lockbox. Opening it, he pulled out a handgun and jogged back to the porch stairs. He placed his foot on the first stair, right against the railing, and put his full weight on it. It creaked, loud in the quietness of the night. He moved quickly up the rest of the stairs. Any surprise he had to his advantage was blown at this point, anyway.

Holding the gun at low ready, he nudged the door open with his foot and backed up to the edge of the porch, as far to the hinged side of the door as possible. Slice the pie. He used the light to illuminate one section of the room at a time while exposing as little of himself as possible to anyone who might still be in the room.

Convinced he'd seen what he could of the room, he passed through the doorway. If there was anyone there, this would be the moment they would attack. Jess knew that doorways are a point of vulnerability, a funnel for incoming attacks of all sorts, and hence, it was always best to stay in them for as little time as possible. He moved to his right, felt for the light switch, and clicked it on. The room was a mess. Someone had turned his apartment over.

Obviously, his data trap had been discovered, and someone had come here looking for anything they might find. Or perhaps this was just another warning, like being framed for Benita's murder. Here was a definite sign he was getting closer to the truth. But there were other rooms in the house. He needed to check those before he started looking at the damage here.

He used the same technique to enter each of the other rooms in the apartment, slicing the pie, turning on the lights, leaving the doors open behind him, and moving through the doorways quickly. Nothing but a big mess greeted him in each room. Finally, feeling confident he had checked all the rooms thoroughly, he zippered the gun back into its case and put it away in a small lockbox mounted under his computer desk.

Now he turned back to the front door. The door had been opened, but there was no damage. The lock still operated correctly; it hadn't been bumped or destroyed. They had finessed their way in, whoever it was, picking the lock rather than forcing it. He closed the door and locked it.

Turning the lights on, he began to assess the damage. His couch was ruined, the cushions ripped to shreds, their white puffy guts scattered around the room. Jess pushed the two bookcases into their upright position, revealing a pile of ripped-out pages and parts of books, along with a group that had fallen out in a row when the cases were pulled down.

Jess moved into the kitchen, shoved aside a pile of debris, opened a closet, and pulled out a box of extra large garbage bags. Moving back into the living room, he sorted out books, throwing ripped or destroyed books into a garbage bag, lamenting over some first U.S. editions of C. S. Lewis and Agatha Christie. Others were in good condition, so he placed them back into the shelf. When he'd cleared the area out, fifteen or twenty books were in the garbage bags, the rest back in the bookcases. He tossed pieces of a guitar into the bag, along with pages and covers, and tied the second bag up. At least they hadn't damaged the apartment itself, nor had they destroyed his other two guitars. The actual damage was lighter than it first appeared, in fact.

There were two or three bags of destroyed items in each room, things to be put back into place, and furniture with new dents and dings. But, overall, it wasn't as bad as it could have been. They hadn't broken open his small upright safe, which contained guns and other things more valuable than anything they had destroyed. They hadn't actually destroyed the bed, just pulled it apart, leaving the pieces all over the place. He righted it and habitually put the sheets back into place.

Finally, he moved into the kitchen. The sink was full of broken glasses and plates, but nothing else seemed to be damaged, just moved around or tossed aside. As he cleared the counter, he uncovered a note.

"Sorry to have missed you. I'm certain we'll catch up to you later."

The note crumpled under the pressure of his anger. He tossed it in the trash can. They had certainly found his modification quickly. The question was, what all had they found? Finishing up the kitchen could wait until later.

He walked out on the porch and retrieved his laptop. Setting it on the kitchen table, he booted it up and tried to connect to the network in his apartment. His wireless signal was gone. Getting up from the table, he walked over to the small closet in the foyer and opened the door. The wireless access point was on the floor, shattered in pieces. He pulled up a step stool and climbed up so he could see, sliding some boxes out of the way. Apparently, they had missed the rest of this closet because his server was still there, and it appeared to be fine.

Retrieving his laptop from the kitchen, he connected it to the network with an Ethernet cable and sat down on the floor. He tried to connect to work—but his account had been frozen or closed. He couldn't connect, no matter what set of usernames and passwords he tried, including the administrator accounts.

Giving up there, he connected to the server sitting up on the top shelf and opened a directory. They had shut down his accounts, but the information he had collected before they had done so was still there. He copied this data onto a USB drive and then shut down the process that was copying data off the server at work. Or, at least, where he used to work. He had to assume his accounts being cut off also meant he didn't work there any longer. He stuffed the USB key into his laptop bag.

It was tempting to spend some time looking through the data, but it would be better if he just acted like nothing had happened. *If I react, whoever it is that's ransacking my apartment for data will know I'm onto something, and redouble their efforts to find it.* That meant getting up in the morning and heading out on the lake as he had originally planned. If he continued working tonight, he'd be too tired to go on the lake in the morning. He closed everything up and headed off to bed.

Chapter 25

Jamie sat at the computer in the security office, playing a game of solitaire. What had made Brian call her in so he could leave early? She couldn't guess, but she really wanted to know. Knowing things was always useful. You could never tell when it would come in handy.

Who could she get out on the lake with her family this weekend? She couldn't imagine a night without visitors or without one activity or another. It would be boring. The phone rang. She sighed as she picked it up.

"Yell-o?"

"Jamie. Where's Brian?" It was Linda, one of those snobbish secretaries from downstairs.

"Like he tells me anything."

"Well, that's okay. I was really looking for Gerard."

"How did you lose him?"

"Very funny. Have you seen either of them?"

"Nope. It's not like the security office would be someplace he normally hangs out."

"His wife just called and said he was going to be late for a party if he didn't make it home soon."

"I wish he'd invite me! I love parties!"

Linda's voice slowed to a drawl. "Don't you have kids?"

"I can always find someone to dump my kids on. It's good to know people."

The draw continued, annoying Jamie even more. "I doubt these parties would be your type of thing."

"Anyplace there's a party, I'm there! Hey, do you know if Gerard's wife likes to boat? I've seen her at some of my son's games, but I've never been able to ask her."

"I've no idea."

"Darn. I was looking for someone to meet us on the lake this weekend. My son needs someone to throw balls to; he has to practice, you know, so he can keep his arm in shape for football!"

"Um, okay. Listen, could you look around the building and see if you can find him?"

"Sure. Should I call you?"

"No, look up Gerard's home number. It's in the directory."

"Okay. You should come out and watch my son play football sometime. He's in camp this week; we have the big blowup bee out for the team to run through and the smoke generator, too!"

"No, thanks. I'm not much of a football fan."

"Okay." Jamie dropped the phone down on the cradle. Well, no harm in going along, was there? As long as she didn't have to get up and wander around the building, that is. What were cameras for?

Using her mouse, she clicked on the security camera application. The controls took her from place to place in the building. Nothing caught her eye. It looked like someone might have left a mess in the data center, but it wasn't her job to clean up messes, so she skipped by it. Finding nothing, she went back to playing solitaire.

I've lost at least twenty games. This is crazy. She glanced up at the clock. Six thirty. Time for dinner. She flipped back over to the cameras and looked at the parking lot. There were two cars there, but one of them was shrouded in the trees, so she couldn't tell whose it was. She sighed. A little walk wouldn't hurt before she used the microwave to heat her dinner up. She pushed herself out of the chair and carefully locked the door to the security office behind her.

At the front of the building, she looked through the large plate glass windows that overlooked the parking lot. She certainly wasn't walking outside to see if she could see that car better. She recognized it from the back; it was the same car she'd seen at so many of her son's football games, normally open, with lots of beer and goodies stashed inside. Must be nice to make a lot of money and live the good life.

Well, he's still here, then. Time to walk around and find him. Probably just got lost in some work someplace and forgot the time. She'd love to be a fly on the wall when he did get home, though. Arguments were always so much fun to watch.

She began a circuit of the second floor, using various keys from the set clanking on her belt to open doors and peek inside. She didn't carry a flashlight—they were too much of a pain to keep around—so she just waved her hands in front of the sensors to make the overhead lights come on.

He wasn't in any of the conference rooms or offices, so she walked along the hallways between the cubicles, looking into each one to see if he might be there. People were funny, the things they put on their cubicle walls. Some of them had Christian stuff—probably hypocrites. She was a better Christian than any of these folks would ever be.

Nothing. *Well, might as well check the first floor, too.* She glanced into each room again, unlocking them and waving at the sensors to make certain no one was there. It would be funny if she found him asleep, his head on the table. Or with a girl. That would be information worth having.

Maybe he had left. She walked out onto the porch in front of the building and peered into the darkness. No, his car was still there. Had he caught a ride home with someone else? She stepped back inside, passed through the lobby, and considered what to do next. Might as well check the basement since she was already up.

She pushed her feelings aside as she traveled down the elevator to the last stop in her search. She hated the basement. She stepped off the elevator and walked down the hall and up the ramp. She fumbled with the keys for a minute, finally inserting one and opening the lock. She stepped into the space, pushing the door in front of her.

There was the mess on the floor, just on the other end of the row of equipment. It looked like a rack had fallen over. What was under there?

It looked like him, but it couldn't be. She walked closer. Recognition spread to her stomach, and it twisted inside of her, rebelling. She backed up until her back pressed against the cold door, and then she fainted.

Chapter 26

Detective Harris stepped from his car into the familiar surroundings of the OptiData parking lot. A woman was sitting on the front steps. He looked her over with his practiced eye. Dark hair, heavily built, dark eyes, no glasses, dressed in a somewhat shabby security guard's uniform. She obviously hadn't handled her encounter with the dead body well.

"Are you Jamie?"

She looked up, a startled look on her face. She was in some sort of shock and would need to be tended to before she would be able to answer any useful questions.

"Yes?"

"Did you call anyone else? Should we expect anyone else to show up at this point?"

She shook her head. "I just called 911. I didn't know who else I *should* call. Gerard..."

"Yeah, probably not a good idea to call Gerard right now."

Her eyes widened as she realized what he had said. That probably hadn't been the best thing to say at the moment, but he would probably never get over his proclivity for gallows humor when he was under stress. "How about you just let us in? I can find our way to the data center."

She got up and turned, her toe catching on the top step. He reached out his hand and steadied her. Taking a ring from her belt, she selected a key and inserted it into the lock. After opening the door, she mutely handed the key ring over.

"When the ambulance gets here, they'll take care of you. We'll call the appropriate people." He wondered who that would be. Brian, certainly, since he was the head of security. He would have to call Leah, but later, once he'd cleared the crime scene. It wouldn't be good to be overheard talking to her.

He hefted the heavy key ring and headed inside, hearing in the background the first emergency vehicle pulling up. Keys. Interesting. When he saw a building all rigged up with electronic entry systems like this, Harris tended to forget about keys. If someone entered the building using a key, they would be undetected, other than the security cameras. But obviously, the recordings on the security cameras could be altered.

Detective Harris turned and headed back out the door, stopping in front of Jamie. "How many people have keys to this building?"

"Well, there's Gerard, I guess. He's manages the whole place, and we call him in case of emergencies. There's Brian. And there are three sets in the security office. I signed one out when I came to work."

"And the other sets? Just spares?"

"No, we sign keys out to people when they need them."

"Are they sets of keys, like this?"

"There are three sets and then two individual master keys that will open most of the doors in the building."

"Hmm...okay. Thanks." A paramedic walked up behind her, ushering her off to be treated for mild shock. It would probably get worse before it got better, once the reality started to sink in. Sergeant Stone came just behind the paramedic. The detective turned back into the door and headed to the receptionist's desk. A piece of paper was taped there with Brian's cell phone number on it. He picked up the phone lying there on the desk and dialed the number.

"Mr. Colonel?"

"This is Brian, yes."

"Could you come down to the office?"

"What's going on? Who is this?"

"This is Detective Harris; we've met before. There's been another death. Your security guard isn't handling it the best in the world, and we need some information."

"Be there in a minute."

"Thank you." Detective Harris hung the phone up and headed through the double doors leading into the hallway.

Pulling the door open, he moved into the data center, the low humming sound from hundreds of fans enveloping him. Sergeant Stone trailed closely behind him. Moving to his right along the textured gray floor, he glanced down the space between the first two rows of equipment. As his eyes adjusted to the brightening of the overhead lights, he could clearly see Gerard's body, trapped under a rack full of equipment.

"Another murder." Sergeant Stone's tone was gruff, irritated.

"Maybe." Detective Harris moved to the second row and pushed on the rack at the very end. Looking up, he noted there were no cables strung between the rack and the ceiling. He pushed gingerly, testing the amount of pressure it would take to make the rack fall, like the one resting on top of Gerard's body. It felt like it would give way if he put his body weight on it. He stood considering this as the medical team swept in, the camera flashes and hubbub of conversation drowning his thoughts.

"Detective Harris! I came as fast as I could." Brian stood at the door, which had been propped open. Harris waved at the officer standing there, indicating Brian should be let through.

"Tell me about these end racks. None of them seem to be connected to anything."

"No, they never are. I think they use them for spare equipment or something like that."

"And the wheels are always locked?"

"Yes."

Detective Harris watched as Brian settled into one of the chairs in the security office. "Now, you wanted to see the tapes, right?"

Detective Harris hovered over Brian's shoulder. "The ones from the camera just over the door in the data center."

"Okay." Brian clicked through several screens and finally brought up a video recording. He pulled a slider on the bottom of the screen over until the time in the bottom right-hand corner read 12:00. "I remember seeing Gerard around lunch time, but not after that, so we might as well start here." He pressed a button, and the video moved forward rapidly.

Suddenly, it changed to a normal play speed. On the camera, Jess walked into the data center, and then he was in front of the camera, making it shake.

"Early afternoon. What was that about?"

"Jess replaced the camera today with a new one."

"Any particular reason?"

"I had opened up a case on that camera when Benita was killed in there. Remember the missing video on the recording?"

"Yes." Brian pushed the button again, and a few minutes of blank recording were skipped. There was Jess on the camera again, now climbing down from the ladder.

"He seems to show up all the time when people are killed in that data center. Maybe we need to bring him in for questioning again."

"Not yet, Sergeant. Let's not make that mistake again. Okay, stop right there, Brian."

He pushed another button, and the picture stopped changing. He couldn't see the rack. He didn't expect to since it would be hidden by the other racks in the row while it was upright. But it certainly wasn't lying on the floor like it had been just a few minutes ago.

"Okay, move to the next scene change."

Brian pressed a button on screen, and the recording moved forward rapidly again. The player stopped on a barely perceptible shudder in the recording.

"Wait, back up and show that part again, at normal speed."

Brian backed up and replayed it. Detective Harris noted the time skip in the lower right-hand corner of the recording. Either the camera had malfunctioned, or the recording had been altered.

"Okay, that's enough."

"Nothing to see, huh?" Neither Brian nor the sergeant seemed to have seen the shift in the time. Harris decided to keep it to himself for the moment.

"What about the building entry records? Can you tell me who came into the building today?"

"Sure." Brian opened another application and printed out a list. Taking the list from Brian, Detective Harris laid it out on a table.

"Does anything here strike you as unusual?"

Brian looked the list over. "Nothing, really. No one that shouldn't be here. Jess badged into the data center just a few minutes before he replaced the camera. Gerard badged in a bit later."

"What time did Mr. Wirth leave?"

"I don't know. We don't record when people leave the building."

"Okay. I need to make a call. It won't take but a minute."

Harris walked out of the room, wandering on the third floor until he found an open conference room. Glancing around to ensure there wasn't a camera mounted on the wall anyplace, he pulled out his cell phone and dialed a number.

"Leah?"

"Yeah. What's up? Something happen?"

"Where is your charge?"

"Sitting at his pastor's house, eating dinner while I'm sitting out here eating a horrible hamburger."

"Oh. It's called paying your dues. Have you tailed him all afternoon?"

"Yes, since he left work. It was supposed to be Thuan's shift, but he's been tied up in some stuff he's trying to find."

"What time did he leave work?"

"Three forty-eight."

"Okay, that corresponds with what I see here."

"Mind telling me what's up?" Leah asked.

"Mr. Mattingly is dead," Harris replied.

"*What?*"

"He was crushed under a rack in the data center."

"And Jess is a suspect?"

"He was the last person to badge in there before Mr. Mattingly."

"So, it's possible he stayed there and waited."

"And then pushed the rack over onto him, yes."

"So, are you going to bring him back in?"

"No."

"Why?"

Harris laughed. It was always fun to catch someone a little off guard. The hamburger was definitely on his side in this case. "Because Mr. Mattingly died after your charge left the office. At least that's what the times on the data center door tell us, and also what the video recordings of the data center seem to show, at least what we have of them. The recording has been altered."

"Interesting. Don't they record the parking lot as well?"

"Ah, good idea. I'll go check."

"Should I do anything here?"

"No, just keep your guard up. If your charge didn't do this, then the person who did is loose. And Mr. Wirth might be the next target."

He ended the call and headed back over to the security office.

Approaching Brian, Harris asked, "Do you record off the camera in the parking lot?"

"Sure."

"Can you bring it up so we can see what happened in the parking lot this afternoon?"

Brian browsed through the files, finally bringing one up on the screen. "This is this afternoon."

"Can you forward to about three forty-five?"

Brian pulled the slider over, releasing it where the recording said 15:45 in the corner so it would play. After a few minutes, Jess's back appeared on camera. The detective traced his progress from when he entered the camera frame until he reached his truck. After Jess had started up the driveway, another car followed, not too close in behind him. Leah, of course. Brian stopped the recording.

"Okay, that confirms Jess left the building, anyway."

Sergeant Stone huffed. "He could have driven around the back and come back into the building just a few minutes later."

Detective Harris looked at the sergeant. *What is going on here? Sergeant Stone never acts this way about a case, fixating on a single suspect like this.* "He could have, but I don't think he did."

Sergeant Stone continued down the path. "How do you know?"

"Well, check the badge records."

The sergeant tapped Brian on the shoulder. In response, Brian tapped for a minute on the keyboard, bringing up a screen showing each person who had used their badge entering the building that afternoon. Jess's name was not there.

Sergeant Stone looked at Harris. "He could have gotten in some other way."

"How?"

"Maybe he has a key."

Detective Harris turned to Brian. "Does Mr. Wirth have a key to the building? Jamie said there were only a limited number of sets."

"No, he doesn't. There are two sets here, the one set I have, and Gerard has, or rather had, a set."

"Are any missing?"

"Just the set you have down at the office as part of the evidence on Benita's death."

"I had forgotten about that. How would she get a set of keys?"

"The cleaning people don't have badges. When they come to work, they sign out a set of keys. When they leave, they sign them back in."

"Can I see the log?"

Brian reached onto the desk and picked up a clipboard.

Detective Harris took it from him. "Why isn't this stored in a file on a computer? Seems a bit old-fashioned to me."

"I get signatures. I could do it on the computer, but it's easier this way. I digitize the sheets at the end of the month, so I don't keep them on paper."

"Ah, okay. It doesn't look like Mr. Wirth has checked out any keys recently. Has he ever?"

"Why should he? His badge opens almost every door in the building."

"Has anyone ever forgotten to bring the keys back or taken the keys home?"

"Usually that happens once or twice a year, but it's not happened this year, yet. Normally it seems to happen around the holidays, for some reason—I think people are just not thinking about what they're doing during that time of the year."

"So they've not been taken home accidentally in the last four or five months?"

"Not that I know of. I could check the back logs if you think—"

"No, that won't be necessary." He stepped out of the office, heading towards the elevator.

"What now?" Sergeant Stone was clearly irritated.

"We go home, eat dinner, and wait until Monday."

"*Monday?*"

"Yes, Monday. There's no rush here, no reason to disturb anyone's weekend, really," said Harris.

"We need to start pulling people in and questioning them now, not on Monday," Stone insisted.

"Nothing will change between now and Monday. Go home and have a good weekend for once."

Chapter 27

Jess peered into his rearview mirrors, adjusting the steering wheel slightly from side to side, trying to keep the small trailer in between the two curbs. The fenders released bubbles as they broke the surface of the water; he set the brake, put the transmission in second gear, and shut off the engine.

Some time on the lake would help him forget the office. He didn't want to wonder about what else was going on, and sitting in front of a computer analyzing the data he'd captured wasn't a good pursuit for a warm Saturday morning. He released the safety chain and winch, waded into the water, and pulled the PWC from the trailer. There would be plenty of time to try and digest what the web had caught tonight.

After tying the PWC to the pier, he pulled the truck out and parked it in one of the long, diagonal spaces painted across the blacktop. There weren't many trailers parked in the lot, which meant there weren't a lot of boats on the lake today. It was probably too early in the season for a lot of families. Smaller children didn't fare as well in the colder water of the early season.

He walked gingerly over the pier's rough boards. Shuffling in water shoes along the coarse wooden boards of the pier wasn't ever a good idea. The long splinters that sometimes peeled away from the wood would puncture water shoes just as easily as they would flesh.

Releasing the lines holding his PWC, he cranked the engine and backed out into the cove. Turning, he throttled it a little, but he tried to keep it slow enough not to rock the No Wake signs posted around the perimeter of the ramp and pier area. There was nothing worse than lining your boat up on the trailer, gunning it for the final run in, and being knocked off to one side or another by the wake from a passing boat.

He navigated through the buoys marked with orange danger triangles, staying in the center of the channel as much as possible. He gunned it more heavily as he passed the island, pushing out into the main lake, heading north towards the Highway 64 bridge. Just past the bridge, he turned to his starboard side and slipped behind the marina's artificial barrier. Pulling up into one of the slots in their dock, he tied up to the cleat and jumped off. Inside the store, he picked out two sodas and walked over to the cashier to pay for them.

"Hey, out watching eagles today? The weather is nice. There should be plenty of them up there fishing."

"I'm going to run into a big cove just up on the other side of the lake for a bit and eat some lunch first."

"Ah, the one up on the port side that has a bunch of smaller coves running off of it? It doesn't look like much from the lake side, so not many people run there. As few people as there are on the lake today, it should be nice and quiet."

"Well, thanks—I'm back out on the water."

"Have a good time."

Back on his PWC, he slipped past the marina's barrier and out into the main lake again. Running up onto plane and pushing the throttle all the way, he shot across the lake, making for the cove. He ran in a little way, just to a point where two of the smaller coves met. No one else was anchored in there, so he backed off the throttle, letting the PWC settle, and he considered where to eat lunch.

His cell phone rang. "Hello?"

"Jess, where are you?"

"Linda, you sound like you've been crying. I'm on the lake. What's going on?"

"It's horrible, Jess. I just found out this morning when I called in to work to check my voice mail. The office is shut down on Monday; Gerard has been killed."

"*What?*"

"Yes. I don't know how it happened. I called Brian, and he said something about a rack falling on him, but I didn't really understand it all."

"A *rack?*"

"That's what he said."

"And the office is closed on Monday? I suppose the owners will have to come in and find someone else to run the place or something."

"Not until this one is cleared up, I think. Brian said they want the place shut down for a while."

"Do I need to go into the police station or something?"

"Brian said they weren't going to be questioning anyone until Monday, at least. He said he and the security folks would be working schedules like usual through the week while the police try to figure out what happened."

"So, they're expecting no work at all next week?"

"That's what it sounds like."

"Are you going to be okay?"

"I think so. Do you think this is related to Carl's death?"

"Yes, I do. Linda, is—" He heard the boat before he saw it. A twenty-five-footer, he guessed, white with blue trim. It was certainly loud, and it was probably fast, too, if the sound of the engine was any guide.

"What, Jess? Is what?"

"Wait a minute, Linda; I can't hear you over the noise out here. Just wait 'til this boat—"

The boat wasn't veering off, though. It was heading straight towards him. Putting the cell phone in a drink holder, he throttled up, trying to get the PWC on plane. If he couldn't get on plane, he'd have to speed. Boats that aren't moving can't be steered.

The PWC responded, the bow lifting, but there wouldn't be time to hit plane. He'd have to do the best he could with the speed he had. He turned towards the boat, preparing to angle off in one direction or another. The boat adjusted, bearing directly down on him. Fast. They were coming in parallel to the shore, angling in from the main lake and heading towards the back of the cove.

He jigged to his starboard side, following the rules of the road and putting the boat between him and the shoreline, on his port side. The boat switched too, again heading directly for him. What was going on? Was his PWC so low in the water that they didn't see him?

Having just a few seconds left to react, he turned the handles to the port side, diving off the PWC in that direction, towards the shore. He hoped that putting the PWC between him and the oncoming boat would give him some space and time to react.

The boat kept coming, making adjustments. Jess struck off in the water as fast as he could, swimming towards shore, still about thirty feet off. The new life jacket restricted his arms and scooped into the water, slowing his progress to almost nothing.

It had to go, no matter what the boat did. He struggled with the buckles along the front, his hands not cooperating.

Bang!

Veering off slightly, the boat side-swiped his PWC, pushing it close to Jess. He pulled at the first buckle, unable to get the plastic catch to click open. At least they had veered off, so they didn't run their keel directly over the PWC. That would have hung their boat up on the PWC itself and killed him in the process.

The boat's engine revved as the man at the helm skidded into a turn, spraying water on the opposite shore. Weren't they going to slow down, to stop, inspect the damage, try and figure out what had just happened? No, it didn't look like it. The boat continued turning, staying on plane, looping around on their port side. Sitting in one of the stern seats, a man stretched his arms out. The movement caught Jess's eye, drawing his attention. The short, black barrel of a rifle hung over the starboard gunwale.

The first buckle on his life jacket popped loose. The reason they hadn't stopped was it wasn't an accident.

They're trying to kill me!

The PWC. If he could make it back on the PWC, he could get some speed. But was it fast enough to outrun that rifle? No. No point in trying it; he'd just have to deal with things as they were. The boat was agile and fast. If the man at the helm knew how to drive it, there was no way for Jess to get away. At this point, he just had to count on someone else making a mistake.

Jess pulled frantically at the second buckle, watching the cutting edge of the keel plow into the water. The helmsman pushed the throttle down more, trying to get the boat to turn faster, but it was too much, too fast. The stern slid out, the starboard side popping up dangerously. The engine settled as he backed off, trying to keep the boat up on the water, losing speed.

The second buckle on his life jacket popped loose. It had to go; they could see him easily, bobbing on the surface like this. The helmsman came off the turn, starting to straighten out and gain speed for another run. He leaned on the throttle, but it was too much; the trim was too low, a rooster tail arching high in the back, the bow being driven into the water. A slight turn would put them over the sides now, the helmsman struggling with the wheel to keep it straight.

A few seconds and they would be on top of him.

The third buckle on his life jacket popped loose. His hands objected with searing pain.

Even with the bow buried in the water, there was no way to out swim a boat. Left or right didn't matter; he couldn't swim fast enough for it to make any difference at this point.

He dove, slipping his arms out of the life jacket, leaving it floating on the surface of the water.

How deep? He focused, digging through his mind. Twenty-five feet long. Probably draws around two feet. The foot and skeg, another ten inches. Three feet, at least.

The loud whine of the prop was getting louder, just seconds away; the keel under the bow was probably just feet away. The last reading on the depth finder was ten feet. How could he stay down long enough to avoid a collision with the prop?

His foot touched something—it was smooth, not a rock, not the bottom. A log.

He went head down and felt for a place to hang on. A branch. He grabbed it and pulled down hard, willing himself to hold his breath for as long as possible.

The engine was louder. Then deafening. He *felt* the prop pass overhead. When he looked up, pieces of his lifejacket were floating on the surface. The prop was whining a different tune now. The boat was in a turn, and the prop was having trouble holding onto the water. It was cavitating, slicing up air bubbles as the water slid by the blades. It wouldn't stay on plane if the helmsman didn't find that trim button. Jess hoped he didn't.

He pulled himself along the log, towards shore, needing air. He let himself bob to the surface, coming up as the boat was on the far side of another turn. The two men in the back were looking for him, but the boat was on its own wake, bouncing as it plowed into the waves. They couldn't see him with the motion of the boat and the distance. It was always hard to see things in the water, the reason skiers always wear bright jackets and put their hands in the air.

Taking a deep breath, he dove again, skimming under the surface of the water towards the shore. His foot touched the bottom, so he lifted his head, putting just his eyes and nose above the surface. There was a shallow cove to his right, probably too shallow for the boat. He ducked under the water, skimming just under the surface as fast as he could.

His head bumped into a tree. *Ow!*

Taking another breath, he swam out, away from the shore, around the trunk, and back in, surfacing just on the other side. The tree would make good cover for a minute, at least until he could figure out what they were going to do next.

The boat had come in, run over his life jacket again, and was back out in the middle of another loop, looking for him. They apparently decided he was gone because the man at the helm dropped the throttle to neutral as the boat came off the turn.

The wake, catching up, pooped the boat, pushing it forward towards the shore. The helmsman pulled the throttle, pulling the boat back, counteracting the wave. They drifted loose, about twenty feet from the shore, right at the point.

They sat in the boat for some minutes, using binoculars to search into the woods and around through the coves. One of them finally said, "Can't wait too long. Someone will be along here soon. We need to get things arranged before that happens."

Jess thought about his situation. No cell phone. No wallet. No camera. He would have a hard time finding his way out of this mess, even if he got out with his life.

Someone grabbed his arm under the water; he opened his mouth to scream, but it was covered by another hand. "*Shut up!*"

"*Leah!*"

In a low, urgent voice, she said, "*I said shut up!* You do want to live, don't you?" She took her hand off his mouth and smiled at him. He nodded and turned to see what was going on.

The man sitting in the stern seat got up, swaying as the boat settled on the water. He dumped the rifle he'd been holding, an AR-15, on the seat, sweeping the muzzle across the two men seated behind the windshield. They were just as sloppy with their gun handling as they were with their boat handling. After dumping the rifle, he tossed a cooler onto the gunwale and pushed it into the water.

Two men then stepped out on the stern swim platform and dove off into the water. Coming back to the surface, one of the men pushed the cooler towards the shore while the other swam out towards Jess's PWC. The helmsman put the throttle down, moving the boat around the point, back towards the main lake;

he was going to block the entrance to the cove while the other two worked.

The man on Jess's PWC gunned it, spun it around, and then took it out into the water a little ways. Spinning it again, he sideswiped a rock, making a hole in one side. Jess started to jump up, unable to control his immediate reaction to do something. Leah squeezed his arm and then released it.

"Leave it!" The sound of the PWC would cover their voices for the moment. He felt Leah release his arm. He looked just in time to see her pull a resealable plastic bag from under the surface of the water. She opened it and slid a semiautomatic pistol out.

He kept his voice low. "Springfield XD. Ever heard of a holster?"

"Stickler, huh? At least I'm carrying something, anyway."

"Okay, so I don't go armed on my PWC. Maybe I will from now on. Why do you?"

She smiled. "For the moment, let's just keep us both alive." They turned back to the man on the PWC. It started to swamp, so he ran the throttle up and got it up on plane, heading straight for the shore. When he hit the shore, he went over the handlebars, rolling along the mud towards the woods. He got up and shook himself off. The man pushing the cooler followed it up onto the shore. He reached inside, pulled out a beer bottle, and took a couple of swigs.

"The boss doesn't like you drinking on the job, you know."

"I'm not driving, so it don't matter. It's not like you can shoot straight with the boat bouncing all over the place, anyway. I wish he'd learn to drive that thing."

"Like you could do better, I suppose?"

The man with the beer snorted in response. "Think he's down there someplace?" He waved towards the water just off the point with his hand.

"Must be. Can't see where else he'd go. I think we got him with that last run."

He grunted. "No blood on the life jacket, though. Could still be around here someplace."

"It's wet, if you hadn't noticed. Would've washed off, probably. We should look around in the woods a little anyway, just to be certain. We can look around from the boat when we're done here, too."

As they tramped up into the woods, twigs snapping under their water shoes, Jess and Leah pulled in closer to the log.

"Snakes."

She whispered back, "I don't care. They're more dangerous than a water moccasin."

The men emerged from the woods a bit past them, heading back towards the PWC piled up on the shore. They ducked under the water quickly.

When they came back up, the men were past them. One of them pulled his rash shirt away from his back and sides. "Can't stand having things stick to me like that."

Leah pulled the handgun out of the water, letting it drain back into the lake. One of the men turned back towards them. "I thought I heard some water dripping."

"Like, duh, you're surrounded by a lake. There's water dripping all over the place. Probably just that log we just walked past."

"We need to check out that PWC we saw a few minutes ago, too."

"We'll check it out from the boat. I'm not swimming across the cove to take a look."

The man with the beer bottle took one more swig and then started pouring it all over Jess's PWC. The other man opened the seat compartment and took some hanks of line out to make room. He opened a few beer bottles, pouring them down into the compartment and on the mud. Once they were empty, he shoved them into the empty space.

"That should be enough."

"Just one final touch." He took some of the shredded pieces of Jess's life jacket from where they had washed up on the shore and tossed them around the PWC. Then he took a walkie-talkie from a waterproof bag hanging from his shoulder and spoke into it for a moment.

A few seconds later, the big boat came purring back into the cove, the driver backing just as he came about ten feet from shore. He put a ladder down, and the two men on the shore swam back over, pushing the cooler ahead of them.

As the first one climbed on the boat, the helmsman said, "Think they'll be convinced?"

"It'll look just like a guy thing—out drinking beer on the lake and ended up having a little accident. They'll find the body eventually, and no one will think to go looking for the boat that shredded him."

The second man climbed up the ladder and then struggled to pull the cooler up onto the swim deck. He turned to the helmsman. "We need to check around the shore some to make certain we got him and to check out that PWC around in the other cove."

"Let's go poke around the lake some before we check the other PWC out. It's a nice day."

"Hang out for a while on the boss's time?"

"Sure, why not?"

The driver pulled the throttle into reverse, turned the boat, and then pushed full forward. The boat leapt onto plane, throwing off a high rooster tail, and faded off towards the main part of the lake.

Jess and Leah crawled up onto shore and lay there. "You often go around saving people's lives?"

"Only guys that I like a lot. Pink roses, you know."

He smiled. "I suppose you've paid me back for those now, haven't you?"

"Yes, I think I have. I normally don't do this. I've broken a few rules here, and I have to sort some things out. Let's swim over towards my PWC."

"Wait, should we try to get mine back into the water?"

"If someone is trying to kill you, what do you think the best thing to be is?"

"Oh, I see. Dead."

"Yes, exactly. Besides which, it has enough holes in it to be pretty useless about now."

Jess glanced over at his PWC, completely out of the water. She was right. "Could I get my camera and a bag?"

"Camera? How long is the lens?"

"Long enough to get a picture of that boat if it comes back."

"Check. Bag? Why a bag?"

"Well, I think you lost yours down there on the shore someplace. I don't expect you want to just shove that thing into your life jacket to get home." He indicated the handgun she was still holding.

"Oh. Hadn't thought of that. Okay, try to be quick. I don't like either of us to be out and exposed if they happen to come back."

Jess jogged to his PWC and opened the back compartment. His spare life jacket was covered in beer. He didn't want to run into any rangers on the lake smelling like beer. He moved to the front and opened the smaller compartment there. Thankfully, they hadn't poured beer all over his camera. He let the cover drop, the sound echoing on the lake. Leah turned and shot him a look, her cell phone glued to her head. He shrugged, pulled his keys and wallet out, and dumped the rest on the ground. No harm in adding to the mess. He headed back to the woods.

"You parked at New Hope, right?"

"Don't you know? I'm guessing you didn't just happen to be out on the lake, or in the same cove, or hiding behind that log."

She rolled her eyes again. "You're impossible, you know. Just checking."

"Are you checking to see if I'm impossible, or are you checking to see where I parked? Hey, what's going on, anyway?"

"I'm arranging to have your PWC found by the appropriate authorities and to have your truck towed before the guys who arranged this little accident get any ideas about taking it."

"Leah, can you tell them to be careful with my truck?"

She ended the call. "Somehow I don't think you need to worry about that. It's not often you see a forest green 1964 Ford pickup in mint condition like yours. You treat it like a baby, you know; I noticed water beads up on it like you wax it every day or something."

"Well, it's a bit of a sentimental heirloom."

"I gathered. If it's an heirloom, maybe you should buy something else to drive. I don't think many people understand the concept of driving an heirloom to work every day." He started to object that he didn't have any place to park another car, but she said, "You know, Ms. Parker would be glad to let you park another car in the driveway, so don't even start."

"How would you know that?"

"Later. For now, let's get out of here. I'll make certain they put it someplace out of the rain, don't worry. I actually like that truck, you know." She smiled.

"I guess I'll have to buy a new PWC now." He sighed. "I just went through this."

"Get a boat this time. Linda says it's time for you to think about starting a family, anyway."

"You talk to Linda too much. So just who are these friends of yours that are being so nice with my truck?"

"Later. Curiosity killed the cat."

"Satisfaction brought him back."

She smiled, but she said nothing. As they emerged from the woods on the other side of the point where they had been hiding, she dumped the handgun into the dry bag and tucked it inside her life jacket. She waded into the water and started swimming across the cove.

Jess could see her PWC pulled up on the shore opposite. It would take longer to walk, so he waded in behind her, carrying the bag with the handgun and the bag with his camera in one arm, using the side-stroke to pull himself along the surface.

On reaching the other side, she popped the seat open on her PWC and handed him a life jacket. "Put this on while I make some calls." It was blue, of course, matching the trim on her PWC.

She flipped her phone open again and read the coordinates off her GPS to someone on the other end. She ended the call and turned back to the lake. It was peaceful sitting on the shore where she had pulled her PWC up, looking out over the cove. His PWC was hidden from sight by the woods on the other side of the cove.

"I spent a lot of my time on the water when I was growing up, too, you know. It's always great being out on a lake, isn't it? Lots of space in to think, and just to stop and listen."

"Leah, how do you know so much about me?"

"I just do, that's all. You'll figure it out soon, I think."

He heard a familiar sound—it was the big white boat, returning.

"Shut up and kiss me." Jess stared at her.

"Geez, I've never had to ask a guy to kiss me twice before!" She pulled him towards her and kissed him. When she broke free, the sound of the white boat was gone.

"You always go around picking up strange men off the lake, giving them a spare life jacket, and then kissing them?"

"I had to hide your face, didn't I? Don't get any ideas."

"And kissing me was the only thing you could think of?"

Her face flushed red.

"You're cute when you're embarrassed, you know."

"Shut up." She pushed her PWC out into the water and tossed him keys attached to a little pink fish floater. "You drive," she said. "I'm riding behind." She slipped the handgun out of the dry bag and shoved it under her life jacket.

Chapter 28

Jess bumped into the side of the pier, grabbing onto one of the cleats to steady the PWC. Leah climbed up onto the pier.

"Vista Point. I could never get used to the waves out in this part of the lake. Mind if I take your PWC for a run while I'm waiting on you to back the trailer in?"

"You won't have time."

"You certain? Girls backing trailers, you know."

She shot him a look. "Boys bumping into piers, too!"

"Touché," he said to her receding back as she walked up the ramp towards the parking lot. A few minutes later, she swept past the ramp in a forest green four-door Jeep and backed the little trailer down without having to pull up and straighten out once. Jess took the PWC out a little ways and ran straight up onto the trailer. She began tying it down as he climbed off into the water.

"Not bad for a girl."

"Told you so."

"I think you used your mirrors, too, instead of turning around to look out of the back of the truck."

She smiled. "You're just jealous because I have a new truck and you don't!"

They climbed in, riding in silence for some time.

"So, where are we going?"

"My place."

"You always take guys home on the first date?"

"Only if I like them."

"Which means you like me?"

"I haven't decided yet."

He laughed. "Okay, you're confusing me."

She laughed as well. "That's my job."

She pulled into a nice apartment complex in Chapel Hill and turned into a small parking lot behind the buildings. She quickly backed the trailered PWC into a covered area beside a number of other trailers parked there, all in various states of repair. She jumped out, and Jess followed her, helping her lift the hitch off the ball and pulling a cover over the PWC while she locked it up.

"So, want to tell me what happened out there on the lake today? Why were you following me? Why did you get in the middle of that mess? Do you always carry a gun?" Jess had a lot of questions pent up, spitting them all out at once.

"Don't you normally carry a gun?"

"Not always—"

"Just most of the time. Let's leave the answers 'til later. It's a long story. I'm too hungry and tired to start on it."

"If it's a long story, starting sooner would be better, wouldn't it?"

"Like I said, later."

They climbed back into her Jeep in silence; she pulled farther into the complex, parking in front of one of the buildings.

"Nice place you live in here."

"It's not my place, really."

"It's not your place, but it is your place. More confusion. I suppose if I ask for an explanation, you'll just tell me to wait 'til later?"

"If you know the answer, why bother asking?" She climbed out of the truck, pulled a few items from the seat, and pressed the key fob twice to lock all the doors.

She walked up the steps through the maze of apartments. She stopped to put a key in a door, and then she pushed it open. Jess stepped in behind her, walking into a large living room area. An open counter area led into the kitchen, and three doors led off into different areas within the apartment.

She headed to one of them and pointed to another. "This is my bedroom. The other one is empty. The guys should have already brought in some clothes and stuff from your place. There aren't any boogey men here to get you; it's pretty safe, being a safe house and all." She laughed at her own humor as she walked into the bedroom and closed the door.

Walking through the door Leah indicated, he found himself in a room filled with heavy modern furniture. It felt more like a hotel room than a place someone would actually live. There was one familiar thing in the room, though; his suitcase lay on the bed.

Opening it, he found three or four days' worth of clothes. They weren't neatly folded, but at least he had something to wear other than a bathing suit.

———

After he had bathed and dressed, he headed back into the living room area. There was a television positioned in a heavy entertainment center along one wall, and a couple of nondescript pictures were along the walls. Where were the books? He glanced around, searching for something to read, but there wasn't a printed page to be found. He sighed and moved into the kitchen.

The green light on the front of the dishwasher was lit. Well, at least there was something to do. Pulling it open, he started emptying it into the cabinets around the kitchen, guessing where things might go. Leah could sort things out later, but at least he'd done a good deed for the day.

Just as he closed the door on the empty dishwasher, Leah came out of the other bedroom. "What, you don't know how to use a television set?"

"Television? I haven't watched television in fifteen years, at least. And there's not a book in this place." He stepped from the kitchen into the living room and looked at her. Her brown hair was down, falling just below her shoulders. Her eyes reflected the blue of her nicely fitted blue dress, the hem falling just to her knees. He stood there staring at her. She was stunning.

"What's wrong? Cat got your tongue? Would you consider this dress pretty or elegant?"

"You're beautiful. You're way out of—"

"Your league. I have a small recommendation to make. Don't ever use that line around me again. I'm a grown up girl, in case you hadn't noticed, and God gave me a brain. I think I'll be the judge of who's out of my league and who's not."

"Um, okay. Sorry."

"Don't be sorry, just don't do it again. The next time you do, I might just give you five little red marks across your cheek to remind you for the future." She held out her hand, flexing her fingers.

"I'm sorry, Leah, it's just—"

"That you think I'm too pretty for you. You told me I'm beautiful. Thank you, but don't put yourself down to make the point, okay? Now, what should we do for dinner?"

"Aren't you going to start that long story about why you were following me and why you got involved?"

"I'm too hungry to talk."

"How do I know this isn't a nefarious plot to poison me?"

She sighed and opened her purse. She dug through it for a moment, finally producing a small white card, which she handed to him. "That's the only question I'm going to answer before I eat."

The card's dimples slid through his fingers as he considered what was written there. The card was printed with raised ink, meant to make it feel engraved in your hand, but much cheaper to print and process. *Department of Homeland Security, Special Operations, Information Systems Investigations Unit.* Why would someone want to investigate information systems?

"You're a government agent?"

"I thought you said you read a lot?"

"There's not a lot here to work from. What are you investigating at OptiData? Is it something to do with Carl's death?"

"I'm *really* hungry."

"Someone is stealing data from our servers?"

"I'm *really, really* hungry. I might just faint right here, and then you'd have to carry me to dinner. I'm certain that would be really romantic and all, but I really prefer to walk, if possible."

"Okay, okay, I get the picture. We can talk about it after dinner. Where should we go?"

"There's a good Mexican place around the corner. I know you like Mexican, so it should do."

"You know, it's creepy going out with a girl who already knows everything there is to know about you and won't tell you why."

"You ask too many questions."

He opened the door and let her pass through first. She handed him the keys so he could lock it, but she refused to take the keys back.

"You're driving. The guy always drives on a real date."

"What if I wreck your new truck?"

"Are you kidding? I've seen the truck you drive. If that's any indication, you drive like an old lady."

He laughed. "Not so much. But I suppose you're about to find out soon enough."

"Don't you think I already know?"

"Creepy."

"Hush. There's one slight issue that I already know you're not going to like. I have to pay."

"Why shouldn't I pay? I know we live in modern times, but I'm a bit old-fashioned. I expect you already know that about me, too."

"I knew you wouldn't like it, but none of that has anything to do with it. I don't think your credit cards are working. The guys I work with have already reported you missing, and they're looking for your body just about now. We should be able to see it on the news when we get back."

"You might actually convince me to watch television just so I can see the reports of my own death."

"Two iced teas and a bowl of queso," said Jess.

The waiter asked, "Sweet or unsweetened tea?"

"Are you serious? You have unsweetened tea? Here in North Carolina?"

Leah cut in. "Don't mind him; he doesn't get out to fancy restaurants very often." The waiter laughed and headed off to get their drinks.

"So, what's it like to work as a secret agent? Is it exciting, like in the movies?"

"It's actually pretty boring. Mostly just paperwork. There's the time spent sifting through complaints to try and find a pattern someplace on which to base an investigation. Then there's the initial report to justify the investigation. There are daily reports, all the evidence gathered during the investigation has to be sifted and sorted, warrants and subpoenas, expense reports, final reports, suspect character buildups—"

"So, nothing like *The Avengers?*"

She laughed. "Mr. Steed with his umbrella and Mrs. Peel in her body suits, running around England? Mrs. Peel ending up tied to a set of railroad tracks, or finding a building that is a bomb? No, nothing like that."

"No cool gadgets no one else knows about?"

"No, there's no department of special research that gives us special gadgets, like Q."

"So, you're telling the movies are just all make-believe?"

"They must be. I don't have guys chasing me around like James Bond has girls, at any rate."

He was startled by her last statement. "There's no one in your life?"

She laughed. "You think because I'm pretty I should have a ton of guys or be married, right?"

"Well, it seems obvious."

"Have you even tried dating nowadays?"

"Oh, I know, it's a mess out there. I was just talking to Linda about this a few days ago."

"And my career doesn't exactly allow me a lot of time to date, anyway. Until I've made my mark as a field agent and can get promoted into a position with more sane hours, there's not much time for dating or for marriage."

"Wow, that's pretty tough. I suppose it must be a hard environment for you to work in if pretty much everyone you work with is single."

"Yes. There's a lot of pressure to build unattached sorts of relationships, to reach understandings with people. Friendships with benefits."

He looked at her. With the flowers at work and the anger in Gerard's words, he had assumed she wasn't that kind of a girl. It was one of the many things he liked about her.

"What are you thinking about?"

"Friendships with benefits."

"Oh. No, I've never gone for that. If I do anything like that, it's going to be in a long-term relationship, something committed, not just for the fun of it."

What did she mean by *committed?* This probably wasn't the place or time to talk about it. "Is that why you wouldn't date me?"

"Maybe. It probably also has to do with Daniel, my mentor, constantly giving me a hard time about my relationship with you. And it probably has to do with your status as a suspect."

"In Carl's death?"

"No, I'm pretty certain you're not involved in that."

"I was arrested for murdering Benita."

"Brought in for questioning. And you should be happy I was tailing you because I was the one who sprung you."

"Oh. I see. You knew when I had left work and what I'd been doing?"

"Yes, and it was taking a risk to talk to the detective about it, honestly. My boss wasn't happy about that one. And he's not going to be happy about this one, either."

"Why not?"

"Because you're still, technically, a suspect in what we're investigating."

"So there's something other than the deaths going on? Are the two things connected?"

"We really shouldn't talk about this here."

"What else should we talk about?"

"What about your church? Most of the churches in my area are much larger than yours, and folks don't normally drop by the pastor's house like you do. It seems old-fashioned. Why do you like it so much?"

"I suppose because I'm old-fashioned. I mean, the music is pretty up-to-date, and folks wear what they like, but the pastor is conservative. I like all those things."

"I noticed."

"You've been there?"

"Remember the girl you chased out of the service?"

"That was *you?*"

She laughed. "Yes, that was me. You weren't supposed to see me, and most people wouldn't have. But you're a bit too observant of your surroundings sometimes."

"A bit too observant for someone who's trying to tail me, you mean? Failed Fieldcraft 101, did you?"

"Something like that. The guys I work with, they say I'm hard to hide."

"I would say that's an understatement. Are we still going to church in the morning?"

"Why?"

"Well, there's something there I need to get."

"Is it *that* important?" Leah asked.

"Yes, I think so. And there's something in my apartment I need. Your folks aren't the ones who trashed my apartment, did you?"

"That wasn't us, no. What is it you need?"

"Some information from the pastor. My laptop from my apartment."

"You want to check your e-mail? You can set up my laptop to do that if you want to."

"No, there's something else I need in my laptop bag as well."

"What is it?" Leah asked.

"Just something I need."

"Are you always this cagey? Do you ever tell anyone anything, or do you live in a self contained world?"

"I don't trust well."

"That's what Linda said. It would be better, at this point, if you just told me what you know."

"I didn't think this was the time or place?"

"Okay, you got me. It could be a big risk going to church in the morning. Can't we just drop by afterwards and get whatever it is?"

"I don't think so. The pastor needs to see both of us, I think."

"He's cagey, too?"

"Generally, yes."

"Aren't pastors usually nice, gentle folks?"

"I wouldn't say Pastor David is mean or anything, but he's been around the block a few times."

"Great. So we have to deal with a pastor who's been burned before and doesn't give things away easily. Okay, so the only way you can get this information is to go to church in the morning?"

"Well, it's the way I'd prefer to get it."

"We couldn't drop by the pastor's house?"

"If someone discovers I'm alive, aren't they less likely to attack me at a church than at his house?"

"I see your point. I'd rather not expose you if possible."

"You mean exposure like going out to dinner with a dead person?"

She sighed. "Okay. Note to self, never mess with someone who's cagier than you are. It might be best if you're armed if we're going out into public. Where is your handgun, so they can get it?"

"You're not going to protect me?"

She shot him a look. "You know you can't be protected all the time. Sometimes you just have to take care of yourself."

"You'd let a suspect go around armed?"

"I've not stopped you up to this point, have I? Besides, I think this little incident today takes you off the suspect list. At least in my opinion."

He took a napkin and drew a figure on it. "It's in a lockbox under the seat of my truck. This is the combination."

"Holster?"

"In the bottom drawer of the desk in the living room. Or rather, what's left of the desk. I'm going to have to replace it at some point."

"What are they looking for?"

"An inside the waistband holster, black, single snap over the belt."

She spoke into the phone for a few minutes and then ended the call. She sat in silence while the waiter placed their plates on the table. When he had gone, she looked over the meal and then up at Jess. "I do hope what you're getting tomorrow morning is the information on Carl's death."

"Do you think it's related?"

"I'm not positive, but it could be."

"This is why you've been bugging me for that information. And why you got so upset when I wouldn't give it to you."

"Yes. You should trust me, Jess."

Jess looked up while continuing to arrange his food. He'd forgotten to tell them not to put guacamole on his plate, so he adroitly scooped it off into one of the small plates originally accompanying the chips. "I suppose I should."

"Then you'll give me what you have on Carl's death."

"Tomorrow morning. I thought you said you were hungry."

She laughed. "Okay, enough talk, let's eat."

Leah unlocked the door to the apartment and walked in. She tripped over his laptop bag, which had been strategically place in the middle of the floor, just in front of the door.

"Very graceful."

"Thanks."

"Why did they put it there?"

"So I would trip over it."

"I thought you said these guys you work with are nice?"

"Did I say that? I don't remember saying it. But now that you say it, they are nice. This is just your typical workplace humor, like you sneaking up on Brian without him knowing you were in the building."

"Oh, you heard about that, did you? You've been talking to Linda way too much."

"How *did* you get into the building without anyone knowing you were there? The badge machines didn't record you, and the cameras didn't record you coming in."

"Trade secret."

"In other words, I'll have to pry it out of you."

"Something like that. Do these guys have keys to this apartment?"

Her face flushed. "It's not like that...it's not my apartment, really. It's just a place the department keeps up for local investigations." She glanced around the room. "You don't think I'd live in a place with this little personality, do you?"

"So, other people could wander in and out of here..."

She laughed. "No. I booted Daniel and Thuan out. They might be nice guys, but I won't sleep in the same apartment with them."

"It's like that?" She nodded, a flush passing over her face again. "Which reminds me, how do I get in touch with you if I need to tonight?"

"You knock on my door?"

"I'm sleeping here, with you?"

"Well, now that you put it that way..." She turned to him and pulled him in close.

Jess started and backed away a little. "I thought you said you wouldn't—"

She looked into his eyes, making him feel like there was no one else in the world. "I've spent a lot of time thinking about it, Jess."

He broke away from her. "Leah, there's nothing I would like more in the world than waking up next to you. But you said not without a commitment."

"I'm willing to make the commitment. You should trust me, Jess."

"I do."

"Then why not?"

"Maybe we mean different things by commitment."

"You have a really hard time trusting, don't you? Why don't you put the divorce behind you?" asked Leah.

"I should."

"Then why don't you?"

"Tomorrow," he said.

"Why not tonight?"

"I'm not in the habit of taking things that don't belong to me."

"I don't understand."

He closed his eyes for a moment and thought about what to say. This was going to be hard to explain, especially in a way that didn't destroy their friendship. "I've been here before. I married a girl I slept with first, and I thought I was in love. It was a disaster, letting my feelings get ahead of where the relationship was. I'm not doing that again." She looked confused, so he continued. "In two or three years, you're going to be established in your career, and you're going to look for a man to marry, to have kids with. If I sleep with you tonight, what are the odds that man is going to be me?"

"I would wait for you."

"Is that the way you feel, or is it what you have decided to do? If you've decided you would wait for me until your career is to the point when you're ready, then the waiting should involve everything, including sleeping together."

"Aren't you worried about losing me?"

"I *am* worried about losing you, but if it's right, then it will wait. This isn't love; it's passion."

"How do you know what I'm feeling?"

"Because if it were love, you'd want the bond in place, in public, permanently, before getting involved in this. Because you'd have thought out the tradeoffs and decided it was worth it, whatever the cost. Love isn't taking one part of the relationship and not the rest."

"But I have decided to love you."

"Then what about your career?"

"Can't I have both?"

Jess smiled; he wasn't about to get into this argument. "I didn't say you couldn't have both. But you can't have it both ways. You can't wait to get married in order to build your career and have the relationship you would have while you're married at the same time. Waiting is fine, or not waiting is fine, but having part of marriage without the rest is not fine."

Anger started to drive out the other emotions on her face. "You're turning me down? I'd never have thought—"

"Leah, it's not like that. I'm flattered. You're truly a beautiful girl, but this is the right way." He could see she was doubtful; the words tumbled out. "It's hard for me to say no to this. But I'm going to respect the choices you've made in your life and where you're going. And I'm going to respect the person who does take your heart. I don't want to lose your friendship or the chance at something more later."

"You don't love me?"

"Please stop, Leah. The real test of my love for you is waiting. Love waits."

She started to turn, her face in confusion.

"Wait. I will kiss you good night." He pulled her to him but she pushed him away.

"Good night, Jess." Her voice was rough, filled with anger. She walked into her bedroom, and fairly slammed the door in his face.

"Good night," he replied to the door.

Chapter 29

Jess's eyes were assaulted by the garish yellow and red flower pattern on the kitchen's wallpaper as he made the coffee. He picked his mug up and moved from the kitchen to the living room, the tan floor blending into the tan carpet under the popcorn-textured off-white ceiling.

Leah was still in getting ready, still obviously upset from last night. He was still certain he had done the right thing, though. Maybe starting a conversation about something else would help ease the tension. "What's your real place like, Leah?" He had to shout to make himself heard over the sound of the blow-dryer.

"Not nearly as neat as this. I usually have to clean for a couple of days before my mom comes for dinner."

"It can't be that bad."

"I didn't say it was dirty, just messy."

"I hope it has more personality than this hotel room."

The blow-dryer shut off. The apartment sounded empty, hollow without the blaring noise.

"I don't know. I don't spend as much time there as I'd like. Most of my time I'm on the road, in hotel rooms or apartments like this one. I've always told myself I'll have a real place when I get off the road. For now, it's just a place to store stuff and spend a few nights in between trips."

"Coffee?"

She glanced at his mug. "It's terrible, isn't it? Worse than the stuff at your office."

"Breakfast?"

"Only if you can stomach cold cereal and milk. How about we stop and grab a bagel? There's a good place between here and the church."

"Sure, but we have to get moving, then, if we're going to make the early service."

"The first couple of hymns and announcements won't hurt. In fact, it's better if we get there a little late. We can scope out the parking lot before we go in, look for anything out of the ordinary."

Jess got up from the kitchen table. "Good idea. Condition orange, I suppose, should be the norm until we figure out what is going on,"

"Perception of threat, but no clear indicative sign to point to one specifically. I would say so. You must have had some training along the way."

"Just a few classes here and there. My concealed carry instructor recommended a couple. Yavapai and Thunder Ranch were the ones I finally settled on."

"Both respected schools. Good choices. Come on, let's get out of here."

He dumped the coffee into the sink, rinsed the mug out, and set it in the sink.

"No wonder your place is so neat all the time," Leah said. She tossed him the keys to her truck, and they headed out the door.

"For here or to go?" The woman behind the counter looked at him, impatient for an answer.

Jess turned to Leah. "Should we eat here, or run?"

"You're not eating that everything bagel in my truck so you can scatter little seeds all over the place. Unless you're volunteering to give it a good detail job once we're done."

"We'll take it for here."

At the table, he decided it was time to clear the air a little. "Leah, about last night. I didn't want to hurt your feelings."

"I don't think I was in my right mind. It wasn't professional at all, and it was wrong. I'm sorry, too."

"I hope that, no matter what happens here, we can still be friends."

"I think I can be certain enough that you're not a suspect to promise that. Even if it is unprofessional. I can just blame it on this being my first real case."

"Really? This is your first case?"

"This is the first case I've ever been in charge of, anyway. The two guys waiting for us at the church comprise the rest of the front-end team. One of them, Daniel, is my boss."

"So we shouldn't kiss in front of Daniel, right?"

"That would be really unprofessional." She laughed, spilling a dribble of coffee on the table. "Now see what you've done?" She dabbed at the mess on the table and started laughing again.

Once the service was over, they walked outside and sat down on the steps, out of the way of the main traffic flow. Pastor David stood at the door, talking to people as they walked by. He finally finished and walked over to them.

"You must be Leah." He shook her hand and turned to Jess. "You didn't tell me she was quite this beautiful."

"Well, I didn't want to say anything. You might introduce her to some guy before I could steal her heart."

"And how's that going?" Pastor David winked.

"Not too well, to be honest," Jess answered.

"Would you two cut it out? I *am* standing right here, you know." Her face was red.

"You're cute when you're embarrassed, too."

"Jess, I swear—"

"Okay, sorry, Leah, just teasing you."

The pastor's wife joined them. "Hi, you must be Leah." She shook her hand. "You just let me know when you've had enough of these two."

"I think she's capable of taking care of herself," said Jess.

Leah shot Jess a look and turned to the pastor. "You really believe love is a choice, don't you? I don't think I've ever heard it argued or explained so elegantly before."

The pastor's wife jumped in, "If love were all just about emotions, my husband here," she indicated the pastor, "would be lucky to have lived as long as he has."

"There are feelings involved, of course, but our focus on that side of our relationships is really a product of our human nature. We really like to *feel* things. Somehow, we don't think an experience is real unless we feel it. Anyway, I think I need to give this to someone, but I'm not certain who since you are both here."

He pulled the envelope Jess had given him out of his pocket and handed it to her. "Maybe it would be safer with you."

She turned to Jess. "An envelope? What's in here?"

"Don't open it here. It's better if you wait 'til we get back to your apartment."

"Okay, there's one point of confusion here. Why the pastor? Why not give it to me directly?"

"I figured Pastor David would get it to you one way or the other, pretty much no matter what happened."

"So this is what you were doing at his house on Friday night. You weren't just over for dinner. But why not just wait until Monday to give this to me, if you'd decided to?"

Pastor David interrupted, "Because he did something at work he was convinced was going to put his life in danger over the weekend. But I'd better leave you to that conversation later. This probably isn't the best time or place to talk shop."

A look of concern passed over her face. "Jess. You're in over your head, aren't you? That's why they tried to run you down yesterday morning. What did you do?"

"Now it's my turn to tell you later." He smiled. Turning to the pastor, he said, "Thanks for covering this for me."

His wife said, "I saw the report of your death. Scared me to death, with all the other stuff that's been going on. I was overjoyed when you slipped into the service, even if it was late."

"I'm sorry about that, Mary. I'll explain it all later."

"I would invite you and Leah over for lunch. Work or no work, you have to eat. But I think you already have an appointment with those two over there, don't you?" She indicated two men in dark suits milling around by one of the remaining cars in the lot.

Leah replied, "Yes, well, there is that to take care of. Maybe we could come over for dinner sometime this week?"

A car screeched in the distance.

"I wish those people would learn how to drive like normal human beings," Mary said.

The pastor laughed. "I always tell you that you have your definition of normal backwards. It's the Christians who are normal, and the rest of the folks in the world who aren't. Anyway, we should be heading off so you two can get to your meeting."

His wife said,"Call me about dinner."

Leah said, "We will. I promise."

The pastor and his wife headed across the parking lot to their car. Just as the pastor opened the car door for Mary, a car roared up the street, bursting into the parking lot sideways. It headed directly for Jess and Leah.

Condition red. He pulled Leah behind him and started to move to the edge of the parking lot, out of the way. The car was moving fast, but there was still time to get off the line of force.

The car straightened and adjusted, turning into their movement. Someone had figured out he was still alive. Instead of being the victim of a boating accident, he was to be the victim of a crazy hit-and-run driver. This time, Leah was to go with him. Two birds with one stone.

He released her hand and pulled his shirt up, ripping it out from under his belt. His right hand reached under, he felt the steel grip frame, and he pulled it up, clear of the holster. One. The gun pivoted, pointing at the oncoming vehicle. Was there enough time for a complete draw? *Don't ask questions, just move.* He slid to the side and away from the oncoming car, gaining space. Two. He pulled his left hand into the front of the grip. Three. The front sight came into his field of vision, up from the bottom. There were only a few seconds left. No way could he move fast enough to get out of the way. He had no choice.

Leah moved behind him, and his front sight jiggled, kicking the alignment off. No time to worry about it. Front sight on the center of the windshield. Press. He felt the shot, but he didn't hear anything. The sights came back into alignment. Nothing was changing.

He saw muzzle flash on his right, in his peripheral vision. Leah had pulled her 45 and was shooting into the car as well. *No time to look, just keep going.* He pressed the trigger again, losing count of the rounds. *Need to find something else to do, the driver is still coming. Smarter, not faster.* What else could he do?

The driver lost control and slid, narrowly missing him. He straightened the car and slid out of the parking lot. Silence. Then he heard police sirens in the distance, heading towards the church.

Leah was shaking his shoulder. "Jess, down. Put your gun on the ground." He could hear her, but she was distant for some reason. His hand shook. He released the magazine, locked the slide back, and set his handgun gently on the ground.

"I'm too fond of you to have you shot by the responding officers." Leah took her hand off his shoulder and sat on the pavement.

Where was the car? He could still see it coming, the scene replaying in his mind. Was there anything else he could have done? Had he done the right thing? Yes, he had done the right thing. There was nothing else. He and Leah were both slated to die, and he couldn't let that happen.

His world was fragmented. Police cruisers, blue lights flashing. Someone scooped up his gun from the gravel. He was being seated in the back of an open ambulance, a heavy blanket placed around him. It was too warm of a day for a blanket. Leah sat for a while, holding his hand, and then she was gone.

Officers were talking to the other two agents. His mind finally settled, and he realized he'd just come as close as he ever wanted to being killed. Twice in two days.

An officer walked up to the rear of the ambulance and sat down next to him. "You okay, son?"

"I think so. It's hard to know."

"You're just coming out of shock. You can take the blanket off if you're hot." Gratefully, Jess pulled the blanket off and tossed it into the ambulance. "It's like living in a time machine, a little film playing over and over again in your head, the shock. Yeah, I know. There's nothing to be ashamed of here, son. You did the right thing—all of you did. I understand you're the one under protection here, but you did better than the rest. You're going to hear a lot about shock and post violence syndrome and all of that. Just remember, you did the right thing. You took care of your friends, the people you love, and that's never the wrong thing to do."

He sat Jess's 1911 on the floor of the ambulance. "I presume this came from a holster someplace, or you have something to carry it in."

"Oh, yes. But shouldn't you be taking it? I mean, I just shot someone, didn't I?"

"Well, we found the car, shot up pretty bad, abandoned around the corner. We can't find the person that belongs to the car, though, so we really don't have anyone to question on the other side of this incident."

"And did any of the shots hit anyone else?"

"Bystanders? No. You and your girlfriend are both pretty good shots, I'd say. Anyway, we won't be filing any charges. We have enough witnesses whose stories match to show it was self-defense. The main thing we can't figure out is how to file the report. We're looking for your body on Jordan Lake, and here you turn up shooting at cars in Apex. Now put that away."

Jess took the gun and pushed it, mechanically, into the holster.

"Hold your hand out." When he did so, the officer dropped several cartridges into his palm. "Interesting choice, 38 Super. I've not seen one of those in a long time. Don't load this in the parking lot; you're on church property, son."

"Do I need to come down to the station for reports or anything?"

"We know where to find you if we need you. Just keep it firmly planted in your head—you did the right thing. Everyone standing in this parking lot agrees, including those three agents standing over there. You did fine. You're alive, and she's alive, and that's what counts."

"Did the other two shoot?"

"Couldn't get a clear line of fire.

What I can't figure out is why someone is trying to kill you. Twice in two days, it seems. Those folks over there won't talk to me about it."

Jess sighed. "If they won't talk to you about it, I can't either. Maybe later."

"I'll take you up on that. This sounds really interesting." The officer got up and moved off towards his patrol car. Jess stood up and headed over to the group of agents.

Mary intercepted him halfway there. "Jess, are you okay?"

"I think so. The officer said they won't be pressing charges or anything."

"I thought David was kidding when he said this envelope was a matter of life or death."

"Apparently, he wasn't."

"Well, at least you and Leah are both okay. I do want you two to come over for dinner this week. It would be a nice return to normalcy."

"We'll call you, I promise." He moved past her, placing his hands on Leah's shoulders.

"What's up?"

Leah turned to admit him into the circle, giving him a look of serious concern. "They think we need to lock you up until this is over."

"Why? Am I still a suspect? I would think two attempts on my life in twenty-four hours would have cleared that up."

The older one spoke. Jess guessed this one was Daniel, Leah's boss. "Officially, you *are* still a suspect. But I think we are all pretty certain, by now, that you're not a suspect, just someone who got involved in something that was bigger than he thought."

"If you're not in over your head, you're not in. Before yesterday, did *you* think this was as big as it turned out to be?"

Daniel was taken aback. "No, we didn't. What we can't sort out is why you're suddenly being attacked like this. Things have been quiet, too quiet, for a while, and then this weekend—"

"Two attempts on my life in two days. That's because I set a trap. Someone discovered it and wants me dead so what I know can't get out. The problem is, I really don't have any idea what I know, at this point."

The three of them looked at him, surprised. Leah spoke first. "A trap?"

"A data trap. I caught something, but I've not had the time to look at it to find out what it is. I'm pretty certain, at this point, that Carl's death is tied into something much larger, but

I don't have the information to know what it is. I set a trap to find out."

Leah continued, "You're still convinced Carl didn't commit suicide?"

"I *know* he didn't. And I'm pretty certain I know now who killed Carl. And Benita. And Gerard. And who's behind these attacks this weekend."

Leah held up the envelope. "The information proving Carl was murdered is in here?"

"Not completely. That is mostly an interesting string of missing information, rather than information."

"What do you mean?" she asked.

"Look, each time something has happened in the data center, the camera down there missed recording it. That has been blamed on the camera. I checked that camera, and there's nothing wrong with it. Someone has been tampering with the recordings. Beyond that, Carl's e-mail was emptied intentionally, and so was his voice mail. Then there are the physical clues."

Daniel shifted at this point, facing Jess directly. "Like?"

"His cell phone broke on the data center floor. I've dropped my cell phone down there a few times, and it never broke into a thousand little pieces like his did. His cell phone was crushed. There was something on it someone didn't want anyone else to find. And the way his body was hanging, the scratches on his neck—it would have been impossible for him to do that to himself. And the lights were shut off in the data center. How did he do that?"

Daniel wasn't convinced. "Okay, but that doesn't prove he was murdered."

"I agree, but that all set me off on the trail of trying to find out what was going on. I got a copy of the suicide note. It wasn't sent by Carl. It was put together from older e-mails Carl had sent, but it wasn't sent by Carl."

Leah held the envelope up. "And all this information is in this?"

"Yes. These are the files you've been asking me about and apparently trying to get off my computer. Well, I know someone tried to get them, anyway. Y'all obviously know a lot more than I do. What we need to do is put everything we know together and see what comes out of the jigsaw puzzle."

Daniel said, "We have the same information you have, now. It might still be safer to put you into protective custody."

"No. I think it's possible that someone on the police force is wrapped up in this as well. Until we know for certain, putting me in a cell there isn't going to help anything. And there is still the information from the trap I set to be analyzed."

Daniel appeared unconvinced, so Jess continued. "Besides, if they haven't been able to kill me with these two attempts, I'd say I'm already pretty well protected. How many more times can they try between here and the apartment?"

"Okay, we'll follow you over there."

Chapter 30

Jess settled on the couch after setting his laptop up to display through the television in the living room. "From the start, there were things that didn't make sense to me." He opened the file on the screen. "Leah knows I can't stand things that aren't elegant." Leah suppressed a laugh. "So it all started with Carl's murder."

Daniel said, "The local police were certainly convinced it was a suicide. It's not something we second-guessed. What led you to think Sparks was murdered?"

"First, his car had water spots all over it. Based on the rain that passed through the night before, he had to have been in the office much earlier than Detective Harris thought. Either Gerard actually followed Carl to the office, rather than following him home, or Carl left home after Gerard had gone and headed back to the office. Something just didn't make sense in that chain of events."

"What convinced you Sparks didn't go home, and then drive to the office early in the morning?"

"I know the rain ended around one in the morning."

"How do you know Spark's car didn't get wet at the party, and he just left it dirty until the next day at work. You're not likely to go through a car wash at two in the morning."

Jess laughed. "You didn't know Carl. Any time it rained he would take his car right to the nearest car wash. He knew where every car wash in the area was. At the least, he would have driven through the car wash on the way to work. No way would he show up at work with a dirty car."

Daniel's tone was unconvinced. "Okay, so maybe he forgot. Maybe he came in the next morning, and committed suicide."

Jess considered this for a moment, as well. "I suppose he could have, but coming in to work to commit suicide? That doesn't make any sense, either. Was he afraid he would disturb his parents, or something, but committing suicide at their house? Why pull up all those tiles? And why hang yourself from an Ethernet cable after pulling all those tiles up? No, none of it made any sense. It's possible, just not elegant. That's what started me down the path of checking his voice mail and e-mail. When I found both of those had been wiped clean—"

"None of this proves he was murdered, just that he committed suicide in an odd way. Everyone in the office has an alibi. Gerard's is the weakest, but it still seems—"

"Benita saw Gerard at the office at around one in the morning, sitting in his office working on something."

Daniel looked startled. "Did she tell the police that?"

"She wasn't questioned. She always said no one ever listened to her."

Daniel moved to the edge of the couch. "They didn't question her? How could you miss someone who obviously would have seen so much? And then she was murdered."

"And I was framed for it, yes."

There was silence for a moment while they took this new information in. "That was actually a pretty slick job. It's no wonder you were getting worried, Jess." Leah's look of concern was genuine, her eyes soft again.

"Yes, but the recordings from the cameras were altered there, as well, placing the blame on the camera. I checked that camera; there was nothing wrong with it. It should be easy enough to get it from the security company to have it tested if you need to prove it wasn't the camera."

"The suicide note?"

"I broke into Carl's e-mail folders and went through all of his old e-mail. First, that note wasn't in his outbox or log files anyplace. Second, the entire note was made up of sentences copied from other e-mails. I searched through all his old e-mail and found every sentence in the suicide note. You'll notice he never said anything about killing himself, just vague phrases that could just as well relate to a project as easily as they related to his life."

Daniel let out a low whistle as Jess flipped between various e-mails and the suicide note. In each email, he highlighted the matching sentence from the suicide note.

As he was showing them where the suicide note had come from, Jess continued. "And note each of these e-mails were received by Gerard. Some of them, in fact, were only sent to Gerard." Jess opened a copy of the suicide email in a different program, one that showed all the information about the path the email had taken through the network. "Finally, notice the origin of the suicide note itself. The IP address of the machine it was sent from wasn't Carl's. I checked. The suicide note was sent from Gerard's computer."

Daniel broke the silence that followed these revelations. "Why do you think Benita was killed?"

"Someone overheard me talking to Benita in the break room."

"Do you think it was Mattingly?"

"I think so, but I'm not certain. The funny thing about her death is the records from the badge reader system in the building don't seem to be right.

"What about them?"

"The only person who badged into that room all afternoon was me. Benita wasn't recorded entering the room, but—"

Leah looked over at Jess. "How did Benita get in, then?"

"She used a key."

"A *key?*"

"Of course. I once got Benita to let me borrow the key. Brian bet me I couldn't get into the building without him knowing it, or being able to tell how I had gotten in. There are a couple of spots where someone can enter the building without being recorded by the security cameras, if you have a key."

Thuan laughed, lifting his head out of the laptop for a second. "Of course, social engineering. A part of the grand tradition of geeks."

Daniel said, "So if Benita got in with a key, why is it odd that no one else badged into the room?"

Jess replied, "Well, that means the killer must have used a key to open the data center door and actuate the halon system."

Leah sat up. "A *key!*"

"Yes, of course. A key. And who has keys? There are only four or five sets to the building. A couple of sets are kept in the security office for general use, like by the cleaning contractors. Brian keeps another set, and Gerard has the last set."

Daniel considered this for a moment before carrying the conversation forward. "So anyone could have signed those keys out and used them."

"No, I don't think so. It wasn't like you could just walk in and take a set of keys or sign them out for any old reason. Employees aren't allowed to sign them out at all. That's why I had to get a set from Benita. They could be used to go places in the building your badge wouldn't allow you to go."

"This is all interesting, but it doesn't lead us anyplace we want to go."

"Why don't you tell me what you're really looking for?"

Thuan looked up from his laptop screen. "Someone is stealing identities off the servers at OptiData. Not one or two at a time, but thousands. They're selling them to a middleman, who resells them on the black market. OptiData isn't the only company that's been hit, of course, but every time we get close, they roll up the network and move someplace else. We were hoping to get the top of the chain here and shut it down."

"Then that's the tie-in."

Leah said, "What? The tie-in?"

Daniel interjected as well. "You've known about the stolen data? And you've not said anything?"

"Well, I've been snooping around in the data center the last couple of days. I kept coming back to those pulled-up tiles and the rack where Carl was killed. There had to be some *reason.* I couldn't imagine Carl being killed just because. I mean, he wasn't the nicest guy in the world, but still. So I just kept looking around until I found it."

"What did you find?"

"I found an alternate path between one of the servers and the Internet."

Thuan looked up from his laptop. "*What?*"

"Oh, it's there alright. It took some work to trace it, but I ran it all the way from one of the servers out to our Internet connection. There's an alternate firewall. From the outside of the company, it would look just like a normal encrypted data stream, nothing special or unusual. Because it's encrypted, I couldn't tell what was being sent."

Daniel said, "But why bypass the normal connection?"

"Because there's a lot of monitoring equipment along the normal links. I would have seen what they were doing, or someone else would have, and it would have been easy to figure out. This way, they took whatever it was they were stealing out of the network early, so no one would accidentally see it before they got it out the door."

Thuan hadn't gone back to his laptop. "How would they know which server to pick?"

Jess laughed. "That's easy—it doesn't matter. You can move data around on the servers in there much like you might move renters around in a hotel. All you have to do is find the data you want, move it to the one server you're taking data from, take what you want, and then move it back off so you can move something else there."

"And why do you think Carl was killed?" Leah asked. The talk had obviously passed Thuan's area of interest. He buried his head in his laptop again.

"I think Gerard set it up before he started managing the place, and he was paying Carl to maintain the connections. Carl had all the floor tiles pulled because he was thinking about exposing the whole thing. He probably had pictures on his cell phone, showing the way the cable ran and what it did."

Leah sucked her breath in. "That's why Gerard was making payments to Carl through the company's bonus system. I looked through the files at Linda's desk and found receipts for bonuses that would double Carl's salary. No one else was getting anywhere near that much in bonuses."

"And why Carl was able to afford those fancy cars, and lots of other things."

"Can you show us where this feed is?"

Daniel answered before Jess could. "I don't know how we should approach this, Thuan. They're likely to just roll the network up again. Gerard and Carl are both dead, so there's probably no contact left with OptiData at this point."

"I don't think the trail has gone cold yet. Or rather, even if it has, I might be able to hand you what you need to find out what's been going on."

Thuan jerked his head back up from the computer. "How can you do that?"

"Well, what would you need to prove your case? A copy of the data, perhaps? A record of it being passed through that alternate connection? Something like that?"

"If we had the data, we could match it with the stolen identities. That might not tell us who was stealing the data, but it would help us start to tie things up."

"Well, we might just be in luck. I not only traced the cable, I tapped the circuit and gathered some of the data being sent outside the network before it was encrypted." Jess clicked on the files he had collected off the network, bringing them up on his screen. "The problem is, I've no idea what's in these things. I can recognize some stuff, but I couldn't get the metadata off the server so I could put it back into a readable format."

"Can you make a copy of that?" Thuan asked.

"Yeah, sure." He tossed the miniature USB drive over to Thuan. He buried his head in his laptop screen, his fingers flying furiously over the keyboard.

Daniel said, "Well, now we know why your apartment was trashed on Friday night, don't we? They were looking for this data."

"Yes, but I led them pretty far astray. I don't know if they figured out I was copying the data to a machine in my apartment, or if they just trashed my apartment as a warning. When I went to the lake like nothing had happened on Saturday morning, I was calling their hand. It was an attempt to rattle someone's cage."

"You certainly rattled some cages. It's a good thing I followed you out onto the lake on Saturday morning. That was a really big risk to take."

"Well, I had already given Pastor David a copy of at least some of the data. I figured he'd get it to you somehow, and you'd know the right person to talk to, or what to do with it." Jess took a drink before continuing. "Once I'd discovered how deep this was, what could I do? Run away? When someone walks up to you and says, 'Your money or your life,' it's pretty cold comfort knowing the only real difference between the two is being charged with robbery or being charged with murder."

Leah got up and moved into the kitchen, leaving Daniel and Jess facing one another. "There are two problems left. Who killed the cleaning lady, and who killed Mattingly?"

"I don't know. I'd like to pull the video files off the network and see what we can find, but my accounts have been shut down."

"My accounts still work," Leah said as she walked back into the living room. "Want to try it?"

"Sure, why not?" Jess let Leah take control of his laptop long enough to get into the company's network. He opened a session to the server on which the video recordings were stored, found the right one, and downloaded it. He double-clicked the file, typed in the password he remembered from the last time he had looked at the recordings, and started to play it.

He skipped forward in the file, stopping just when the clock in the lower right-hand corner read 3:40. He pushed the play button again. The time skipped from 15:40 to 16:18. In the frame before the skip, there wasn't anything out of place. In the frame after the skip, the fallen rack was visible at the edge of the camera's range, slightly out of focus.

Leah sighed. "Well, that didn't work out."

"Wait, let me think. The backups on this server run around that time every day. I had forgotten about that when I went to look for the other video files. I wonder if the original file was backed up, or the altered one?"

Jess connected to the backup server and quickly navigated through the directories. "Here it is. The file size is different, so it might be a different version of the same file." They all waited while the file downloaded, the progress bar moving slowly across the screen.

Once it was done, he double-clicked the file, typed in the password, slid the position control over until the clock's amber digits read 15:40, and pressed the play button. This time, the recording didn't skip. They could clearly see Gerard walk into the room, followed by Brian. They could see the two of them get into an argument and Gerard pushing Brian out of the way. They traced the rack as it fell silently on Gerard, and then they saw Brian leaving the room.

They sat in shocked silence. Brian was the last person Jess would have expected to be playing a part in all of this. Gerard was the obvious suspect in the entire scheme.

Leah spoke first. "It was an accident. Why cover up his death?"

Jess said, "Thuan, you've been quiet. What do you have?"

Thuan looked up from his laptop screen. "You guys seemed to be having fun. I didn't want to interrupt. Toss me the cable from the television."

Jess unplugged the cable from his computer and tossed it to Thuan. Thuan plugged it in, pressed a few buttons, and brought up a copy of the data Jess had collected from his trap.

"This is what you handed me. I happen to have some of the data that's been sold on the black market. I compared this to what we've seen elsewhere, and I tried finding a format that would fit. Now look." He pressed a few buttons, and the data was reformatted on the screen. It was a complete medical record for someone. It was perfect information on which to base an identity theft since very few people would doubt who you were if you could note specific injuries, operations, and other information.

Jess stared at the data on the screen. "So there we have it. There are still some questions, but that just about wraps it up."

"Not quite," Daniel said. "We still don't know who was running this operation. We're no closer to the top than we've ever been before."

Jess turned to Thuan. "Can you look up the name of Brian's mother? I'm certain you have access to it through some sort of police records or another."

Thuan glanced up after working for a few minutes. "Sylvia Hartwell mean anything to you?"

"That's the name of the private investor who bought OptiData and put Gerard in charge of the whole mess. Things fall into place now. The servers the data is being sent to, they all belong to Sylvia Hartwell, but I couldn't place the name. That's why Brian's office is actually nicer than Gerard's and why Brian can leave the company and come back as often as he wants, always assured of his job as the head of security." Jess turned to Leah. "I think I would investigate his employment records and see where all he's worked in the last several years. I'll bet he's the common link between the different identity thefts."

Leah looked startled. "*Brian?*"

"That's my guess. He's not your murderer, though; he's just the data thief. Gerard was the heavy, along with someone else, I'm guessing. Do any of you have any suspicions about the local police department, as well?"

He saw Leah hesitate, thinking about her answer. "Yes, we do, actually, but why do you say that?"

"It's just a hunch, but I'm betting Sergeant Stone is your other heavy. Those were his guys out on the lake yesterday and his folks in the car today."

Her eyebrows arched. "Why do you think that?"

"Just a hunch."

Daniel turned to Leah. "What do you think? It's your case?"

Leah replied, "I think we have enough to round up some warrants and arrest Brian and his mom. If nothing else, we can start with destruction of evidence and stolen data, and we can move on from there as we start to untie this thing."

"I agree. I'll get some warrants. We should move on this in the morning before anyone has a chance to cover their tracks. We move in the morning." Daniel suddenly looked tired. "We've been at this for a few hours. Why don't we break up for the night?" He looked at Jess and then back to Leah. "You want us to take him back to his apartment?"

"No, he's fine. Just leave him here. He's better off with me, at least until we get Brian off the streets." Then, turning to Jess, she said, "I forgot to tell you, Mary asked us over for dinner. We still have time, if that's okay?"

"Sure, why not."

Daniel shot her a look. "You think that's wise?"

"I think we'll be okay. We'll be careful."

"Since we're heading over to Pastor David's, mind if we call Linda and let her know I'm okay, and not to come to work tomorrow morning?" Leah handed Jess her cell phone as she herded them all out of the apartment.

Chapter 31

Jess looked around the parking lot. There were only two cars there, Brian's and another one he didn't recognize. It made sense; Detective Harris had pretty much shut OptiData down until this third death could be investigated. It would take time for someone else to put the place back into operation. He was certain the owners weren't too happy about it, but it was only supposed to be for a couple of days, and the servers were still up and running for the moment, in compliance with OptiData's contracts.

They had gathered in the parking lot of an adjacent building at nine thirty. After this, they had trudged through the woods to a position where the cameras couldn't see them.

Detective Harris was the last to make it over from the other building. "That's Sergeant Stone's car! What is he doing here?"

Jess replied, "He's the mole from the local police department. That's why he went after me so hard. He mostly used his position to slow down any investigations into the ring until they could roll their network up."

Detective Harris shook his head, disbelief written on his face. He turned to Leah. "This is your call. Are you ready to go in?"

"We have a cordon laid down, thanks to your guys coming in to back us up. I don't think anything bad is going to happen here since we're going to catch them by surprise, but it's always better to be safe than sorry."

"Okay, Daniel, Thuan, and I will enter the back using the key I took from the evidence locker. You two okay in the front by yourselves?"

"Sure. We should be fine. They already know Jess is still alive, so there shouldn't be too much surprise there. The main problem is going to be if they see y'all entering from the back."

"Well, we'll offset by a few minutes, say two. That should give you time to get positioned outside the security office in case they decide to flee."

"Okay, let's go in."

"I hope he's playing solitaire rather than watching the cameras!"

Jess and Leah moved up the steps to the front door, being as casual as possible. She slapped her badge against the reader by the door and waited. The light turned green, the reader emitted a soft beep, and the door clicked open.

They moved into the lobby. An intercom on the receptionist's desk clicked on. "Hey, what are you two doing here? This place is closed until Detective Harris has finished up his investigation."

"I just wanted to get a couple of things out of my cubicle is all. My accounts don't seem to be working, so I asked Leah to come with me since her badge is still working."

"Well, you might as well clean your cubicle out while you're here. Gerard was going to fire you on Monday anyway. If he wasn't murdered."

"Well, I think I'll let the police sort that out. I just want to get a couple of things, and then I'll be on my way."

"We'll be watching you in the cameras."

Leah said, "Since I'm here, I'm going to pick something up I left in Linda's cubicle, as well."

"Okay, well, get with it, and get out of here. I'll call the police if I see you snooping someplace you shouldn't be. Don't even try going down to the data center."

Leah badged from the lobby into the main hallway, and they headed for the elevator. She pressed the up button. The doors opened, and they stepped inside. She giggled when the doors closed. "He'll call the police. Sure, why not? Sounds like a good threat, anyway."

As they exited the elevator, Leah used a fireman's key to send it to the first floor. There wasn't any point in making the other three wait if they could arrange it so the elevator would stay down there for them.

Leah stopped and turned to face them. "There are four of us. Let's split up. We'll go different ways and approach the door from different angles."

"Okay." Jess headed off to his right, losing sight of Leah in the maze of hallways between the cubicles.

He heard a familiar shout. "Hey! What are you doing here?" Jess accelerated, jogging through the maze, coming out just in time to see Leah standing off to one side of the door to the security office. Sergeant Stone was facing her, his back to Jess, and Brian was framed in the doorway. Jess watched as the conversation continued.

"I should ask what *you* are doing here," Leah said.

"Visiting an old friend. Brian and I go way back. Now, I thought you and your boyfriend were just coming in to get a few things, and then you were leaving. Then I look up at the cameras, and you're heading straight for the office here. And where *is* your boyfriend?"

The sergeant was dressed in civilian clothes rather than his uniform, but Jess was certain he was concealing a firearm someplace. Sergeant Stone swiveled, looking around the hallways surrounding him. Jess ducked into a cubicle and pulled his gun out. This could get ugly; better to be ready. He held it out at low ready and pulled the badge the detective had given him from his pocket, holding it like he'd been shown.

Leah turned to Brian, still hanging out in the doorway. "Brian Colonel, I am placing you under arrest for the theft and sale of identities. I'm certain Detective Harris, when he arrives, will have more charges to proffer, as well. You have a right to remain silent—"

The sergeant grabbed her hair from behind, jerking it down unmercifully. She screamed and reached for her sidearm, but it was too late. Sergeant Stone pinned her arms to her sides, preventing her from reaching it.

"Brian, take the gun!" Brian stood there, either uncertain of what to do, or unwilling to go to this point. "*Brian! I said take the gun!*" Brian didn't do anything.

Jess watched in horror as the sergeant pulled out his service auto with his free hand and placed the muzzle against Leah's temple. "Now, little lady, drop the gun on the floor." Leah did as she was instructed. "We're going to walk out of here and right through whatever cordon you have set up. You don't think I know the procedure?" He laughed. "Come on, Brian, we'll take our insurance policy and get over the border. We don't need any more to be rich in Mexico."

Jess considered what to do. Could he take the shot? He'd made smaller shots before, but not under this much pressure. His adrenaline kicked in, his vision narrowing to just the sergeant and Leah. He couldn't let her get hurt, no matter what.

He stepped out and raised his 1911, the front sight coming into his field of view.

Brian saw him. "*Stone! Watch out!*"

"Oh! There's your boyfriend. You want this, buddy, you have to come and—" He collapsed.

"Hey, Jess, can you holster that thing?" Daniel filled Jess's sight picture, a baton in his hand. He had crept up behind the sergeant and knocked him out while Jess had him occupied. It had been a dangerous game, but they had come through it. Jess holstered his gun.

Brian ran. His cell phone was in his hand. Calling his mother to warn her, most likely.

Daniel shouted, "Get him! Don't let him finish that call!"

Thuan jumped out from in between the rows of cubicles and somehow converted Brian's forward motion into a tumble onto the floor.

"Nice job. I'm glad we've scooped up Sergeant Stone, as well. Internal affairs will probably find a lot of obstruction and other problems once they start really investigating." Detective Harris turned to Jess. "Good job for your first day as an auxiliary. I think we'll let you keep the badge in case we need you in the future."

"Thanks, Detective. It might come in handy one day."

Chapter 32

Jess and Leah sat in rocking chairs on the porch leading to his apartment door.

"Well, I'm glad this case is all wrapped up," Leah said.

"Where will you go now?" Jess asked.

"I'll have to go back to Reston and do the normal pile of paperwork. Probably take me a few months. What are you going to do? OptiData is shut down, it looks like, permanently. It's never good to be without a job. Maybe you should join our little team?"

"Oh, I don't think I could work in your job. I'm pretty tired of working for someone. I have a little money saved; I might just incorporate as a consultant and see what sort of work I can drum up."

"Hey, there's an idea. Mind if we call on you from time to time? We always run into cases where Thuan gets overloaded with the work and can't keep up. It would be nice to have another geek to help out with different problems, someone we could farm work out to. That way, Thuan could focus on other things."

"Absolutely not. It would be good to have such a high-profile client, even if I can't talk about the work." They rocked in silence for a while before he spoke again. "I'd really like to see you again. To take you out on a real date."

"You mean one where you're not shot at? A date where we can actually just hang out?"

"Yeah. It's going to be hard with you in Reston and me here."

"It's a short flight, you know. And I'm all over the place, anyway. We can sort out how to see each other, I think."

"Long-distance relationships don't work."

"We're not kids anymore. You know I'm not out running around chasing boys. I'm way too busy to be going out on a lot of dates. Besides, I don't want to get married right now. So I think you're safe in that direction. The question is, what will you do?"

He laughed. "Come on, Leah, you know me. I've not been on a date in years. I'm not in a rush. I'm not likely to meet anyone."

"I hope not."

"You mean that?"

She got up and moved across the deck. Pulling him up and out of the chair, close to her, she kissed him. This time, she wasn't looking for boats over his shoulder.

Made in the USA